KAVANAGH *QC*

Kavanagh, for the benefit of the court, infused his voice with a touch of sarcasm. 'So, there *was* a tussle now, was there?'

'Yeah. He was trying to get hold of the knife.'

'Which knife?' The question was lightning-quick.

'*My* knife.'

'Which hand was it in?'

Instinctively, Parry raised his right hand. 'This one.'

'Your right hand?'

'Yeah.'

'Not your left?'

Parry rolled his eyes. 'No, man, it was in my right hand.'

Then it dawned on him and he opened his mouth in silent horror. The exchange between the two of them had been so instinctive that he hadn't paused for thought. Now, too late, he realized he had well and truly incriminated himself.

James Kavanagh took the words out of his mouth. 'I think the word you're looking for, Mr Parry, is "Oops".' With that, he allowed himself a small smile and sat down. He had so confused Parry with his relentless questions that the latter had quite forgotten the basis of his defence – that the other man had been the one with the knife.

Also by Tom McGregor

BETWEEN THE LINES,

The Chill Factor
Close Protection

Peak Practice

KAVANAGH
QC

Tom McGregor

PAN BOOKS

First published 1995 by Pan Books

an imprint of Macmillan General Books
Cavaye Place London SW10 9PG
and Basingstoke

Associated companies throughout the world

ISBN 0 330 34131 6

1 3 5 7 9 8 6 4 2

A CIP catalogue record for this book is available from
the British Library

Phototypeset by Intype, London
Printed and bound in Great Britain by Cox & Wyman Ltd,
Reading, Berkshire

To Susie

CHAPTER ONE

James Kavanagh had his back to his mother as he rose to question the man in the witness box. It was just as well: no matter that Marjorie Kavanagh was well into her seventies and that her son had already celebrated half a century, she still couldn't help seeing him as her little boy.

Jim Kavanagh, aged six, hadn't fluffed his lines. And, several decades down the line, James Kavanagh, QC, was hardly likely to do so in the middle of Manchester Crown Court. Yet that didn't stop his mother frowning as she watched him get to his feet and adjust his glasses. Her frown was due partly to motherly pride and worry – and partly to what she perceived as the extraordinary garb he was obliged to wear: the dark cloak and the white wig were only the most obvious of the mysteries that surrounded her son's profession.

James made the customary bow to the judge and then turned to address the man in the witness box. His mother, he would have been appalled to know, had already decided that the man was lying. It had nothing, she told herself, to do with his colour; it was simply his attitude. He had, as far as she was concerned, no manners.

'Now, Mr Parry,' James began in his friendly yet authoritative manner. 'You say that when you reached your car, Mr Gardiner came out at you. Is that right?'

Parry looked out from the witness box with a mixture of antagonism, disdain and nonchalance. 'Yeah.'

Marjorie Kavanagh shuddered. Definitely no manners. She still wasn't sure where her son's brains had come from, but manners were something she and her husband, Alf, had instilled into him from an early age. And look where that had got him.

'And,' continued her son, 'Mr Gardiner said—' here he looked at his notes, ' "I'm going to do you." Is that so?'

'Yeah.'

Marjorie exchanged a meaningful look with her husband. Neither of them had warmed to Parry or Gardiner, and it went unspoken that they would like to see both of them found guilty. Still, that was impossible.

The case had been brought by The Crown Prosecution Service, accusing Gardiner of beating up Parry and knifing him in a dark car park. And prosecuting counsel had already put forward a fairly convincing case that Gardiner had indeed stabbed Parry in an unprovoked assault. Kavanagh, defending Gardiner, was going to have an uphill job.

'It was very sporting of Mr Gardiner,' he continued, 'to give you fair warning. But then, he's a sporting man, isn't he? A boxer, in fact.'

Parry looked down his nose. 'So they say.'

Kavanagh ignored the sarcasm. 'Do you know what a Southpaw is, Mr Parry?'

Parry, taken aback by the unexpected question, looked up in surprise. ''S a fighter who leads with his right.'

Kavanagh nodded. 'Now, did Mr Gardiner have the knife in his hand at this point?'

'Yeah.'

'In which hand?'

2

'His right.'

Kavanagh paused before his next question. Almost involuntarily, both his parents leaned forward. Neither was sure yet where this line of questioning was leading, but both were aware of a subtle change of atmosphere in the court. Clearly their son, with his rapid-fire questions and pregnant pauses, was getting somewhere.

'Are you sure of that?' he asked at length.

Parry shifted uneasily in his seat. 'Yeah. But ... it might've been his left.'

'Well, which one was it?'

Parry avoided Kavanagh's questioning gaze. 'You're trying to confuse me.'

'It's not a difficult question, Mr Parry. Two choices.'

Parry glared back. 'It was hard to tell.'

'Hard to tell left from right?'

'It was very dark.'

'Very dark?' Again Kavanagh looked down at the notes he had made while the opposing barrister had been questioning the witness.

'You told prosecuting counsel that you saw "a flash of something in his hand shining". Now, I take it you didn't mean he was holding a torch?'

'The—'

'Because,' Kavanagh interrupted, 'unless the blade was coated with luminous paint, there's no way you would have seen the glint of a knife, is there, Mr Parry?'

But the witness glared defiantly back. 'That,' he said, 'is what I saw.'

Kavanagh hardly paused as he moved swiftly on to a different line of questioning. 'This so-called car park is little more than a piece of waste ground, isn't it?'

Parry shrugged.

'It has no street lighting whatsoever. That's right,

3

isn't it? It was also, incidentally, the dark of the moon. Is that, perhaps, how you got so terribly lost?'

'Lost?'

'Well, you weren't found by *your* car at all, were you? You were found by Mr Gardiner's vehicle. Some forty yards from your own.'

The sharp intake of breath was clearly audible throughout the court. Marjorie Kavanagh, looking to her right, saw consternation on the police benches in the corner. And as she shifted her gaze to the witness box, she recognized in Parry the haunted look of a trapped animal. 'I don't know how I got there,' he replied weakly.

'Don't you? Let me suggest that it wasn't Mr Gardiner who ambushed you, it was *you* who ambushed *him*.'

Again Parry avoided eye-contact. 'You dunno what you're talking about.'

'How did you come to be by Mr Gardiner's car?'

'It must have been in the tussle.'

'The tussle?' Something told Marjorie Kavanagh that her son was feigning his surprise. The seemingly innocuous, almost irrelevant questions, the carefully studied theatricality of his responses; they were, she knew, all part of the performance. Being a barrister was, in many ways, similar to being an actor. The difference lay in the results: often spectacular, always unexpected.

Parry, now looking distinctly flustered, merely mumbled a 'Yeah' in response.

Kavanagh, for the benefit of the court, infused his voice with a touch of sarcasm. 'So there *was* a tussle now, was there?'

'Yeah. He was trying to get hold of the knife.'

'Which knife?' The question was lightning-quick.

'*My* knife.'

4

'Which hand was it in?'

Instinctively, Parry raised his right hand. 'This one.'

'Your right hand?'

'Yeah.'

'Not your left?'

Parry rolled his eyes. 'No, man, it was in my right hand.'

Then it dawned on him and he opened his mouth in silent horror. The exchange between the two of them had been so instinctive that he hadn't paused for thought. Now, too late, he realized he had well and truly incriminated himself.

James Kavanagh took the words out of his mouth. 'I think the word you're looking for, Mr Parry, is "Oops".' With that, he allowed himself a small smile and sat down. He had so confused Parry with his relentless questions that the latter had quite forgotten the basis of his defence – that the other man had been the one with the knife.

Kavanagh's parents felt like clapping. They, like the astonished jurors sitting on the right of the judge, realized that the rest of the proceedings would be a mere formality. Parry, not quick enough for his opponent, had turned the entire case on its head. Not only had he all but admitted that he was the guilty party, he had, when being questioned by prosecuting counsel, perjured himself. He wouldn't, they reckoned, be brandishing knives in car parks for some time to come.

Half an hour later, the jury had unanimously found Parry guilty, a delighted Gardiner had been vindicated, the prosecuting counsel had departed with a rueful look at his adversary, and the case was over. For the court professionals, it was all in a day's work. For the elder Kavanaghs, it was yet another indication of just how different their son's life was from their own. They had never moved from Bolton, the Lancashire town where they had raised their three children. Their eldest son, on the other hand, had always shown signs of going places.

Yet while his lifestyle was different, his personality remained unchanged. While his years of living in London had given him wealth and sophistication, they had not robbed him of his gentle warmth and his forthright, down-to-earth manner. Even his marriage – 'that' marriage as it had been referred to at the time – had not dislodged him from his roots. Marjorie and Alf, had they ever cared to think about aristocrats, would have considered them to be a species apart. Twenty years ago, they had been in for a rude awakening: they had acquired one as a daughter-in-law. It was strange, thought Alf as he waited in the court lobby for his son, that it was his *other* daughter-in-law who was the roaring snob. And aristocratic Cynthia most certainly was not.

'I thought you were pulling my leg,' he said as his son approached, 'when you said it'd be over by lunch. Didn't think you stood a chance.'

Marjorie shot him a mock-disapproving look. 'We thought you were very good, Jim. I was saying to Dad, wasn't I, that you should do more of your cases up here.'

Kavanagh smiled fondly but didn't reply. It wasn't the first time he'd heard that particular refrain from his mother. And today wasn't the first time he'd taken on a badly paid, low-profile brief just so that he could come north to see his parents.

His father nodded. 'Aye. Home turf.' Then he

frowned slightly and looked at his son. 'How'd you know Gardiner was a Southpaw?'

Kavanagh grinned. 'He isn't.'

'But you said he was!'

'No, Dad. I asked Parry if he knew what a Southpaw was. From then on he thought I knew something he didn't. He was so busy trying to work out what it was, that he stopped listening to what he was saying himself.'

His father gave him a warm look. 'Cheating.'

Again Kavanagh grinned. 'Winning.' Then, putting a hand to his head, he added, 'Look, give me a minute to get out of this fancy dress and then we'll go over to the hotel.'

'Em . . . we've said to Grahame to come.' Alf smiled uncertainly at his son. 'That was all right, wasn't it? Can't come up and not see your brother.'

Kavanagh's hesitation was but brief. 'Sure. It'll be great to see him.' They made eye-contact in mutual understanding. Grahame wasn't the problem. He never was. It was his wife: she never let her husband anywhere near his family unless she, limpet-like, was there as well. Cynthia liked to make her presence felt.

She made her presence felt in a big way over lunch. As usual, she treated her parents-in-law in a slightly off-hand, dismissive manner. The message, as it had been for many years, was that they weren't good enough for her. Her attitude to her brother-in-law, however, was an entirely different matter. She tried at every opportunity to provoke him, to needle him into losing his temper, and, as ever, she made no bones about her dislike for him. Kavanagh, who had always tried to like her for Grahame's sake, could read her like a book. It wasn't dislike that motivated her – it was intense jealousy.

Cynthia had married the wrong man. In Grahame Kavanagh she thought she had found a better-looking version of his older brother; she had assumed that the ambition that had taken James from lower-middle-class Bolton to high-life London was also present in Grahame. Yet to her eternal disappointment, she had watched the smart, funny and attractive young man she married turn into affable and indolent middle age. He had achieved the rank of middle manager in a computer software firm, and, at the age of forty-seven, was unlikely to go any further. The fact that that didn't bother Grahame in the slightest only served to fuel Cynthia's anger and resentment.

The Kavanaghs, and especially James, would have been hugely embarrassed to know that Cynthia's dislike of her brother-in-law and his wife transformed itself into something akin to slavish adoration when she was outwith the family circle. She never missed an opportunity to let slip the fact that Lizzie, James's wife, came from a titled family. 'As dear Lady Probyn told me' was one of her favourite ways of referring to Lizzie's mother whom Cynthia had, in fact, met only a handful of times. She was also in the habit of referring to 'Elizabeth's invitations to her family seat', the intimation being that Lizzie and she were firm friends and that Cynthia was in the habit of hob-nobbing with the aristocracy. She never, however, mentioned that the family seat had never been graced by her presence and that Lizzie and James actually lived in a fairly modest house in Wimbledon.

Cynthia also made mileage out of James's status as a QC. 'It means,' she would say to the puzzled faces that greeted this information, 'that he's a Queen's Counsel. One of the country's most eminent and experienced barristers. You have to have an unblemished record for *at least* fifteen years to become one.' As most people were barely aware of the difference between a solicitor and a barrister, let alone of the finer points of becoming a QC, they would merely nod and silently reflect that however grand James Kavanagh might be, his sister-in-law was even grander in her pretensions.

Yet Cynthia was no fool and it irked her to realize that James and Lizzie's attitude towards her went no further than tolerance. She watched from afar as they raised two good-looking, well-behaved children with apparent ease, as James's career went from strength to strength, and as Lizzie herself began to acquire a reputation as a high-profile and highly professional fund-raiser for charities. Their lives, it seemed to her, were perfect. It had taken her completely by surprise when she had discovered, six months ago, that their domestic situation was in fact nothing of the sort. When the chink in their armour was exposed, Cynthia, with something approaching glee, lost no opportunity to rub salt in the wound.

'And how *is* Elizabeth – now?' she asked her brother-in-law over lunch.

She pursed her lips as Grahame shot her a warning look. James, scarcely pausing, adroitly changed the subject.

Cynthia hadn't been the only one to be astounded when, six months before, Lizzie left her husband. Her departure, seemingly coming out of the blue, was subsequently explained by the fact that she had been having an extramarital affair for months. That affair, so Cynthia had managed to prise out of a reluctant Grahame, had started as a direct result of James's prolonged absences from home due to his almost total absorption in his work. It was a bitter irony lost on no one that Lizzie had met her paramour through her husband and that he was, of all things, a fellow-barrister. Miles Petersham was younger than James, better looking and outwardly more dynamic. He was also madly in love with Lizzie.

Yet Lizzie was not so much crazy about Miles as furious at her husband: the affair, as she herself had realized shortly after leaving her husband to live on her own, had more to do with anger at James than passion for Miles. James himself, belatedly realizing that his zest for work was destroying his personal life, had also arrived at that conclusion, and had made strenuous efforts to woo his wife back. His motivation was increased by the reaction of Matt and Kate, their teenage children, to their mother's departure. They wanted her back. Very badly.

In the end, and after many agonized discussions and tearful recriminations, Miles had been given his marching orders and Lizzie had returned to the fold. Cynthia, who beneath the burdensome weight of her airs and graces was a family person at heart, was glad for her in-laws and for the children in particular. Yet her jealousy proved a difficult monster to tame, and she couldn't help making barbed remarks to the effect that James, however brilliant a barrister, had proved himself a rotten husband. Nor could she stop herself making the odd snide remark about Lizzie. Her sister-in-law, she hinted, was flighty: it came, she explained to a friend, from her unstable mother and her inbred background. The friend had been more than a little alarmed at Cynthia's sudden departure from her allegiance to Lizzie's grand family, and had pressed her for more information. Cynthia, however, had refused to divulge anything further – for the simple reason that she didn't know any more.

10

After the family lunch, Cynthia still remained in a position of ignorance about the state of James's marriage. The subject of Lizzie remained closed throughout the meal, and only afterwards, as they prepared to leave the hotel, could James be drawn on the subject. Yet it was his father, not Cynthia, who mentioned Lizzie. As the men waited in the vestibule while the women fetched their coats, Alf Kavanagh approached his elder son and, in that hesitant yet sincere manner common to people not accustomed to discussing emotions, he asked how 'everything' was.

'Everything's fine, Dad.' James was, in many ways, very like his father. Emotions were things that happened to other people. He was still, after twenty years, finding it difficult to understand that Lizzie, despite her background, thought differently.

'And Lizzie?' asked Alf with what he thought was a meaningful look.

'Yes. Fine.'

'And you?'

James sighed in embarrassed exasperation. 'We're *both* fine.'

'Right. Well. You'd best . . .'

'Yes.' James said nothing more, but his body language told his father that the subject was now firmly closed.

At that moment James's taxi, destined for the airport, drew up in front of them, and the family confidences, such as they had been, came to an end. With handshakes, kisses and a tear from his mother, James made his farewells.

As they sped through the urban sprawl, he reflected that he himself was in much the same position as Cynthia: he knew very little about the present state of his marriage. Lizzie was back – but they still had a long

11

way to go. It was, he felt, like a second courtship. Both of them were slightly wary of each other, still discovering new things about the other, and all too prone to flare into tempers over the most trivial of things. Yet something told him that they were now heading in the right direction – together.

Two hours later, as James emerged from the main concourse of Heathrow's Terminal One, his feelings were confirmed. Among the ranks of taxi-drivers bearing cards with the names of their fares was a very familiar face: a face that still made his heart beat slightly faster every time he saw it. The short brown hair, the elegant arch of the eyebrows above the penetrating blue eyes and the well-defined cheekbones were as familiar to him as his own features. But it was the instantly recognizable smile that affected him most: it suggested mischief. Sure enough, as soon as she saw him, she came forward and held up a cardboard sign with the name 'Kavanagh'.

They exchanged a look more vocal than any words. It was she who broke the silence. In imitation of the taxi-drivers around them, she asked, tentatively and in an unconvincing Cockney accent, if he were Mr Kavanagh.

'Yes, Mrs Kavanagh, I am.'

CHAPTER TWO

'We can't just not go to parties. Especially *this* party.'

'No. True.' James sounded unconvinced.

Lizzie shot him a quizzical look. 'You're not upset, are you, that you didn't accept Head of Chambers?'

'God, no. Lot of bloody nonsense. I don't want to spend any more time than I have to pushing bits of paper about and worrying about how the damned place is run.'

Lizzie didn't reply. She still remained to be convinced that her husband had genuinely *not* wanted to be Head of Chambers. She wondered whether his turning down the post had been a decision prompted by their domestic situation rather than by his own vision of his career. Most senior barristers would jump at the chance. It meant, basically, being the boss. Yet James did have a point about the administrative duties associated with the position. About the only thing barristers had in common with any other profession was that being promoted meant you spent less time doing what you were actually trained to do. And James, she knew, held little truck with titles. Peter Foxcott, also a QC, had accepted the job, yet it was still to James that other people looked for guidance.

Lizzie knew a great deal more about the mysterious organization called the Bar than did Marjorie Kavanagh, but she still marvelled at the almost impenetrable rules, customs and hierarchies with which the profession was riddled. In defiance of her upbringing and her class, she had always been left-wing and, in her younger days, had viewed the Bar in much the same way as she regarded gentlemen's clubs and masonic societies: as arcane, divisive, elitist and hopelessly out of date. It had greatly surprised her, then, when she had met James Kavanagh, a Northern boy with working-class roots and left-wing views, and discovered that he was hell-bent on becoming a barrister or, as it was properly known, being called to the Bar. Initially, and with the fervour of the radical she had been twenty years ago, Lizzie had accused him of wanting to dissociate himself from his origins and attaching himself to the very people who perpetrated Britain's class system. Much to her annoyance, James had put forward a perfectly sensible argument to the effect that the reason why Britain's legal system hadn't changed for so long was because it worked. He had agreed with her that while solicitors came from a variety of backgrounds, barristers were predominantly upper-middle-class. And the only way to change that, he had argued with maddening logic, was from within: for people like him to gain a foothold on the ladder and rise, against the odds, to the top.

And James had certainly had to struggle against the odds. Gaining a law degree was the easiest part. After that, prospective solicitors and barristers parted ways; the former to do their articles at a firm of solicitors, the latter to do the equivalent, known as a pupillage, at a set of chambers. And after twelve months of working on this lowest rung of the ladder – sometimes for nothing, never for much – it was the ambition of every pupil to be taken on as a tenant and thus as a fully fledged barrister at their chambers.

Nowadays, it was less uncommon for people from James's background to qualify as barristers. It was still, however, an uphill task. Apart from the fact that the competition was fierce, dyed-in-the-wool, conservative senior barristers had a habit of looking after their own. If James genuinely didn't want to be head of River Court Chambers, it was, thought Lizzie, all the more admirable, considering where he had come from.

After a moment's silence during which James concentrated on negotiating the heavy commuter traffic, Lizzie spoke again. 'The position was yours by right. You had the earlier call.'

James turned for a moment and looked at her. 'The idea was that we should see more of each other, not less – wasn't it?'

So, thought Lizzie, he *has* made a sacrifice. She caught his eye and smiled. 'Family will come first,' he had said when they first became reconciled. Evidently he was prepared to practise what he preached.

Once more they lapsed into silence – a contented silence – as they drove along the Embankment. A mere two hours after returning from Heathrow, they were on the move again, this time to the party celebrating Peter Foxcott's becoming Head of Chambers. It was the first time for months that they would appear together in front of James's colleagues: and both of them were slightly nervous about it – not least because of one of the other guests. Miles Petersham, while not a member of River Court Chambers, was a friend of Peter Foxcott, and he would undoubtedly be there. Although Lizzie's affair with him had not been widely broadcast, it was known to all James's colleagues. And while neither Lizzie nor James had mentioned Miles, they both instinctively knew what the other was thinking: tonight was going to be both an embarrassment and a trial.

The venue for the party was a riverboat moored on the Thames. Always a scenic location, it only came into its own in summer, when one could walk on the decks and admire the illuminated sights of St Paul's, the Houses of Parliament and other, more architecturally questionable London landmarks. It was not surprising that on walking across the gangplank and on to the boat, the Kavanaghs should see a couple enjoying the balmy night air. It was, however, extremely disconcerting that the couple turned out to be Miles Petersham and an unknown but very beautiful young girl hanging on to his arm and, seemingly, his every word. Lizzie, her heart pounding, caught Miles's eye and then looked away. She tightened her grip on her husband's arm and leaned closer to him as they descended into the bar.

The first person they ran into was Jeremy Aldermarten. 'Elizabeth!' he shouted delightedly as he stepped forward and gave Lizzie a clumsy, rather wet kiss. 'It's been far too long. I think you've been hiding from us.'

Lizzie smiled her mischievous grin. 'From you, perhaps.'

Jeremy roared with laughter. Little do you know, thought Lizzie, that I half meant what I said. Then, looking at him, she chided herself for being so uncharitable. Jeremy Aldermarten was not the sort of person to arouse strong feelings in anyone, and on the rare occasions when Lizzie thought about him, it was with nothing more than mild irritation. The man was harmless. And that, she thought, was his problem. In his early forties, balding but pleasant-looking in an anodyne sort of way, he was also the butt of most of the jokes at River Court Chambers. If anybody was going to put their foot in it, that person would be Jeremy Aldermarten. And if anyone was to cast around looking for a buffoon, they would have to look no further than him. There was no doubt that he always meant well – just as there was no doubt that he always seemed to do rather badly.

'How's the charity business?' he continued when he'd stopped laughing. 'Hearts still bleeding?'

Lizzie, unsure how to take that remark, hesitated. She was saved from having to reply by Peter Foxcott's arrival on the scene. A big man with a booming voice, he tended to dominate every conversation. Lizzie, who like her husband was fond of him, was immensely glad that he looked like dominating this particular one.

'Ah, James! How was Manchester? Natives still painting themselves blue?' Then, as usual not waiting for a reply to his salvo of questions, he turned to Lizzie and beamed. 'Lizzie! How nice to see you.'

'Hello, Peter.' Then, noticing that Peter Foxcott was accompanied by, and rather overshadowing, a tall, elegant and extremely self-assured girl, she smiled even more warmly. 'Hello, Julia.'

Julia Piper returned the smile and the greeting with equal sincerity. At twenty-six, she was nearly twenty years younger than Lizzie, yet the two of them had always got on extremely well on the few occasions they had met since Julia joined River Court three years previously. Julia, in direct contrast to Jeremy Aldermarten, was someone who was clearly destined for great things. Attractive and extremely intelligent, she was the rising star of River Court. She was also the unwilling object of Jeremy's attentions.

'The gang's all here then,' said James to no one in particular as he surveyed the room.

'Oh yes,' agreed Jeremy. 'Quite a few old faces.' He indicated an elderly man at the far end. 'There's dear old Uncle Humpty. Sir Neville's here, of course. And then there's that young Miles Petersham.' He looked around vaguely. 'I'm sure he's here somewhere.'

There was a brief and very loaded silence. It was Julia, quick-witted as ever, who dived in to save the day. 'Jeremy,' she commanded, 'I really do need a hand with the canapés. Will you come and help me?' Without giving him a chance to reply, she grabbed him by the arm and hauled him away. When she was out of earshot of the others, she turned and glared at him. 'Jeremy,' she said with emphasis, 'you really are a total shit.'

Jeremy looked at her in surprise. Had he put his foot in it? he wondered.

An hour later, the party was in full swing as Julia again approached Kavanagh at the bar. 'You'd make a better Head of Chambers than Peter, you know,' she said without preamble. Beating about the bush was a concept alien to Julia.

'I'm sure Peter will do the job admirably.'

'I know – but you'd do it better. You could've dragged River Court into the twentieth century.'

Kavanagh grinned and took a sip of his whisky. 'The nineteenth would be a start.'

Julia was not to be deflected. 'Why didn't you take it?' But Kavanagh was not to be drawn on that one. Again, and with a slight shrug, he smiled at his companion.

'Aldermarten's cock-a-hoop,' she continued with a grimace.

'Well, Jeremy's always pleased to see his friends get on.'

Julia shuddered. 'Dreadful toady.'

'That's no way,' teased Kavanagh, 'to speak of one whose heart you hold in your hand.'

Julia glared at him. 'He just wants to get into my knickers.'

Kavanagh reached for the drinks that the barman had just deposited in front of him. Then he turned back to Julia and grinned. 'Tell him to buy his own. In fact,' he added as he looked over Julia's shoulder, 'you could tell him now.' Swiftly making his escape, he went off to find Lizzie, as Jeremy, now thoroughly inebriated, wove towards Julia.

'Ah, Julia,' he said with what he hoped was a winning smile but was in fact a drunken leer. 'Did I tell you I managed to get hold of tickets for *Don Giovanni*?'

Not for the first time, Julia felt wrong-footed. Trust him, she thought as she looked at Jeremy's eager, flushed face, to hit upon my favourite opera.

Kavanagh, failing to find his wife amongst the throng, decided to try the deck. The night was still warm and, Lizzie or no Lizzie, a breath of fresh air wouldn't go amiss. And anyway, he was getting fed up with holding two glasses. If Lizzie didn't materialize he would just have to drink them both. He grinned to himself as he registered the thought. He only drank a lot when he was happy. Things were obviously looking up.

A minute later the smile was instantly wiped off his face. Lizzie was standing leaning over the balcony rail, evidently lost in a world of her own. Yet Kavanagh, still in the shadows, was just in time to witness her rude awakening by Miles Petersham.

'Hello, Elizabeth,' he said as he sidled up to her.

Kavanagh had to admire his wife's composure as, without taking her eyes off the water below, she replied calmly, 'Go back to the party, Miles.'

'I was just saying hello,' said Miles, peeved.

This time Lizzie looked at him. 'Well, now you can just say goodbye, can't you?'

Miles raised his eyebrows. 'Or what?' he challenged. 'Fisticuffs?'

Before Lizzie had time to reply, Kavanagh was at her side. He looked at Miles without expression. 'Come near her again,' he said, 'and I'll kill you.'

Miles grinned and, in a bad imitation of a broad Yorkshire accent, made a disparaging remark about 'the lad from oop North'.

Neither Lizzie nor Kavanagh replied. Shrugging his elegant shoulders, Miles left them and retreated into the bar.

It was Kavanagh who broke the silence. 'You weren't thinking, were you, that we could shake hands and it would all be water under the bridge?'

Lizzie had in fact been thinking along those lines. 'You were friends once,' she said. 'I can handle it.'

'Well, I can't. Not yet. I'm sorry.'

Lizzie straightened and looked her husband in the eye. 'Jim, it's over. I made *my* choice. Miles is in the past. *I* decided that. It's you I'm with – for always.'

Kavanagh looked at his wife, wishing that he could match her confidence, wishing that he could be as certain as she was that they had finally negotiated the rocks and were sailing full steam ahead.

CHAPTER THREE

In most professions, the term 'clerk' suggests a menial position. The Bar, however, has things differently. A barrister's clerk wields enough power to make or break the barristers themselves: it is he who assigns cases to individual barristers. Someone of James Kavanagh's calibre was sought after on his own merit, rather than on the reputation of his chambers, but for junior barristers – those who hadn't or wouldn't make it to QC – it paid to keep on the right side of the clerks. It was a lesson that Jeremy Aldermarten had yet to learn.

Tom Buckley was the senior clerk at River Court Chambers. Tall, well-built and not to be trifled with, he looked, as Aldermarten had once remarked, like the sort of person to be found at the other end of a pit-bull terrier. But as far as Kavanagh was concerned, Tom Buckley was worth his weight in gold. As well as assigning cases to barristers, clerks had the unenviable task of chasing solicitors to pay barristers' fees. Most solicitors tried to defer payment for as long as possible: when Tom was on the other end of the line, they tended to pay up.

When Kavanagh walked into River Court the morning after the party, Tom was on the telephone. It wasn't difficult to tell that he was in the process of familiarizing some unsuspecting soul with his attitude to late payments. His manner was impeccably polite; his words were not. As Kavanagh nodded a greeting, Tom finished his conversation and, with a satisfied smile, replaced the receiver. 'Morning, sir. Good party?' Then he peered closely at Kavanagh. 'Doesn't look as if it was.'

Kavanagh laughed. Tom judged the success of any party by the severity of the next day's hangover. Kavanagh had no trace of one. 'Good enough, Tom. Good enough.'

'Hmm.' Tom looked unconvinced. Then he looked down at his desk and extracted a file from what looked like the fall-out from a burglary. It was a mystery to everyone else how Tom managed to be so organized when his desk was such a mess.

'I've got something for you here, sir. A new brief.'

'Oh? What is it?'

Tom grinned wryly. 'Oh, it's right up your street, sir. A nice little rape.'

One of Kavanagh's most spectacular cases of recent years had been the successful defence of a well-known public figure accused of rape. The trial had caused a sensation, and the Old Bailey had been packed to the gunwales with both the press and the public. In all the conflicting comments and media gossip about the case, there was only one point on which everyone agreed – Kavanagh didn't stand a chance. He had proved everyone wrong. His client had been acquitted and he himself became something of a public hero for several weeks thereafter.

The case with which Tom Buckley had just presented him would, he hoped, have a lower profile. Kavanagh hated the muck-raking aspect of trials that the press so relished. To him, it was a necessary evil, not a topic for general conversation and public dissection.

As he read through the papers he realized that, once again, this case would have the press panting. The man accused of rape was David Armstrong, the student son of the founder and chairman of Armstrong Chemicals. Jock Armstrong was always in the news. Vociferous and combative, he was, as he was fond of telling the world, a self-made man who stopped at nothing to get what he wanted in business. Kavanagh wondered if his son was cast in the same mould: if he had wanted to have sex with one Eve Kendall and had refused to take 'no' for an answer.

Eve Kendall, the complainant, was wealthy, middle-class and married. A housewife who worked part-time in a bookshop, she had been at home overseeing the construction of a swimming-pool in the substantial garden of the Kendall family home. And David Armstrong, together with a builder called Gary Porter, had been preparing the foundations for that pool. David, so Kavanagh read, was simply doing the job to supplement his allowance during the long vacation. A Cambridge education and a millionaire father indicated that he was destined for great things in life. On the other hand, if he was found guilty of raping Eve Kendall, his career was going to be severely curtailed.

After reading the brief, Kavanagh phoned through to Julia Piper in the office next to him. Tom had said he would be leading her in the defence, and that she was already well-briefed on the case.

'Julia? Have you got a moment to come and talk about this Armstrong thing?'

'Sure,' came her friendly voice down the line. 'Give me ten minutes.'

She entered his office, almost exactly ten minutes

later, looking, as was necessary in chambers, rather more demure than she had the previous night. Then, she had been wearing a mini-skirt and a brightly patterned jacket. Today she was wearing a black suit and white blouse. Yet, being Julia, she managed to lend the severe attire a fashionable bent. Her skirt, Kavanagh noted, was a great deal shorter than was the norm. He rather approved of that: he was one of the few male barristers who joined their female counterparts in thinking the dress codes for court completely archaic. Yet judges were all-powerful within the private domain of their courts and they were quite within their rights to expel a barrister for being improperly dressed. And as some judges, relics from a bygone age, still quivered with indignation at the very existence of female barristers, it was most definitely not politic to antagonize them by flaunting femininity.

Kavanagh smiled at Julia and indicated the seat opposite him. 'Tell me,' he said, 'what you know about the case. Have you met the boy?'

'Briefly. Nice. Middle-class. Very good-looking as well. Should come across well to the jury.'

'Mmm.' Kavanagh, after all his years at the Bar, still had conflicting thoughts about the vital role that PR played in the defence or prosecution of an individual. From the barrister's point of view when preparing the case, guilty or not guilty was not the issue. The exception to that was if a defendant who was going to plead not guilty told the barrister defending them that he or she actually *was* guilty, then the barrister, 'professionally embarrassed', would have to step down and a replacement would be found. Otherwise, the entire business of defending or prosecuting was about convincing juries rather than about justice.

Kavanagh looked down at his notes for a moment. 'His father's something, isn't he?'

Julia grimaced. 'Yes. Armstrong Chemicals.' Then, rapidly changing tack, she smiled. 'If there's one certainty about this case, it's that money won't be an issue. He'll spend everything he's got to prove his darling son's innocence. And he's got millions.'

'Try telling that to Tom,' said Kavanagh drily. Then he leaned back in his chair. 'Anyway, tell me what you know.'

The story, or at least the version of events as related by Eve Kendall, was simple enough. David Armstrong, Eve claimed, had raped her one hot day in June after she had invited him into the house for a beer and a sandwich at lunchtime. His fellow-builder Gary Porter had, at some point in the morning, been called away on another job, leaving David and Eve Kendall alone at the property. There were therefore no witnesses. But nor was there any doubt that sexual intercourse had occurred. For one thing, Eve Kendall's husband had returned home that evening to find his wife in a state of hysterical collapse and had taken her to hospital, where a full examination had been made. For another thing, David didn't deny that he had had sex with Eve. Yet he vehemently denied that he had raped her. *His* story was that she had seduced him and that, being a hot-blooded twenty-one-year-old, he had been unable to resist.

Kavanagh looked at Julia after she had recounted the basic elements of the story. While they exchanged no words, they both knew what the other was thinking: this was going to be an uphill challenge. Juries tended to sympathize with middle-class housewives more than with arrogant youths, regardless of how good-looking or well-mannered they were. Still, as yet they had only the bare bones of the story. There was a great deal more to learn.

'Jock Armstrong,' said Julia, 'is pushing his solicitor for a meeting with us this afternoon. Shall I arrange it?'

'Yes. Best to get on with this as soon as possible.'

'OK.' Julia stood up and looked at her watch. 'You won't forget that you've got the pupillage conference in half an hour, will you?'

'Oh God.' Kavanagh *had* forgotten. One of the benefits of being a QC was that one no longer had to take a pupil under one's wing. He looked imploringly at Julia. 'Do they really need me there?'

'Yes. It's Jeremy's pupil. He's only seen the CVs so far but he's already shortlisted to two.' She paused for emphasis. 'And they're both female.'

'Ah.' There was no need to say any more. They both knew that Jeremy Aldermarten's criteria for the selection of pupils – of female pupils – had very little to do with academic qualifications or finding a face that fitted. He was only interested in the length of leg, the marital status (single, preferably) and the possibility of extending the boundaries of the pupil–master relationship. And for Julia Piper there was an extra – very worrying – dimension to this particular choice. One of the two shortlisted candidates was an old friend from school.

As Kavanagh and Julia were winding up their preparations for the meeting with the Armstrongs, Jeremy Aldermarten was already in Peter Foxcott's office, anxious to put forward his case before the others arrived.

'They're both highly promising, of course,' he was

26

saying. 'But I really think Alexandra Wilson has the edge. Cambridge double first.'

'And the other?'

Aldermarten frowned. 'Glenda Evans.' Aldermarten, thought Foxcott, had obviously decided that anyone called Glenda would not be suitable for River Court. 'Red-brick university. But very good for all that,' he added charitably.

Foxcott was silent for a moment. 'Who would Kavanagh go for?'

'That's not relevant. You're Head of Chambers.'

Foxcott shrugged. 'More by default.'

'Nonsense.' Aldermarten wasn't going to let Foxcott be swayed by what Kavanagh might think.

'No,' continued Foxcott, 'I might have the title, but it's still Kavanagh people look to for advice. However, if I can make my mark with the pupil intake . . . set the tone in chambers. D'you see?'

Aldermarten did see. Foxcott, while bearing no animosity whatsoever towards Kavanagh, wanted to make sure his choice would be different. 'Well,' he said, 'Kavanagh will push for the red-brick. Glenda. Wimmin's issues written all over her.' Warming to his theme, he hurried on. 'Bound to be. Battered wives breast-feeding all over the place. The smell of smoking D-cups assailing our noses.' He leaned forward in his chair. 'I don't think we want that, do we?'

There wasn't, thought Foxcott, much he could say to that. And neither was there the opportunity. As soon as Aldermarten finished speaking, the door opened and Kavanagh walked in. Before he closed the door, the other two had a chance to see the two smartly dressed women sitting nervously in the hallway. The candidates had arrived.

'Ah, James,' said Aldermarten, quickly recovering

his composure. 'We've been waiting for you.' He inclined his head in the direction of the hall. 'Do you have any thoughts?' From his brief glimpse of the candidates, his suspicions about Glenda Evans had been confirmed – and had deepened. She was black.

'Well, Julia's just shown me their letters. I must say, I thought Wilson's was the better.'

'Did you?' Aldermarten was astonished. 'Well, that does surprise me.' He smiled. 'Coming from you. You didn't prefer the . . . the, er, you know . . . red-brick?'

'No, I didn't. And of course, it must go on merit. I understand Ms Piper's also very keen on Wilson.'

'Is she? Is she really? Quite. Quite.' He hadn't expected victory to be quite this easy. With a satisfied smile, he stood up and went to the door. He opened it with a theatrical flourish and looked squarely at the white applicant. 'Miss Wilson? Would you come in, please?'

After a brief pause, Alexandra Wilson stood up. Tall, elegant and self-assured, she came forward and extended one perfectly manicured hand to the dumbstruck Aldermarten. It was all he could do to return a mumbled greeting. Alexandra Wilson was the black candidate.

She was also, it soon transpired, by far the more suitable; and Jeremy Aldermarten remained uncharacteristically quiet during the interviews with both girls.

After the two meetings he sought out Julia Piper. 'I've just seen Miss Wilson,' he said.

'Alex?' Julia deliberately affected nonchalance. 'Oh yes?'

'Very personable, I thought.'

'Did you?' Julia was fighting hard not to giggle.

'Peter,' continued Aldermarten, 'is not quite so keen, but, er . . . he can, of course, be a little stuffy.'

He hesitated. 'I naturally said that it must go on merit and,' he shrugged, 'well, my voice does carry some weight in these matters.'

Feeling distinctly uncomfortable by now, he added, 'Friend of yours, is she?'

'From school, yes.'

'Popular girl, I'd imagine. Very vivacious.'

Piper grinned. 'Oh yes. The whole dorm had the most frightful crushes on Alex.' That was a lie: day-schools didn't have dorms, but she was enjoying this quiet torture of Jeremy Aldermarten. He was, she noticed, positively squirming now.

'Yes,' he said. 'Did you . . . did they? I mean, well . . . um. Quite. Yes.'

Julia, in silent stitches, suddenly had a brainwave. 'What's the situation vis-à-vis those tickets for *Don Giovanni*?'

Aldermarten, glad that she had changed the subject, was pleasantly surprised that she still seemed keen on the idea of the opera. She hadn't exactly been over-whelmed with enthusiasm last night. 'Oh,' he said. 'I, er . . . I didn't think you were . . .'

'Well, I was thinking, you see, that perhaps we could make it a threesome. I know Alex is a big fan.'

'Is she?' This, for Aldermarten, was really too much for one morning. 'Yes . . . well, I'm sure something could be . . .' He trailed off and then, finally getting a grip on his conflicting emotions, he leaned forward. 'You know, the more I think . . . yes, the more I think, I think . . . I really do that she'd do very well at River Court, don't you? Certainly bring some much needed colour to chambers.'

'So it's a deal, then?'

'What?'

'*Don Giovanni*.'

'Oh! Well, yes. Yes. Absolutely. In fact, I'll just go and find out if I can get another ticket.' With one last and now quite genuine smile at his colleague, he bustled out of the room.

'Prat,' said Julia to the closed door.

CHAPTER FOUR

Jock Armstrong arrived at River Court Chambers that afternoon with his son David and Fiona Marshall, David's solicitor. It quickly became apparent to Kavanagh and Julia that Armstrong senior thought the presence of both son and solicitor something of an irrelevance. This was a man who was used to dealing with everything on his own terms and, they wouldn't doubt, always getting his own way. To Kavanagh in particular, the latter consideration carried with it an extra dimension. For Jock to have his own way – to get his son acquitted of the accusation of rape – he would have to rely on Kavanagh's performance in court. And that performance was going to prove a strain: the junior prosecuting counsel acting for Eve Kendall was, so Kavanagh had discovered earlier in the afternoon, none other than Miles Petersham.

As they talked through David's version of the events at the Kendall household, Julia found herself increasingly fascinated by both father and son. Armstrong was clearly of the opinion that everything his son did was right: so much so that if David had admitted raping Eve Kendall he would somehow have managed to find a justification for that rape. Julia found it difficult to conceal her dislike for the man.

David, however, was an entirely different matter. He was, thought Julia, an extremely attractive young man and if, as he claimed, Eve Kendall had deliberately set about seducing him, then Julia really couldn't blame her. Either David was an expert liar or he really was charming, gentle and honest, if a little naïve. He also, she knew from her first meeting with him, had a steady girlfriend; the equally attractive, personable and well-bred Sophie. That Sophie was prepared to stand by him spoke volumes about their relationship: no self-respecting girl would cover for a rapist. The impression the Armstrong clan were giving was that they couldn't blame poor, frustrated Eve Kendall for seducing David, nor could they blame David for capitulating. He was a healthy young man, and Eve, although twenty years his senior, was a handsome woman. The whole episode had been regrettable, and all the more so because Eve, plagued with guilt about her husband, was trying to absolve herself by crying rape. Kavanagh, Jock Armstrong implied, would easily sort the whole thing out.

Kavanagh wished it was as simple as that. As David described what had happened that day and went into the background of the whole story, Kavanagh, as was his custom, was mentally calculating both the strengths and the weaknesses of David's argument. There were, he thought, rather more of the latter.

'The police surgeon's report', he said as David finished talking, 'goes on to mention bruising to Mrs Kendall's face. Can you suggest how she might have come by those injuries?'

'No.' David looked expressionlessly at him. 'No, I'm afraid I can't.'

'In the statement you made to the police,' continued Kavanagh, 'you said that she'd asked you to be rough with her.'

'But not to hit her.' David sounded genuinely horrified. 'I wouldn't have even if she'd asked me to. It's just . . . the idea is . . . I mean, it's repugnant.'

'All right. Don't worry.' Kavanagh went back to his notes. 'The surgeon,' he continued after a moment, 'also notes some chafing to her wrists?'

David squirmed in his seat, opened his mouth to reply, and then clearly thought better of it.

'Ms Piper and I,' said Kavanagh gently, 'aren't here to make any judgement on you, David. Moral or otherwise.'

David then looked him in the eye. 'She asked me to pin her arms down.'

'Mmm. Was her shirt on or off during intercourse?'
'Off.'
'Who removed it?'
'She did.'
'Right.' Kavanagh wrote something on the pad in front of him. 'Did you engage in much foreplay?'

'No. It was a bit wham-bam – but that's how she wanted it.' He shrugged apologetically. 'I can't say we made love. It was just sex.'

'Yes. I see.'

David, clearly feeling awkward, leaned forward over the desk. 'Look, I know this sounds . . . well . . . but you will go easy on her, won't you? I think she's a nice woman – basically.'

At that his father snorted derisively. 'This nice woman has just accused you of rape, David.' He looked in disgust at Kavanagh. 'I've tried to tell him, Mr Kavanagh.'

Kavanagh wondered privately just what else Jock Armstrong had tried to tell his son. Yet before he could reply David turned and tried to remonstrate with his father. 'Dad, she's got problems . . .'

That was too much for Jock. He put his hands in

the air in an irritated gesture of mock-defeat. 'Oh well, then, plead guilty, why don't you? You'll save me a fortune in fees.'

Ignoring his outburst, Kavanagh addressed David again. 'What sort of problems?'

But it was the hitherto silent solicitor, Fiona Marshall, who replied. 'Her husband's having an affair. A stock-controller with his firm. Our enquiries suggest it was going on at the time we're concerned with.'

Jock Armstrong looked at her in appreciation. 'And the thing with the other lad, don't forget. Christopher Roberts.'

Kavanagh and Julia looked at each other. Neither had a clue what the father was talking about. He noticed the look and added, as if to enlighten them, 'He's the feller at the bookshop where Eve Kendall worked part-time.'

'I'm not entirely sure,' said Kavanagh coolly, 'what you're getting at.'

'Well, she had an affair with him, didn't she? That's what the manager of the bookshop said. Roberts,' he added, 'wouldn't talk to the agent I hired to make enquiries. But I'm sure if things were made clear, he could be persuaded to go to court.'

Several warning bells rang in Kavanagh's head. Jock Armstrong had obviously hired a private detective to 'further his son's case'. Any information gleaned from him would, they both knew, only serve to complicate the issue further. And Jock Armstrong himself, it was clear, needed to be taught a few lessons.

Kavanagh put down his pen and looked across the desk at his clients. 'All right, let's just pause there for a moment. Our defence – and I want us to be crystal-clear about this – is that she consented to intercourse . . .'

'Correct,' said Jock.

'So – how do we feel that introducing this Roberts would help us with that? With consent?'

Jock thought the answer to that was obvious. 'He's a young lad – like David. He could show her up for what she is. I mean, if she's done it before—'

'Perhaps,' interrupted Kavanagh with barely concealed irritation, 'I'm not making the point well enough. Let's say – and remember this is hearsay – that Mrs Kendall had an affair, that she was consenting to intercourse with Christopher Roberts. How does that go towards confirming she consented to having sex with David?'

'Well, it's . . .'

'Say a wife consents to intercourse with her husband,' continued Kavanagh. 'Is she, by that, consenting to sex with any man?'

'Well . . . no.'

Kavanagh looked Jock Armstrong straight in the eye. 'Exactly. No. We have to be very careful not to muddy the waters in any way. As far as the court is concerned, Mrs Kendall's sexual conduct with anyone other than the accused is held to be irrelevant.'

'What?' Jock was outraged.

'It's called rape shield,' interjected Julia. 'And the prosecution also can't go for us in a similar fashion.'

'We could apply for leave to introduce such evidence,' said Kavanagh, 'but only insofar as it relates to this case.'

'I don't follow you.' Jock, not used to this sort of rebuttal, was looking distinctly annoyed.

'It would have to be something specific,' explained Kavanagh. 'If, for example, David had green hair and we could show that she had a string of liaisons with men with green hair . . . Believe me,' he finished, 'we're on much firmer ground with consent.'

There was a brief silence as both father and son digested that information. 'Am I', asked David at length, 'going to be asked to go into detail about the er . . . intercourse?'

'Are you worried about that?'

'Well, yes. Not for any . . . I mean, it's . . . it's embarrassing.'

'God Almighty!' roared his father. 'You're charged with *rape*, David. Of course they're going to ask you the details.'

'Look, Dad, it's me who . . .'

'*They're* not going to be bloody coy about it, are they?'

'I think,' said Kavanagh mildly, 'that David needs our support and reassurance at this time, Mr Armstrong. Not . . . well, really, this doesn't help, you know.'

David looked at Kavanagh with grateful understanding. 'It's Sophie, you see, Mr Kavanagh. My girlfriend. She'll have to hear . . .'

'Can't you ask her to stay away?'

'No. She wants everyone to know she's sticking by me.'

'Well. What d'you make of him?'

Julia Piper, walking beside Kavanagh as they left River Court an hour later, grimaced in distaste. 'I think his old man's an ocean-going shit. Should imagine he's a total bully in the boardroom.'

'And in the bedroom?'

Julia looked thoughtfully at her colleague. 'Like father, like son? Hardly. No. I thought David was . . .

36

Well, he's really going through it, isn't he? Can't be easy for him.'

David Armstrong, thought Kavanagh, certainly knew how to bowl them over.

'What'll you go for with Mrs Kendall?' Julia asked. 'Tit for tat? Getting back at hubby?'

'Mmm. But why, then, cry rape?'

'Perhaps she thought it might shake him up.'

'Bit extreme, isn't it?'

'I don't know. Perhaps it's a touch of the "You've neglected me and see what happened".'

'You think so?' Kavanagh didn't sound too convinced.

'A little guilt goes a long way.'

'Yes.' Kavanagh looked thoughtful. 'I suppose it does.'

They were silent for a moment as they approached their respective cars. 'Well,' said Julia as she fished for her keys, 'we've got the weekend to think it over.'

Kavanagh looked at her to see if she was serious. Her impish grin told him she wasn't. 'Quite. What're you doing – apart, that is, from worrying about the Armstrongs?'

'Oh, this and that.' Julia was notoriously coy about her private life. 'And you?'

'Down to the country. Lizzie's father's been doing the "Goodness, it's been a long time" bit. Anyway, kill two birds with one stone. Haven't been on the boat for ages either.'

Julia looked at him in surprise. Kavanagh's elderly Nicholson Sloop, she knew, was one of his grand passions. Things must have been difficult at home if he hadn't been able to indulge it for some time. She reached her car and raised a hand in salute. 'Well, have fun.'

'You too. See you on Monday.' With that, Kavanagh

went over to his own car – and back to his own thoughts. He wished Julia hadn't mentioned the word guilt. Since the meeting with Miles the previous evening, all his old doubts about the state of his marriage had resurfaced; all his feelings of guilt about not noticing the cracks in his relationship with Lizzie had returned. While he believed her when she said her affair with Miles was well and truly over, the afternoon with David Armstrong had unsettled him in more ways than one.

He had been acutely aware of the effect that David had had on Julia: he was younger than her, conveyed a lethal mixture of charm and vulnerability, and was very good-looking to boot. The parallels between that scenario and Miles Petersham's relationship with his own wife were all too startlingly obvious. Lost in thought, he turned out on to the Embankment and began the long commuter-locked drive to Wimbledon.

The house was ominously quiet when Kavanagh let himself in three-quarters of an hour later. The day before, on his return from the airport, Matt had been noisily playing a computer game in the drawing-room while Kate had been in her customary pose: curled round the telephone making the sort of social arrangements that her father still found alarmingly sophisticated for a seventeen-year-old. Neither of his children had paid him much attention: a brief, friendly smile had been his lot. But today the house appeared to have been invaded by something altogether more threatening. Silence.

He went into the drawing-room and looked, puzzled, at the blank television.

'What's wrong?' Lizzie, having heard the car, came into the room to greet her husband.

James turned round and smiled at his wife. 'No loud music? No Super Mario Lanza on the TV? Don't tell me the kids've been repossessed.'

Lizzie laughed. 'They've gone down to Dad's with Luke.'

'Luke?'

'Kate's Luke.'

'Oh. Kate's Luke.'

Lizzie went up to Kavanagh and put her arms round his neck. 'You look as if you've just had a limb amputated, my darling. They're not *married*. He's just her boyfriend. It happens, you know.'

Kavanagh grinned. 'Yes. I s'pose it does. It's just that I thought they were all coming down with us tomorrow.'

'They were.'

'Oh.'

'But now they're not.'

'Oh.'

Lizzie was aware that her husband was looking at her in a most peculiar way. 'What is it?' she asked gently.

'Nothing.'

'Jim . . .'

'Am I . . . well, I mean . . .' Kavanagh, embarrassed, trailed off into silence.

'Are you what?'

'I'm, er, not . . . *boring* . . . am I?'

'No.'

'You're sure? You're not bored? With me? With, um . . .' Kaleidoscopic visions of David Armstrong and Eve Kendall, of Lizzie and Miles disturbed his train of thought.

'No.' Lizzie was adamant. And deadly serious.

'Good.' He looked back at her in silent, relieved understanding. 'Good.'

Lizzie walked towards the corner of the room and turned her attention to the half-wrapped present sitting on the table. Part of the reason for this weekend's visit, Kavanagh now remembered, was Lizzie's father's birthday. 'What's brought this on?' she asked.

'Oh. Nothing. Nothing. No. Good.' Visions of the bumbling Jeremy Aldermarten suddenly leaped out at him. He straightened himself and walked briskly towards the drinks cabinet. 'So,' he asked in a different, positive voice, 'what have you cooked for me tea, then?'

Lizzie looked as if she had been hit. She turned round, ready to launch into angry invective. Then she noticed his teasing expression and grinned. 'Actually, since we're the only hungry mouths to feed, I rather thought we could let someone else do it for us.'

'What a very good idea.' James made for the telephone. 'Shall I see if we can get a table at Nino's?'

'I already have.'

CHAPTER FIVE

The family seat about which Cynthia Kavanagh claimed to be so knowledgeable was even larger and grander than the mansion she had built in her mind. Durford House had been built in the reign of Queen Anne, added to throughout successive centuries and was, James had once calculated in an uncustomary moment of spiteful glee, thirty-five times the size of Cynthia's own house. When James himself had first set eyes on it, he had assumed Lizzie had been joking. 'Nobody's father,' he said, 'lives in grandeur like this.'

But Lord Probyn did – and all alone save for his housekeeper. Mrs Hunter, cast in the Cynthia mould, was always on the point of leaving because she found the house 'impossible'. She found Lord Probyn equally impossible, yet she was also inordinately fond of him. The two of them enjoyed a relationship that would have destroyed lesser individuals years ago: while they would have balked at the use of first names, they didn't bat an eyelid about sometimes being quite astonishingly rude to each other. Yet the real reason why they got on so well was because they were both lonely. Mrs Hunter was a widow and Lord Probyn had, for years, been separated from a wife who – if Mrs Hunter were to be believed – preferred young men and gin to her husband or even, she suspected, to her only daughter.

Lord Probyn often affected uninterest when his family came to visit – only because he was too proud to admit that he counted every second until their arrival. Lizzie, of course, knew this, and it was for that reason she had sent Matt, Kate and the increasingly limpet-like Luke to Durford on Friday instead of Saturday. Her father, she knew, doted on his grandchildren and they, likewise, adored him. Even fifteen-year-old Matt, normally bored rigid by adults unless they happened to be called Arnold Schwarzenegger, relished his grandfather's company.

There was, however, another reason why Lizzie had engineered the weekend that way. While James admired Lord Probyn, he often found the older man's company extremely trying. Ted Probyn was a dyed-in-the-wool Conservative and he enjoyed teasing both his daughter and his son-in-law about their allegiance to the Labour Party. While they generally accepted that in good part, it was his other pet subject that really irritated Kavanagh. His father-in-law never stopped asking him when he was going to go to the bench, or, in layman's terms, become a judge. While Kavanagh had the ability to be a judge, it was not part of his game-plan. What had drawn him to the Bar in the first place, and what still motivated him, was the drama of the combat on the court floor. The isolation of a judge's life, the fact that it would remove him from where he felt he belonged, held no appeal for him. Lord Probyn, however, was not impressed. As far as he was concerned, the whole point of a career was that you started at the bottom and then went right to the very top.

Lizzie could read her husband's mind as they turned into the gateway of Durford House. As they approached the final bend of the drive, she covered his hand with her own. 'C'mon,' she urged, 'it gets better.'

42

Kavanagh looked at her with a wry smile. 'Yes. When we leave.'

Two minutes later, they were out of the car and surrounded by barking dogs, their children and, loitering in the background, a teenager who seemed unable to decide if he was Lord Byron or James Dean. So that, thought Kavanagh, is Luke. What a mess.

'Good run?' asked Matt as he took his mother's suitcase.

'Two hours.'

Matt was unimpressed. 'Should've put your foot down.'

Kavanagh cuffed him playfully on the head. 'Yes. With you. Firmly and years ago.'

Kate, for once shy, sidled up to her father, the poet-rebel in tow. 'Er, this is . . .'

Jim smiled and extended his hand. 'Luke, isn't it? Pleased to meet you. James Kavanagh.'

Luke, without grace, returned the gesture. 'Yeah,' he said, 'I know.'

At that moment Lord Probyn, with a spry step that belied his seventy years, came out of the house. He went up to his daughter, kissed her fondly and, with a twinkle in his eye, turned to Kavanagh. 'I see you've brought that no-hoper of a husband with you again. About time he made it to the Bench, isn't it?'

Lizzie laughed and hit him gently on the arm. 'Happy birthday, you fraudulent old bugger. When're you going to hurry up and die . . .'

'The day you vote Tory.'

Lizzie laughed again. She put an affectionate arm through her father's and walked with him into the house.

Behind them, Kate, still ill-at-ease, caught her father

looking at the loitering Luke. 'He's nice,' she said tentatively.

'Yes.'

'Once you get to know him.'

'I'm sure.'

Kate, with a placatory smile, then turned and went over to Luke. In a curiously intimate manner, she tugged at his arm – and at her father's heart. Kavanagh, alone beside the car, felt that something had been lost for ever.

The rest of the day, however, passed pleasantly enough. Both Kavanagh and Lizzie were pleased to escape the still-humid London autumn; Lord Probyn delightedly showed them both around the grounds which, he insisted, were looking much better than they had last time. To Kavanagh, they looked exactly as they had always done, yet he was aware that that was not the point. The object of the exercise was the undercurrents swirling beneath the gardening conversation. Lord and Lady Probyn were fiercely competitive for their family's affections. The latter, James knew, had recently taken to gardening in a big and highly successful way. It was therefore par for the course that her estranged husband should try to do the same thing – only more successfully. The whole thing was, he reflected, extremely pathetic and deeply sad. It would be awful, he thought with a sudden pang and a covert glance at his wife, to spend one's old age on one's own.

It wasn't until they were gathered round the dinner-table that Kavanagh had a chance to further his acquaintance with Luke. He must, he told himself, try to like the boy. To alienate him would be to alienate Kate – and that was the last thing he wanted. If his daughter was blessed with her mother's looks, she was cursed with her father's more volatile temperament. It wouldn't do, Kavanagh thought, to get on the wrong side of her. But Luke, with the arrogance of youth, appeared oblivious of any social niceties – and overburdened with opinions. His studies of English literature made him, he reckoned, an expert on everything – and everyone.

' "A society of men," ' he was now quoting, ' "bred up from their youth in the art of proving by words multiplied for the purpose that white is black and black is white according to how they are paid." Isn't that how Swift described your profession?'

Kavanagh couldn't help being impressed. 'I won't argue with my bread and butter.'

But that only made Luke see red. 'Come on, if you know some guy's a murderer, how can you still defend him?'

Lord Probyn was delighted. 'We've got a budding radical amongst us,' he chuckled. Then, addressing Luke but with a nod in his son-in-law's direction, he added, 'He used to be like that once, you know. Wouldn't think it to look at him now. But once upon a time . . .'

'I know it's your birthday, Ted,' said Kavanagh irritably, 'but do we have to?'

'Lord Probyn to you,' replied Ted with an impish grin. 'Bloody proles. That's how they met, you know, Luke. In court. Back in the swinging sixties.'

Luke twirled his earring and announced, with authority, that the sixties had been a much overrated decade. 'We did it,' he explained, 'in the fifth form.'

'When were you born, as a matter of interest?' asked

Kavanagh, who had just noticed his daughter's doe-eyed expression.

'Seventy-seven. My mum and dad were punks.'

'Ah. Heredity.'

Lizzie, listening with amusement, stifled a giggle, drawing herself to her father's attention. 'Madam here,' he said, 'was – what was it, dear – women's rights?'

'Pro-abortion lobby,' corrected Lizzie, deliberately not rising to the bait.

Lord Probyn snorted. 'Ended up in the dock with the sisters. Breach of the peace. Some damned rally or other. Then up pops the radical barrister—'

'The starving barrister,' interjected Kavanagh with a grin. 'I'd have taken anything then.'

'. . . rides to the rescue on his white charger. All charges dismissed.' Again Lord Probyn snorted in mock disgust. 'Wacky baccy and free jiggity-jig all round, one would imagine. Love at first sight, she said. Humph! And did you know – until a week before the wedding, he hadn't a clue about me,' here Lord Probyn waved an excitable hand around the grand, ornately gilded room, 'about all this—'

'I knew all I needed to,' interrupted Kavanagh.

Lord Probyn, now fully in his stride, turned to him. 'Oh, spare us the Patience Strong, or else I shall hurl.'

Matt, who loved seeing his grandfather in full spate, didn't want the show to stop. 'Party on, Garth,' he said to Lord Probyn.

'Party on, Wayne,' replied the older man with glee.

'Oh God,' said Kavanagh to Lizzie, 'I knew it was a mistake to let him have cable TV.'

Luke, despite his pretensions to worldliness, was finally lost for words.

The next day it was Kavanagh who, while they were all out in his beloved boat, was nearly dumbstruck.

'Dad.' Kate, gazelle-like, sidled up to her father.

'Mmm.'

'Luke and I . . . well, we were thinking . . . would it be all right if I brought him along to watch you at work?'

Kavanagh tried to hide his astonishment. 'Of course. You don't even have to ask.'

Kate smiled, pecked her father on the cheek, and then retreated to the prow of the boat where her hapless boyfriend, in a most un-Byronic manner, was throwing up over the side. Well, thought Kavanagh, I wonder what I did to earn that little piece of respect?

CHAPTER SIX

'David Robert Armstrong, you are charged that on the
twenty-third of June last, at 38 Fairmile Road, London
SW19, you did rape Eveline Marie Kendall, contrary to
Section One of the Sexual Offences Act 1956. How do
you plead? Guilty or not guilty?'

David Armstrong rose to his full height and
addressed the Clerk of the Court. 'Not guilty.'

Kavanagh turned to look at Julia behind him and
whispered, 'Eyes down for a full house.'

It was indeed a full house. The public gallery was
crammed to overflowing and the court itself seemed
even fuller than usual. Perhaps, reflected Kavanagh, it
was because of the power of the personalities involved.
On the bench, hawk-like, sat the dreaded Judge Granville. Tom Buckley had tried to make a joke about the
fact that one of the most disapproving and reactionary
members of the Bench was presiding over the case.
The joke had backfired. Granville was known for his
extreme views on rape: he regarded it as a hanging
offence and, as some members of the Bar had been
known to whisper, he was probably not aware that hanging had been abolished.

Kavanagh's opposite number, gowned and bewigged
like himself, sat near him. The female of the species,
it was said, was deadlier than the male, and Eleanor
Harker QC was one of the deadliest opponents of all.

A tall, attractive yet slightly severe-looking woman in her early forties, she was, like Kavanagh, one of the most capable criminal barristers in the country. Yet it was her junior who made his presence most felt to Kavanagh. He could almost feel Miles Petersham's eyes boring into the back of his head. He found it extremely disconcerting. If there was one thing he was determined should not happen, it was to let this case spill over into some sort of personal vendetta between himself and Petersham.

Kate, in the gallery with Luke, was unaware that Petersham was even in the court. She knew of her mother's affair, yet she had never met the man involved. Her father thought it was just as well: the last thing he wanted was for Petersham to cast his spell over his nubile daughter. But now, since the advent of Luke, that was extremely unlikely. If there was one thing to be said in Luke's favour, it was that he rendered Kate oblivious to the existence of any other man.

Kate watched Eleanor Harker make an opening speech to the jury in which she stated her intentions of making a case 'without prejudice' that would present the jury with all the facts, after which they would have to decide for themselves if David Armstrong was guilty – or not – of raping Eveline Kendall on the said date. Then her father made a speech which sounded remarkably similar, except that he declared his intention of proving Armstrong's innocence. Kate looked with interest at the members of the jury. 'Twelve men good and true,' she remembered from her history books – except five of this lot, she was glad to see, were women. Still, she thought, they were a pretty motley crew. Three of them were already looking completely baffled while another three looked bored sick. From the little Kate knew of her father's profession, she had decided she was unsure of the ability of a jury to reach a proper decision. What did they know, she thought, of the wiles and the tricks employed by barristers; of the subtle ways they tried to influence their audience and – although they would vehemently deny it – their witnesses? Kate knew that 'leading' questions were not allowed when questioning witnesses. This piece of information she had imparted, with great authority, to Luke, who had immediately asked her for an example of one. Not entirely sure of what constituted 'leading', she whispered for him to wait and see.

It was not until later in the afternoon that, from a spectator's point of view, things began to get interesting. Eve Kendall, accompanied by prurient gazes and an expectant hush, was called to the witness stand. She was, thought Kate, quite an attractive woman; probably of much the same age as her mother, yet far less assertive in her bearing. It took Eve several minutes to get over her stage-fright and into her stride. Harker, conducting her examination-in-chief, steered her expertly through the proceedings and, eventually, towards the crux of the matter. Kate leaned forward in her seat as Eve, gently prompted by Harker, began to talk about the afternoon in question.

'I had been weeding – in the garden. It was a very hot day. Mr Armstrong was also working in the garden. It was coming up to lunchtime. I asked him if he would like a beer.'

'Why was that?'

Eve looked surprised. 'I thought he might appreciate

a drink. I was going to have something myself. I didn't want to be impolite.'

'And how did he respond?'

'He said that would be very nice – or something along those lines.'

Harker paused for a moment. 'I see. And did you bring him a beer?'

'No. He came into the kitchen for it.'

'He came into the kitchen. Was that at your invitation?'

'Yes.' Eve looked up in wide-eyed innocence. 'I said I was making a sandwich for myself and could make him one too – if he was hungry. So he came to the house.'

'So, in offering him something to eat and drink, you were merely being thoughtful?'

Luke, rather to Kate's irritation, leaned towards her and whispered, 'That must be a leading question.' At the same time, Kate saw her father lean towards Harker. While he didn't actually voice an objection, his expression indicated that the question was, in fact, out of order. It was, his look implied, up to the jury to decide for themselves if Eve Kendall was a thoughtful woman.

Harker noted the look and, with a brief smile, acknowledged it. 'Sorry.' Then, turning back to Eve, she continued, 'Mrs Kendall, why did you invite David Armstrong into your house?'

'To provide him with food and drink.'

'Did you trust him?'

Eve looked thoughtfully at David Armstrong. He was sitting expressionlessly at the back of the court, accompanied by a police officer, and behind a half-height glass partition. 'I had no cause not to. He was

51

quiet. Well-spoken. I knew he was a student – doing the pool for a summer job. I never thought—'

'Yes.' Harker interrupted her client in mid-flow. 'As I understand, since he'd been in your employ, his manner towards you had been consistently polite and respectful. Is that right?'

'Yes.'

'So, he came to the house. Where were you?'

'We were in the kitchen.'

'In the kitchen. Could you tell us, please, what happened next?'

'We were talking. I . . . er – he ate a sandwich. And we were talking.' Eve, again, was beginning to show signs of distress. Even though Eleanor Harker was on her side, even though they had gone over the questions Eleanor would ask her, answering them for the benefit of the court was both different and unpleasant. 'Then, er . . . I . . . he reached over and – touched my face.'

'He touched your face?'

'Yes.'

'How? In what way?'

'The palm of his hand.' Eve, raising a hand to her face, imitated the gesture. 'On my cheek.'

'What did you do?' asked Harker with a hint of sympathy.

'I said, "Don't" or "Stop".'

'You said to him, "Don't" or "Stop". What did you mean by that?'

Kate and Luke exchanged a look. This, they thought, was going painfully slowly. But then, as they looked at the expressions of the members of the jury, they realized what was happening. Harker, by forcing Eve to relive the experience, was painting a picture of a kind, trusting woman whose trust had been betrayed in the most brutal way.

'I wanted him,' replied Eve, 'to stop touching my face.'

'Did Mr Armstrong remove his hand?'

'No.'

'What did he do?'

'He . . . er . . . he said I was lovely.'

'Lovely?' Harker let that sink in for a moment. 'Yes. And then?'

'And then he put an arm round my waist and pulled me towards him.'

'What did you do?'

'I tried to pull away from him. It was . . . I was embarrassed. And . . . I was starting to feel frightened.' Kate looked across the court at the jury. The elderly woman who had at first looked bored was now glaring in disgust at David Armstrong.

'You tried to pull away from him,' repeated Harker. '*Did* you pull away from him?'

'No. He's very strong.'

'Too strong for you to push him away?'

'Yes.'

'I see. Go on.'

Eve took a deep breath. 'He pressed . . . my bottom – pushing me against him. Then . . . then he said, "Feel that. That's for you." '

'What was he referring to?'

Eve looked down at her feet. 'He was referring to his penis.' This time all the female members of the jury looked at Armstrong.

'And what did you do,' continued Harker after a moment's pause, 'when Mr Armstrong said, "Feel that, that's for you"?'

'I didn't know what to do.' Eve's voice rose to a wail as she continued. 'I was shocked. I pushed my hands against his chest. I said, I think, "Stop it. Now." '

'You said, "Stop it. Now." *How* did you say it?'

Eve looked straight at Armstrong as she replied.

'Forcefully.'

Kavanagh, hearing this, allowed himself a small smile. It was, he suspected, a word that Harker had hinted to her client.

Harker shot him an irritated glance and then looked back at Eve. 'You were adamant?'

'Yes. I wanted him to stop.'

'Was there anything about those words, or the way you said them, which could have been misunderstood by Mr Armstrong?'

This time it was Kavanagh who looked irritated. He turned to his opponent. 'You're leading,' he said in a quiet yet firm tone. Judge Granville, noticing the exchange, nodded in agreement.

Harker looked towards the bench. 'I apologize, Your Honour.' Then, again turning to Eve, she continued her questioning.

'Did you make it plain, Mrs Kendall – as far as you were aware – that you wanted Mr Armstrong to stop?'

'Yes.'

'And did Mr Armstrong stop?'

'No. He said, "I know what you want . . . and I'm going to give it to you." '

'What did you take that to mean?'

In the public gallery, Luke nudged Kate and grinned.

'Sex,' replied Eve in a small voice.

'*Did* you want sex with Mr Armstrong?'

'No!'

'Had you given Mr Armstrong any cause to believe you wanted sex with him?'

Kavanagh, again, was irritated by his opponent's question. He looked at her, drummed his pen on the pad in front of him, and tutted. Judge Granville, however, was more irritated by Kavanagh's reaction than Harker's question. 'If you have a problem, Mr Kavanagh, or are concerned about the way questions are being put, perhaps you'd stand up and tell me about it.'

Kavanagh dutifully rose to his feet. 'Your Honour, I do apologize, of course . . .'

'And please refrain from fidgeting. It's most disconcerting for those of us trying to follow the evidence.'

'As Your Honour pleases.' Kavanagh, duly chastised, sat down again. His daughter grinned as she looked at him. It was strange, and rather amusing, to see her father being treated like a naughty schoolboy.

Granville then looked at the defence counsel. 'Miss Harker. Please continue.'

'I'm obliged, Your Honour. Mrs Kendall, did you flirt with Mr Armstrong?'

'No.'

'No. Very well, go on.'

'He removed . . . he took his hand away from my face and started to touch my breasts.'

'What did you do?'

'I said, "Please, David. Don't." '

'Again you were asking him to stop?'

'Yes. But he tried to pull my shirt open and—'

Again Harker, bent on her task of establishing David Armstrong as a monster, stalled her client. 'He tried to pull your shirt open,' she repeated. 'Did you make any attempt to stop him opening your shirt? Physically, I mean.'

'I . . . I tried to hold my shirt together. To keep it closed.'

'And what happened?'

Eve took a deep breath and looked Harker straight in the eye. 'He hit me.'

Harker didn't reply at first. She wanted the words to sink in; wanted the jury to be fully aware of their impact. Then she repeated them in a flat tone: 'He hit you.' After another, briefer pause, she added, 'Where?'

Eve raised her hand again. 'Across the face. Quite hard.' She flinched. 'And then he said, "Stop it. You're spoiling it." '

'What did you do?'

'I . . . I froze. I was scared. I didn't know what he would do.'

The eldest woman juror extracted a handkerchief from her bag and dabbed at her eyes.

'What happened then?' asked Harker.

'He pulled me through into the hall – by the wrist – and told me to lie down – on the floor.'

Kavanagh, evidently finding that point important, turned to Julia behind him and whispered urgently to her.

'And did you?' asked Harker.

Eve bit her lip. She didn't want to reply, didn't want the jury to misconstrue her answer.

Judge Granville gave her a moment and then leaned forward and, in a sympathetic, avuncular manner, looked towards the witness box. 'Please answer the question, Mrs Kendall.'

'Yes,' said Eve.

'You were in the hall?' continued Harker.

'Yes.'

'Yes. Could you tell the court where you stood in relation to Mr Armstrong and the front door?'

'He was between me and the door.'

Again Harker, willing the jury to form a picture in their minds, repeated the words. Then she addressed Eve once more. 'What were you thinking at the time?'

'I'm not conscious I was thinking anything.' Eve

twisted her hands in front of her. 'Not rational thoughts, anyway. I was very afraid. I thought he might kill me. His eyes were – they weren't looking right.' She paused and took a deep breath. 'I didn't want to die.'

Kate, to her consternation and even greater surprise, felt tears welling. Angrily, she wiped her face with her sleeve. This, she thought, was getting rather horrid. Eve Kendall, only a few feet away from her in the witness box, was by now a pitiful sight.

'Did you at any time,' continued Harker, 'call for help?'

'I couldn't,' wailed Eve. 'I couldn't catch my breath. I thought . . . if I did what he wanted, I'd be all right . . . that he wouldn't hurt me.'

Harker's face was now a picture of concern as she looked at her client. 'What did you do?'

'I lay on the floor and . . . and Armstrong got on top of me . . . and . . . and . . .' Unable to continue, Eve bowed her head and sniffed loudly. Her hands, fumbling for a handkerchief, seemed to have lost their co-ordination and her shoulders slumped in weary defeat. She looked utterly desolate, completely alone. Again Kate found herself blinking fiercely as she fought to contain her own tears. Then, as suddenly as she had bent her head, Eve raised it and, with tears trickling down her face, looked straight at David Armstrong. 'He raped me.'

Although the members of the jury had known what was coming, they were all taken aback by the ferocity of her words. Some of them flinched; all of them looked appalled – even guilty – at witnessing this woman being reduced before their eyes. Eve herself, unable to muster any more self-control, started to sob; great heaving, silent cries that racked her whole body.

Harker, after remaining silent in order to let the entire court witness the scene before them, asked her if she would like a glass of water. Eve, her face now hidden in front of her, shook her head.

Then Harker looked at Judge Granville. If he was moved by the scene before him, he wasn't showing it. He was, however, aware of Eve's distress.

'Will the witness,' he asked Harker, 'be able to continue if we adjourn for a while, Ms Harker?'

Harker, very pointedly, looked at the court clock. Everyone else followed her gaze. It was ten to four. Then Harker looked imploringly up at Granville. 'Perhaps, in view of the hour, Your Honour . . .?'

Granville needed no prompting. 'Yes. Very well, I think that might be best.' He picked up the papers in front of him, looked to his right, and began to rise. 'Until tomorrow morning, then, members of the jury.'

The court usher leaped to her feet. 'All rise,' she commanded. A collective sigh of relief washed through the court as everyone stood in acknowledgement of the judge's departure. Then Harker, no longer bound by etiquette to stand in her place, went over to the witness box. Julia Piper, clearly put out at the abrupt ending of the session, leaned forward to Kavanagh. 'Bloody hell,' she whispered. 'She opens the floodgates and Granville goes for it hook, line and sinker.' She nodded in the direction of the jury. 'And *they're* going to go home with "He raped me" ringing in their ears.'

Kavanagh, however, was more sanguine. 'Give them half an hour, Jools, and they'll have other things to think about.' He grinned. 'Like what's for tea and how long it's going to take them to get home.'

'Humph.' Julia was unimpressed – and unconvinced. 'I just hope our defence is good enough.'

'So do I,' said a voice behind them.

Kavanagh and Piper turned in surprise: they had both forgotten about Miles Petersham, acting as Eleanor Harker's junior. 'I suppose,' he continued, 'your defence is consent.' Then, with a particularly piercing look at Kavanagh, he added, 'The old ones are always the best, isn't that right, Jim?' With a swagger, and before the other had a chance to reply, he walked out of the court.

'What a pity,' said Kavanagh as he watched him leave, 'that Miles isn't leading the prosecution. I actually *like* Eleanor Harker; and they say . . .'

' . . . that a good old dog-fight between rivals always gets the best results,' finished Julia.

Kavanagh looked slightly sheepish. 'What do you say,' he asked, 'that we do tomorrow's briefing and then I'll treat you to an Indian?'

'Is that an offer of a meal, or something rather more exotic?'

CHAPTER SEVEN

It was an offer that Kavanagh would live to regret. Not because there was anything wrong with what they ate – but because they shouldn't have been eating it in the first place. While they were tucking into their curry, Lizzie Kavanagh was looking at her watch with increasing frequency – and increasing irritation. This evening was one of the most important events in her fund-raising calendar, and she had worked extremely hard to ensure that it all went without a hitch.

She stood in the middle of the art gallery, silently cursing while trying to keep a smile on her face. The pictures around her were stark black and white photographs of life in the underbelly of London. If the people who were milling around her in the smart Mayfair gallery were expecting to see pretty still-lifes or Post-Modernist masters, then they were in for a rude awakening. The charity for which Lizzie worked had one aim and one aim only: to increase and administer the funds of a trust set up to help sick and needy children worldwide. And her latest idea had been to show prospective donors exactly the sort of people the trust helped. The photographs were not pretty. They were not meant to be.

An overdressed, middle-aged woman with violently

painted nails and an unwisely short skirt sidled up to Lizzie and looked with distaste at the photograph behind her. 'A bit grim, isn't it?'

Lizzie mustered a smile. 'It was taken,' she explained, 'at Temple Underground Station where . . .'

' . . . where lots of beggars hang out,' finished the woman.

Lizzie wanted to hit her. Instead she smiled sweetly. 'If you want to contribute, you don't actually have to buy a picture. The photographs are primarily to raise awareness, but . . .'

'Oh, I think we're *aware*, aren't we?' With the triumphant smile of a self-styled do-gooder, the woman turned to her husband. 'We're very aware of the world around us, aren't we, dear?'

'Oh yes,' said the dear, who was evidently cast in the same mould as his wife, 'but you don't want to be aware all the time, do you?'

Lizzie gritted her teeth. Where the hell, she asked herself, is he? She was useless at this sort of thing; at being charming to people whom she instinctively loathed. James, on the other hand, was brilliant at it. But James, who had promised on pain of death that he would attend, was noticeable only by his absence.

The man looked at the photograph, seemingly lost in contemplation. 'Temple,' he said at length. 'That's where your husband works, isn't it?' He smiled brightly at Lizzie. 'I must say I'm looking forward to meeting him. Will you let me know,' he added after a brief glance at his watch, 'when he arrives?'

Lizzie could only nod as the couple walked off. As they disappeared into the throng at the bar, she registered the opening of the door and the arrival of more people. She turned, a hopeful, expectant smile replacing her earlier frown.

She found herself smiling at Miles. He, also smiling, walked straight up to her and kissed her on the cheek. Then he stepped back, looked at her admiringly, and pulled a crumpled invitation from his breast-pocket. 'You did,' he announced, 'give me an invitation.'

'But that was . . .'

'I know. Don't be mad.' Then he moved closer and grabbed her arm. 'Look, I had to come. Can we talk somewhere?' He gestured wildly at the walls. 'I'll *buy* one of your pictures. Just give me five minutes.'

To her intense annoyance, Lizzie found that her heart was beating faster. 'What for?' she asked.

'I miss you.'

Damn you, thought Lizzie. Bugger you. Why must you always catch me feeling like this? She tried to avoid his eyes.

'It's finished.'

'Just like that?' Miles's voice was too loud. Lizzie was sure heads were beginning to turn. 'Don't I get a say in the matter?'

'No. No you don't.' Desperate to get rid of him, to get herself out of an increasingly embarrassing situation, Lizzie started to propel him towards the door. 'You must go. Jim's about to come.'

'You're just staying for the kids, aren't you?' Miles, although evidently prepared to leave the premises, was not going without a fight. 'You don't love him, do you?'

'Yes. I do.' The force of her conviction surprised her. 'Now, please. You can see I'm up to my neck.'

They were at the entrance of the gallery now. Lizzie reached forward and held the door open for Miles. 'I'm just trying,' he said, 'to sort things out. What's more important, me or your bloody homeless?'

Lizzie's expression was answer enough.

'I thought,' persisted Miles in a wounded tone, 'I meant something to you.'

'So you did,' replied Lizzie. 'Once.'

She didn't know how she got through the rest of the evening. Miles had upset her more than she cared to admit, and as a result she knew she had been less than charming to the very people she was supposed to impress. She received fewer donations than she expected; only a handful of the photographs were bought and, infinitely worse, she was acutely aware of several muttered conversations along the lines of 'Oh, didn't you *know* their marriage was in trouble?' James's complete failure to turn up only served to lend credibility to the gossip. By the time she ushered the stragglers out at half-past ten, Lizzie was exhausted and very, very angry.

'I'm really sorry,' said a breathless voice behind her as she dimmed the lights. She turned, startled, and stared at her husband. He was carrying his pilot's case, his hair was dishevelled, and his raincoat, badly in need of a clean, was hanging off one shoulder. 'I forgot,' he rasped. 'What can I say?'

'How about,' said Lizzie with icy calm, ' "it's you and the kids – all the way"?'

Kavanagh looked as if he had been hit. 'I know. I know. Look . . .'

'You said you'd be here.'

'It slipped my mind.' Kavanagh tried a tentative smile.

'When you've got a meeting with a client it doesn't slip your mind.' Lizzie glared at her husband. 'I only ask you to do one thing – and you forget.'

'All right. I'm sorry. I'll be at the next.'

'No!' The smiles were only serving to fuel Lizzie's anger; she was almost shouting now. 'That's no good.'

'Why not?'

'I didn't want you to be here for being here's sake. Look, I know you hate these things as much as I hate your bloody chambers dos—'

'Then—'

'But,' continued Lizzie, 'there were people I wanted you to meet. Important people. They won't be at the next one, Jim. I've been trying to crack them for a donation. You could've made all the difference. Just five minutes with you . . .'

'I've said I'm sorry.'

Lizzie's expression implied that still wasn't good enough. Then she dug the knife in. 'Even Miles remembered.'

'*What?*'

'I mentioned it to him in passing four months back. I reminded you this morning.'

They were standing only two feet apart, but the distance between them seemed infinitely greater.

'My mind,' said Kavanagh icily, 'is on this case. What do you mean, anyway? He came here? Tonight?'

'Yes. He came here. Tonight.'

'Why?'

Lizzie shrugged. 'He values my work.'

'*I* value your work!'

'Obviously.'

Kavanagh sighed in exasperation. 'I do. Of course I do.' Then, more to himself than to his wife, he added, 'That bastard came here. I don't believe it.'

Lizzie ignored him. She fished in her handbag for the keys to the gallery and fiddled again with the light switch. 'Where have you been, anyway?'

'I went for a quick drink with Jools.'

'A quick drink? It's half-past ten.'

'We . . . er, we ended up going for an Indian. I've got to eat.'

Lizzie stared at him. 'It's starting again, isn't it?' she said quietly.

'No.'

'Me or the job, Jim. You can't have it both ways.'

That was too much. 'Nor can you,' he snapped. 'Have I ever – *ever* – complained about the time you put into *your* work? The times you're away, or late home? Times *I've* needed you? It can't all,' he finished, 'be a one-way street.'

Lizzie was more than a little taken aback by his outburst.

'You said . . .'

'No. That stops here and now. No more "I said" or "You promised". That's no basis for anything. I am trying, Lizzie, but I'm not spending the rest of my days walking on egg-shells.' His face was deadly serious as he added, 'We start with a clean sheet or else we just knock it on the head. Well?'

Lizzie stared at him for a moment. She had been about to remind him of what he had 'promised' and 'said'; but now she realized he was right. He had never once complained about her job – and she didn't want him treading on egg-shells for the rest of their married life. A life that she wanted to continue.

CHAPTER EIGHT

Kate looked with interest at the pretty girl who, seconds before the court session began, slipped into the public gallery and into the row behind her and Luke. She knew the girl wasn't David Armstrong's girlfriend. She, along with Jock Armstrong, was sitting, as she had done yesterday, in the front row, making a very public display of support for David. Probably, Kate mused, a university pal of David's; or perhaps a friend of Eve Kendall's. Maybe even a member of the public who got a kick out of going to trials. Kate couldn't blame her if it was the latter: this was certainly good theatre. Then, as the court usher told them to rise for Judge Granville, she lost interest in the new arrival. The second act was about to begin.

After the formalities of beginning a new day, Eleanor Harker rose to continue her examination-in-chief. Eve had recovered her composure after yesterday's outburst, but she was, thought Kate, looking paler and decidedly more apprehensive.

'Did you, Mrs Kendall, resist Mr Armstrong?'

'Yes. As much as I could. When I realized it wasn't any use, I covered my eyes, but he took me by the wrists and pinned my hands above my head. I shut my eyes, but he told me to open them.' She spoke the words with a certain awed detachment, as if she were describing something that had happened to someone other than herself.

'The rape itself,' continued Harker. 'How long did it go on for?'

'I don't know. I remember thinking . . . I thought it would be quick, but it seemed like it went on for ever.' She lowered both her head and her voice as she added, 'It was very painful.'

Harker allowed a brief pause before continuing. 'What happened when it was over?'

'Armstrong left.'

'Did he say anything to you?'

'He wanted me not to tell anyone. He said no one would believe someone like him would go for someone like me.' Eve flinched as she spoke the painful words. 'Then he laughed.'

'He laughed,' repeated Harker. Then, without another word, she looked, searchingly and at length, straight at the jury. And then she sat down.

Kate's heart began to race as her father stood up, bowed slightly to the judge, and began his cross-examination of Eve.

'Mr Armstrong,' he said, 'had been working on building this swimming-pool at your house for about three weeks, hadn't he?' The expression on his face was kind and open; his stance was unthreatening and the question itself was delivered in a friendly manner. He could, for all the world, have been a friend of Eve's.

She smiled at him. 'About that, yes.'

'About three weeks.' Then he looked down at his notes. 'In June. It was rather a good June, wasn't it? Weatherwise?'

'Yes. Yes, I suppose it was.'

'As I understand it, both Mr Armstrong and his

workmate, Mr Porter, had come along on all of those days?'

'Yes.'

'And they'd arrive at about eight-thirty to begin work. Is that right?'

'Yes, that's right.'

'And would they work through till lunch, or would they stop for coffee, or—'

Eve, slightly flustered at the increasing speed of Kavanagh's questions, interrupted him. 'They'd stop for coffee. At about eleven.'

'Yes.' Again he looked down at his notes before continuing, 'There's a sandwich bar about five minutes up the road from your house, isn't there?'

'Yes.'

'They'd go there, would they?'

'No. One or the other would go and fetch the coffee.'

Kate, from her vantage-point in the gallery, looked round the court. Most people in the room were looking bored. The judge, she noted with amusement, looked as if he was having difficulty keeping awake. Even Eve Kendall herself seemed uninterested in the questions she was being asked. Yet, as with Eleanor Harker's questions yesterday, these were evidently leading somewhere.

'And at lunchtime, as I understand it,' continued Kavanagh, 'the two men would eat in the shade of the trees at that far end of your garden, wouldn't they?'

'Yes.' Eve, suddenly, was looking wary.

'Mr Armstrong had a yellow rucksack he'd bring his lunch in, didn't he?'

'Yes. Yes. I think so.'

Kavanagh leaned back for a moment and looked at the jury, silently urging them to digest that information.

Then he turned back to Eve. 'On the days leading up to the one we're concerned with, Mr Armstrong and Mr Porter had worked together and been there all day, hadn't they?'

'Yes.'

'There'd never been just one of them there on his own, had there?'

'No.'

'On this particular day, as I understand it, there was a telephone call. Mr Porter was called away. Is that right?'

'Yes.'

'What time was that?'

'After their coffee break. About half-past eleven.'

'Mmm. About half-past eleven. So, there was about ninety minutes between the telephone call and lunch. Is that right?'

Eve looked at him as if he were stupid. 'Yes.'

Suddenly Kavanagh changed tack. 'When the men were working in your garden, you'd go out there sometimes, would you?'

'Yes.'

'In fact, you'd been out there earlier that morning. Before Mr Porter's phone call.' Again he looked down at his notes. 'You'd been hanging out the washing, is that right?'

Eve nodded. 'Yes. I had been hanging out the washing.'

'And when you were hanging out this washing, Mrs Kendall, you were, as I understand it, wearing a shirt and a pair of jeans. Is that correct?'

'Yes.'

In the gallery, Kate and Luke exchanged a puzzled look. So did some of the members of the jury. This was

69

all old ground. Surely Eleanor Harker had covered it all yesterday?

Kavanagh paused again, looked at the jury, and changed tack once more. 'Now, why was it that on this day, you invited Mr Armstrong in for lunch?'

'As I said, I thought it would be rude to prepare something for myself and not offer him something also. Not to share it.'

'But he had his own lunch, didn't he?'

'No . . . well, I didn't *know* whether he did.'

With quiet deliberation, Kavanagh reminded her that she'd just told the court about the yellow rucksack. There was an audible intake of breath from both the public gallery and the members of the jury. Eve, realizing the position she was now in, looked trapped.

'So every day for, how long was it, three weeks, he'd been having his lunch in the shade of the trees and you chose this day to ask him in?'

'Well . . . yes . . .'

'Despite the fact he had his own lunch?'

Eve bowed her head. 'Yes.'

'Why did you choose *this* day?'

'Well, it was hot. I thought a drink . . .'

But Kavanagh, relentlessly, pushed home his advantage. 'Was it because there'd been a phone call for Mr Porter?'

'What do you mean?'

'Well, Mr Porter had been called away, hadn't he?'

At that point, one of the women jurors shot Kavanagh a thoroughly nasty look. It was the same woman who yesterday had been reduced to tears by Eve's display of emotion.

'Yes,' replied Eve. 'He had.'

'He hadn't been called away before, had he?'

'No.'

'So, this was the first day that Mr Armstrong had been there on his own, wasn't it?'

Kate silently urged her father to be quiet, to desist from torturing the poor woman. He had, she felt, made his point abundantly clear.

But Eve was obliged to reply. 'Yes,' she sighed.

'Is that a coincidence?'

'Er . . . I don't know what . . . I wasn't always there when they were doing the swimming-pool. Mr Porter may have been absent before – or Mr Armstrong. I simply don't know. I work, you see . . . I worked part-time in a bookshop—'

'Yes,' interrupted Kavanagh. 'Of course. We'll come to the bookshop in a moment, but if we can just deal with this. I'm asking why this – the first time you had been alone at the house with Mr Armstrong – was the first time you invited him in for lunch.'

Eve shrugged. 'I don't know. I just did.'

Kavanagh nodded. 'You just did.' Then he looked at her again. 'Because this was also the day, wasn't it, that you'd rung up the bookshop to say you wouldn't be in for work. Is that right?'

This was the first time the jury had been made aware of that fact. All twelve of them looked with new interest towards the witness box.

'Yes,' said Eve, 'it was.'

'What time was that?'

'I'm not sure.'

'Well, was it before or after Mr Porter was called away?'

'Before.'

'Before? Are you sure of that?'

'I think so.'

'Why were you not going into work as usual?'

'Because I had a severe headache.'

'When,' continued Kavanagh, 'did this start? Before or after Mr Porter's departure?'

'I woke up with it and it had been getting worse all morning.'

Kavanagh nodded sympathetically. 'Yes. I believe you described it in your statement to the police as "a migraine", did you not?'

'I may have.'

Kavanagh picked up the piece of paper in front of him. 'I have in front of me the statement you made to the police, Mrs Kendall. You told them you had – in your own words – "called in sick with a migraine".'

Eve glared at him. 'If it's in my statement – then that's what I said.'

Kavanagh stopped for a moment and rearranged the papers in his file. Kate suspected nothing needed rearranging: her father was just making sure that the jury had properly digested all the information.

'Now,' he said with a friendly smile, 'let's move on to the house, Mrs Kendall. You've said that Mr Armstrong raped you in the hall.'

'Yes.'

'You asked him into the kitchen, didn't you?'

'Yes.'

'He could have raped you there, couldn't he?'

'There was nowhere to lie down.'

'Nowhere to lie down?' Kavanagh looked at her in surprise. 'The floor of the kitchen would have done just as well for his purposes as that of the hall, wouldn't it – if he was intent on raping you?'

'I . . . I don't know.'

'You don't know?'

'I was pushing him away,' said Eve with vigour. 'Somehow we ended up in the hall.'

'Somehow? Is the hall adjacent to the kitchen?'

'No. It's through the lounge. . . . But . . . but he had me by the arms.'

'He had you by the arms?'

Eve nodded and, in illustration, raised her hands to her biceps. 'Gripping here,' she said, 'pushing me back into the hall.'

Kavanagh quickly turned to Julia Piper behind him. She, equally quickly, handed him a notepad. 'You told my learned friend,' he continued, 'that Mr Armstrong had you by the wrists. "He pulled me by the wrist", you said. Which was it, Mrs Kendall, arms or wrist?'

Eve, showing both arms and wrists, gestured in exasperation. 'That was later. When we reached the hall and he pushed me down on to the floor.'

Kavanagh frowned. 'Were your arms bruised, Mrs Kendall?'

'My . . .'

'Yes. If Mr Armstrong had gripped your arms in a manner such as you've demonstrated, one might reasonably expect them to be bruised. Were they?'

'They hurt for some time afterwards.'

'Were they bruised?'

'They had red marks where . . .'

'Were they bruised?'

Eve gave up. 'I don't know,' she answered feebly.

'So, as you would have it, Mr Armstrong, intent on rape, ignores the kitchen, ignores the lounge and presses on through to the hall where he pushes you down to the floor. Is that right?'

Eve nodded. 'Yes. Pinning down my wrists.'

'I see. He's let go of the bicep area now, has he?'

Kate, at that moment, was torn between wanting to cheer her father and wanting to hit him. Suddenly, it all seemed so unfair; as if Eve Kendall had walked into a tiger's lair rather than a court of justice.

'Yes,' mumbled Eve.

'Was it you who removed your jeans, then?'

'No.'

'Oh. Perhaps you can explain to the court how Mr Armstrong managed to remove them while simultaneously pinning your wrists to the ground?'

'I wasn't wearing jeans.'

'I'm sorry? I'm not sure the court heard that.' The court, of course, had heard every word – and was riveted.

'I'd changed,' explained Eve, 'into a skirt.'

'You'd changed into a skirt. Yes. You had, hadn't you? I was coming to that in a moment, but – let's deal with it now. Why did you change?'

'For weeding the borders. In the garden. Jeans were too hot for that sort of work.'

'You were wearing them to hang out the washing.'

'That,' said Eve with a defiant nod, 'was earlier.'

'Before Mr Porter was called away?'

'Yes, but . . .' Too late, Eve saw the trap.

'So you changed into a skirt after Mr Porter had left. Is that right?'

'Yes.'

'How soon after?'

'Perhaps half an hour. I don't recall.'

'So half an hour after Mr Porter left, you changed into a skirt to weed the garden? Is that right?'

'Yes.'

'And, as you told prosecuting counsel, you drank two bottles of beer at lunchtime?'

Most of the court, including Eve, looked surprised at the different line of questioning. Only Eleanor Harker and Miles Petersham looked as if they knew what was coming.

'Yes,' said Eve. 'That's right. I did.'

'Did working in the hot sun and drinking alcohol improve your migraine?'

Those of the jury who had forgotten about the migraine now recalled it – with a great deal less sympathy than before.

'I was feeling better by the time I started work in the garden.'

'Within ninety minutes, a migraine headache – so severe that it prevented you from attending work – had cleared?'

'Yes.'

Kavanagh paused for so long that Judge Granville leaned forward to admonish him. But just as he opened his mouth, Kavanagh resumed his questioning. 'You also told counsel that Mr Armstrong pulled open your shirt. Is that right?'

'Yes. He pulled it open in the kitchen.'

'Pulled it open,' mused Kavanagh. 'Was it not buttoned?'

'I had it tied at the waist.'

'No buttons done up whatsoever?'

'Yes. One or two, perhaps. I can't remember.'

'One or two. Then Mr Armstrong must have pulled at your shirt with some force to get these buttons off and break a knot. Is that right?'

Eve shifted uncomfortably. 'Yes. Well, I don't remember clearly.'

'Were the buttons torn off?'

'I've told you! I can't remember.'

Kavanagh turned to address the court usher. 'Could the witness be shown exhibit C, please?'

The usher rose and went towards the table in the corner of the court. She picked up an evidence bag from the neatly arranged objects on it, and went over to Eve.

'Would you be so good,' continued Kavanagh, 'as to examine that exhibit? Do you recognize it?'

'It's the shirt I was wearing that day.'

'Could you take it out of the bag?' He waited until Eve, with an expression of profound distaste, had extracted it from the bag. 'Are there any buttons missing, Mrs Kendall?'

'No.'

'Any rips or tears?'

'No.'

'It's not damaged in any way at all. *You* took it off, didn't you?'

Eve looked at him in horror. 'No, I didn't.'

'You took it off because you wanted to have sex with David Armstrong . . .'

'That's not true . . . !'

' . . . and you had sex with David Armstrong because you wanted to get back at your husband. Isn't that the truth of the matter?'

'No!'

'Your husband was having an affair at the time, wasn't he, Mrs Kendall?'

'Yes, but . . .'

'And you had quarrelled with him that morning?'

'We'd had words.'

'What sort of words?'

'A row. Of sorts.'

'A row. Of sorts. Mrs Kendall, isn't the truth of this matter that you had sex with David Armstrong of your own free will in an attempt to pay back your husband for his infidelity?'

'No.'

But Kavanagh, with not a trace of the friendly manner in which he had begun his cross-examination, pressed on. 'There was no migraine, was there? You manufactured this headache as an excuse not to go to work, because you wanted to spend the afternoon having sex with David Armstrong.'

'No. No. No!'

'And then, regretting your action – fearing your husband's anger, perhaps, or to provoke his sympathy – you concocted this rape allegation.'

'No.'

'David Armstrong had made it clear to you that there would be no repeat performance, hadn't he?'

'No.' Eve's answers were barely audible now. Her head was bowed and she looked miserable, defeated, and utterly wretched.

'You flirted with David Armstrong over a number of weeks, didn't you?'

'No.'

'And when the first opportunity arose – with Mr Porter out of the way – you took it. Isn't that the truth?'

Eve raised her head. Again she was crying, yet it was impossible to tell if they were tears of anger or of distress.

'No. It isn't. That's not what happened. I . . . The truth? I've *told* you the truth. The truth is he raped me.'

As her impassioned words rang through the court, the expressions on the faces of the jurors were a strange mixture of bafflement, pity, distaste – and uncertainty.

Kavanagh noted their indecision. 'Are you and your husband,' he enquired politely, 'still together?'

Again Eve bowed her head. 'No.'

Kavanagh also inclined his – but in the direction of Judge Granville. Then he sat down.

CHAPTER NINE

Kate didn't want to go to court the next day. During Eve Kendall's cross-examination she had seen her father in a new and unfavourable light; and afterwards they had had a blazing row. 'How could you?' she had shouted when they got home that evening. 'I can't believe the way you treated her! It was disgusting.'

'It was called', replied her father with maddening equanimity, 'testing the evidence.'

'God! You're an unfeeling . . . No wonder . . .' Realizing where she was and what she was about to say; realizing that her mother as well as her father was listening to her, she had changed tack. 'What if it was me? What if I was in her place?'

'What if Luke was in *his*? Would you have me spare her feelings, or would you want me to defend him?'

At that, Kate had stormed out into the hall. Her anger needed an outlet: directing it towards her father would only serve to intensify it. But Kavanagh had followed her. 'Come on, you started this, Kate. Kate? What would you want me to do?'

But Kate, knowing she hadn't a hope of winning the argument, responded by slamming her bedroom door.

A night's sleep had calmed her somewhat. Her father, she reasoned, was only doing his job, and an extraordinary one at that. Of all she had learned in the past two days about his profession, the thing that registered most was the enormous element of theatricality. The deferential manner in which everybody treated the judge, the archaic clothes, the almost absurdly formal language; they all suggested fiction rather than reality. But it was, she knew, anything but make-believe: and most real of all was the insidious manipulation of the witnesses by the barristers. Kate was both repelled and intrigued by that and by the realization that the whole procedure had, at the end of the day, more to do with the art of presentation than the pursuit of justice. It was ultimately a question of who could paint the most convincing picture of what had happened – Eleanor Harker or her father.

Kate, having got over her fury with the latter, was nevertheless hoping he would lose. David Armstrong, as she had told him with utter conviction, was guilty. She could tell. So her curiosity, in the end, got the better of her, and the following day, again accompanied by Luke, she found herself in the public gallery. And now she was listening to her father cross-examining the forensic medical examiner who had attended to Eve after the alleged rape. By her confident manner, it was apparent that Dr Green was no stranger to the witness box.

'Now Dr Green, if someone had been gripped very tightly by the arms, it would be reasonable to expect to find bruising, wouldn't it?'

'It's a possibility.'

'It's more than that, isn't it?' persisted Kavanagh.

But the doctor wasn't going to let the barrister put words in her mouth. She remained silent.

'Doctor,' he continued, 'Mrs Kendall's been dragged from the kitchen, through the lounge and into the hall

– by her arms. Are you seriously suggesting to this jury that there'd be no bruising?'

Dr Green shrugged. 'Well, not in this case.'

'You examined Mrs Kendall thoroughly?'

Dr Green looked distinctly put out at this implied professional slight. 'Yes,' she said through pursed lips.

'And were there any bruises to her upper arms?'

'There were not.'

'No bruises to her upper arms whatsoever?'

'No.'

'What about her thighs? Any bruises there?'

'No.'

'Dr Green, in a rape you would normally expect to find bruising to the victim's thighs, wouldn't you?'

'Not always.'

'But commonly?'

'Yes,' conceded the doctor.

'Any friction burns to her back or buttocks?'

'No.'

'Such injuries are not uncommon in rape cases, are they?'

'No.'

'Indeed, apart from some slight chafing to her wrists and a bruise to her face, Mrs Kendall was not injured in any way, was she?'

'She had some internal abrasions.'

Kavanagh looked momentarily at his notes. 'Which you described in your report as minor?'

'Yes.'

'Would such abrasions be solely attributable to rape?'

'No. Not necessarily.'

'No. In fact, there needn't be rape at all, need there?'

'Well . . . no. There needn't be.'

'And one case where there wouldn't be rape would be a bit of roughness during intercourse, wouldn't it?'

'It might be.'

'Come on, Doctor. If the situation in this case was that it was to be done roughly, then this could be the result?'

'Yes. It could be.'

'Even when she was fully aroused?'

Again Dr Green shrugged – this time in annoyance. 'Yes,' she said eventually.

Without another word, Kavanagh sat down.

The appearance of Alan Kendall, Eve's husband, caused quite a stir in court. As he took his oath in the witness box, all eyes were upon him. This was the man who had come home to find his wife in a state of acute distress; this was the man who had been having an extramarital affair; this was the man who was no longer living with Eve. He was, however, still her husband.

'You have been married to Mrs Kendall for – how long?' asked Eleanor Harker.

'Fourteen years.'

'Yes. Fourteen years. And you enjoyed normal physical relations with your wife in that period. Is that right?'

'Yes.'

'Tell me, Mr Kendall, in all those fourteen years, did your wife ever ask you to be rough with her during sex?'

Alan Kendall replied with total conviction. 'No,' he said, 'never.'

Harker, allowing herself the briefest of smiles, sat down. Behind her, her junior, Miles Petersham, also smiled. Eleanor, he felt, had scored a vital point there.

Then Kavanagh stood up to cross-examine the witness. 'Mr Kendall, you said you found your wife in the bathroom. And that she appeared distressed. "Hysterical" was the word you used?'

'Yes.'

'Yes. As I understand it, she struck out at you. Is that right?'

'Yes.'

'How did you stop her doing that?'

Alan looked distinctly uneasy. 'I . . . er, I don't remember.'

But Kavanagh remembered. 'You grabbed her by the wrists, didn't you?'

'I suppose . . . yes, I suppose I would have done.'

'And she kept on struggling to hit you, didn't she?'

'Er . . . Well . . . Yes. Yes, she . . .'

'Did you do anything else?'

Alan looked surprised. 'How d'you mean?'

'To try and shock her out of her hysterics?'

'Er, no . . . not really.'

'What do people normally do to stop other people being hysterical?'

Alan shifted uneasily in the witness box. 'Well, they, er, I . . . I don't know.'

'Take yourself out of this case for a moment, Mr Kendall. What would you expect people to do? What do you see them do on the television?'

'Well . . .'

'They slap them, don't they?'

'Er, yes. They, er, slap them.'

'Now, what about on this afternoon – did you have to slap your wife to stop her hysterics?'

Alan remained silent.

'You slapped her, didn't you?

Still no reply.

'Mr Kendall?' prompted Kavanagh.

'I might have done.'

'Where might you have slapped her?'

Alan bowed his head. 'Across the face. Possibly.'

Kavanagh looked thoughtful for a moment and, as if to himself, repeated the words 'across the face'. He had no further questions.

Gary Porter, David Armstrong's ex-workmate, called into the witness box after Alan Kendall, was, in marked contrast to the witnesses who had gone before, breezy, cheerful and full of life. He looked slightly older than David, and was clearly from a different sort of background. Yet it spoke volumes for his character that he had had no hesitation about appearing as a witness: and he made it abundantly clear that he thought accusing David of rape would have been laughable had it not been so serious.

'Mr Porter,' asked Kavanagh after Gary had taken the oath, 'did David Armstrong ever give you any indication that he found Eve Kendall attractive?'

Gary grinned. 'No. If anything he was the other way.'

'What do you mean by that?'

'Well, I'd make the odd comment about her, Mrs Kendall. Summing maybe with a bit of an innuendo in it.' He grinned again, this time a little sheepishly. 'Rude, like. David – he'd give me a look. Like I was out of order.'

'He didn't approve?'

'No. I used to pull his leg. You know, "You're one of them new men" sort of thing.' He paused, as if struggling to come to terms with something. 'Dave's a bit more respectful than me with women,' he finally added.

Eleanor Harker was on her feet a split second after

Kavanagh sat down. For the first time, her manner was almost aggressive. 'Mr Porter, the reality is, Mr Armstrong's attraction for Mrs Kendall grew as you were both working on the site, didn't it?'

Gary looked amazed. 'No.'

'He took every oportunity to ingratiate himself with her, didn't he?'

'Nah.' Gary shook his head vehemently. 'If anyone made the running it was her. She was . . . she was always, you know, coming out to him – bringing him jam jars and that to open and, you know, cups of tea and "Couldn't have a look at my car, could you?" sort of thing. And wearing . . . like low-cut stuff – making sure she had to bend down so's he'd get an eyeful.' Gary spoke with conviction – and not without a hint of something that sounded suspiciously like resentment.

'Well,' said Harker, 'let's just have a look at that, shall we? Bringing him jars to open. How do you say that's a come-on?'

'Well, it is, isn't it?'

'Bringing him cups of tea. How do you say that's a come-on?'

Gary avoided her gaze. 'Well, er . . .'

'Did she bring *you* a cup of tea?'

'Now and again, yeah.'

'Was that a come-on to you?'

'Well,' said Gary with an impish grin, 'I wasn't interested, was I?'

The court, warming to Gary, erupted into gales of laughter.

The next witness could not have been more of a contrast. Sober, neat and distinguished in appearance, Professor Bellamy declared himself to have been David's tutor at Cambridge for the past two years. When asked to describe his character, he could not have been more flattering.

'David,' he said gravely, 'is courteous, well-mannered and intelligent. One hesitates to use the term in this day and age but really, with David it's quite justified.' Then he looked straight at the jury. 'He is a gentleman.'

The high drama, however, was to come after lunch. The accused was taken into the witness box and Kavanagh was extremely gratified to note the effect he had on the jury. David was attractive, extremely well-dressed and scrupulously polite.

'She asked me in,' he replied simply to Kavanagh's question about how he came to be in the house. 'For a beer. I'm not a great drinker at the best of times – especially in the afternoon – but it was hot and . . .'

'Yes,' said Kavanagh. 'So, you went into the kitchen. Then what happened?'

'We were just talking about this and that. The weather. She started talking about her husband, that he didn't treat her properly. She said . . . she said they hadn't slept together for about six months.'

'She said they weren't sleeping together. What did you reply?'

David shrugged. 'I didn't know what to say. I said, "Oh," or something like that. Then she asked me if I thought she was unattractive.'

'Did you think she was unattractive?'

'No. Well, she's not. She's – for her age, I mean.' Clearly embarrassed, David then added, 'Quite attractive.'

'Yes. Go on.'

'She gave me another beer. I said I'd better not drink too much as I had to go back to work. She said, "Oh, you don't have to go back to work." ' He paused and looked round the court. Everyone looked as though they were holding their breath. 'Then she came over and put her arms around me. She said, "Why don't we have some fun?" '

'What did you do then?'

'I told her I had a girlfriend. She said she wasn't going to tell her if I wasn't – and then she took my hands and put them on her breasts.'

'She put your hands on her breasts?'

'Yes. And she kissed me. I was . . .' David shuffled uneasily and then continued. 'Well, it was sexy. Perhaps it was the beer – whatever – but I started to kiss her back and . . . well . . . one thing led to another and we ended up having sex.'

'Where?'

'It started in the kitchen and then the living-room – but we ended up in the hall.'

'Who would you say initiated the sex?'

'Mrs Kendall.

'Mrs Kendall.' Kavanagh paused for a moment. 'Was there,' he added, 'much foreplay?'

'No.'

'Why was that?'

David frowned. 'I don't . . .'

'How did Mrs Kendall want you to be with her?'

David frowned again. 'In what way?' he asked, puzzled.

'How did she want you to have sex?'

'Er . . . with me on top.'

Clearly, client and counsel were misunderstanding each other.

'Let me put it another way,' said the latter. 'Did Mrs Kendall express any preference as to . . .'

86

'Oh, I see. Yes. She wanted me to be quite rough with her. Dominant.'

'How did she make that clear to you?'

David shrugged. 'She asked me. She said she liked to be pinned down. Kind of overpowered.'

Mindful of the statements made by Eve Kendall's husband, several of the jury were beginning to look doubtful.

Undaunted, Kavanagh pressed on. 'She asked you to do that?'

'Yes.'

'So you had sex. What happened afterwards?'

'She started asking if I could get rid of Gary – my workmate – another day, so we could do it again. I said I didn't think I could – and that I didn't think we ought to do it again.' He paused, lowered his head slightly and then looked to the public gallery. 'My girlfriend,' he explained in a small voice. Several other heads turned towards the gallery, but none of the jurors knew to which girl he was referring. There were three young women sitting impassively in the enclosed space: one was Kate Kavanagh, another was indeed Sophie, and the third, sitting on her own at the end of the front row, the girl Kate had noticed before, appeared to be a stranger to everyone.

'And how did Mrs Kendall react to that?'

'She got annoyed. I said that I didn't want to fall out over it. Then I left.'

There was complete silence in court. Then, capitalizing on the total attention that David was receiving, Kavanagh asked his final question. 'Mr Armstrong, what was Mrs Kendall's demeanour during intercourse?'

'She was wholly willing.'

*

Kavanagh had told David that, whatever he did, it was imperative that he did not enter into a slanging match with Eleanor Harker. He warned David that she would seek every opportunity to wrong-foot him, to upset him, and to go for the jugular. She would only, he could have added, be doing her job.

If David was unsettled by the look she gave him, nobody in the court was close enough to him to notice the slight quivering of his Adam's apple. The formidable prosecution counsel stood up and addressed him in a formal, slightly icy tone.

'Mr Armstrong, how did you come to be working for the Kendalls?'

'I took a summer job. During the long vac. Trying to earn a few quid.'

'Mmm. Yes. I see. And you come from a fairly affluent background, is that right?'

David looked annoyed. 'I . . . yes, I suppose so.'

'Your father is the chairman of a multinational chemical company, is he not?' Kavanagh turned to Julia Piper. Her expression told him that she too was reflecting on the conversation they had had about the Armstrong family. The words 'spoiled brat' and 'used to getting what he wants' echoed in her head. She looked towards the jury and wondered if they, prompted by Harker, were thinking similar thoughts. David, impassive, confirmed that his father was chairman of Armstrong Chemicals.

'And yet,' replied Harker, 'you took employment as a casual labourer. Why was that?'

'I don't get much of an allowance or . . . well, it was my father who suggested I took the job. He thought it would be character-building.'

'Yes. What did you think of the Kendalls?'

David shrugged. 'Just people I was working for.'

'They were of no consequence to you?'

'No.'

'No. And Mrs Kendall? How did you feel about her?'

'I thought she was very pleasant.'

'Yes. I see. As Mr Kavanagh has already taken pains to establish, your habit was to bring your own lunch with you. Is that right?'

'Yes.'

'And you had done so that day?'

'Yes.'

'Why, then, if you had your own lunch, did you accept Mrs Kendall's invitation to go into the house?'

David sighed. He was clearly finding this boring rather than upsetting. 'For a beer.'

'But as you've told the court, you're not a great drinker.' Looking down at her notes, she added, ' "Especially not in the afternoon." '

'It was hot. I fancied a beer.'

Harker leaned archly towards him. 'Indeed. Was that all you fancied?'

'No.' David, unflinching, met her gaze. 'There was also the possibility of a sandwich.'

'But you could have had both beer and sandwich in your usual spot in the garden, couldn't you?'

'She asked me in.'

'Why did you think she asked you in?'

'For lunch.'

'That was all?'

'Yes.'

'Nothing more?'

'No.'

'Now,' continued Harker without a pause, 'when he left, Mr Porter told you that in all probability he would not return that day, didn't he?'

'No. He said he *might* be back.'

'But not for some time?'

'I suppose so.'

'Thank you.'

Miles Petersham, in his seat behind Harker, frowned slightly as she consulted her notes. Eleanor, he felt, wasn't getting very far – and the jury, he could tell, was still sympathetic towards David. But Eleanor was about to change all that.

'As you've told the court,' she said, 'you were involved in a relationship at the time. One that evidently meant something to you.'

Again David – and most of the jury – looked towards the public gallery. 'Yes,' he said, 'it still does.'

'And yet you had sex with Mrs Kendall?'

David hesitated. Then he grinned. '*Noli equi dentes inscipere donate*, I suppose.'

Judge Granville, privately amused but professionally annoyed, was as quick as a flash. 'I hardly think,' he said with a caustic edge, 'that's what St Jerome had in mind, Mr Armstrong.'

Eleanor Harker, like everyone else in the court, looked puzzled. 'Your Honour?'

Granville smiled. 'Never look a gift horse in the mouth, Miss Harker.'

Harker nodded. 'I'm obliged, Your Honour.' And, like the jury, she thought, I'm pretty unimpressed. A quick sideways glance told her that the jurors hadn't appreciated David's little joke. 'A gift horse, Mr Armstrong? Is that how you viewed Mrs Kendall?'

David shrugged. 'She'd made it plain she was interested. She'd been, well, I don't know . . . coming on a bit. Flirting.'

'In what way?'

'She used to watch me work . . . she didn't think I

knew she was watching, but I caught her out once or twice. I'd catch her eye and then she'd look away.'

'And what did you take that to mean?'

'To mean? I don't . . .'

'Well, did you take it to mean she would be happy to have sex with you?'

'Er, no. It . . .'

'What then?'

'That she thought I was attractive.'

'You believed she thought you were attractive?'

'Yes.'

'Might you have misread the situation?'

'No.' David, suddenly, was back on firm ground again. 'She complimented me on my physique. Said I was obviously very fit. Things like that.'

'What did she say exactly?'

'I can't remember the exact words.'

'But you *were* under the impression that she found you attractive. Is that right?'

'Yes.'

'Yes. Then why were you so surprised when, as you allege, she made her advances towards you more explicit?'

'I just was.'

'You were either aware that Mrs Kendall found you attractive or you weren't?'

'I . . . I wasn't sure . . .'

'You weren't sure?'

'I wasn't sure if she would do anything about it.'

Eleanor Harker cast him a pitying look. 'Very well. Now, you say she wanted you to be forceful with her. What does that mean?'

'To be, er, I don't know, a bit masterful. To take the lead.'

'To take the lead?' Harker was on to him like a shot.

'Yes.'

'I see.' She paused. 'You had sex in the hall?'

'Yes.'

'What was wrong with the bedroom?'

'Nothing, I suppose.'

'Then, why . . .'

'She didn't want to. I thought we were going to go upstairs, but we got as far as the hall and she said she wanted to do it there.'

'You say it was Mrs Kendall's idea to use the hall?'

'Yes.'

'You didn't think the hall likely to prove un-comfortable?'

'No.'

'What did you think?'

'I didn't think anything.'

'*Was* it uncomfortable?'

'Not particularly.'

'The lounge would have been preferable to the hall, wouldn't it?'

'I suppose so. Yes. I, er, didn't really . . .'

'You could have pulled her through to the lounge, couldn't you?'

David, now looking flustered and irritated, spread his hands in a wearied gesture. 'She wanted it in the hall.'

'She'd asked you to be forceful, hadn't she?'

'Yes.'

'To, in your words, "take the lead"? That's right, isn't it?'

David, realizing what she was getting at, yet unnerved by the increasing speed of her questions, merely nodded.

'Then if, as you say, it would have been more comfortable, why didn't you take her into the lounge?'

David just looked at her.

'Mr Armstrong?' she prompted.

'I . . . I don't know.'

'Are there windows in the lounge, Mr Armstrong?'

'Yes. Of course.'

'And the curtains were open. Is that right?'

'I suppose they must have been.'

'Are there windows in the hall?'

David thought for a moment. 'No.'

'No. Did you remove Mrs Kendall's underwear?' Harker had now abandoned her tactic of creating strategic silences. She was going hell-for-leather after David, and the court knew it. Every face was trained upon him; all ears were hanging on to his every word.

'No,' mumbled David. 'I don't think so.'

'You can't remember?'

'I . . . I think they were left on.'

On cue, Miles Petersham leaned forward and handed Harker a copy of David's statement to the police.

'In interview,' she said as she picked it up, 'you told the police Mrs Kendall had removed them herself. "She took her pants off and we had sex." Your words, Mr Armstrong.'

'I can't remember the police interview in any great detail at all. I was in shock. They were asking me all sorts of questions, one after the other.' Just as, he could have added, you are doing now.

'But you remember now that Mrs Kendall's underwear was left on?'

'Yes.'

'How then did you effect intercourse?'

David shrugged. 'I must have pulled them to one side.'

'Wouldn't it have been easier to remove them altogether?'

'I don't know.'

'Or would that have proved difficult?'

David, puzzled, looked at her. 'What do you mean?'

'To remove Mrs Kendall's underwear would have meant releasing her wrists, wouldn't it?'

'Yes. Well, no. Not like that. She asked me,' he almost wailed, 'to hold her by the wrists.'

'You must have let go of them long enough to remove your own shorts.'

'Yes.'

'Then why didn't you remove Mrs Kendall's underwear at the same time?'

'I, er . . . I don't know. We . . . I can't remember if she wanted them left on or . . . I don't know.'

'So, she demanded you have sex in the hall?'

'Yes.'

'And she requested you hold her by the wrists?'

'Yes.'

'And she ordered you not to remove her underwear?'

'Yes.'

'Mr Armstrong, are you always so dominant?'

David didn't reply. Harker didn't need him to. She had, she knew, made her point very clearly and very convincingly – and purely for the benefit of the jury. 'Now,' she continued after a moment, 'you allege that after intercourse had taken place, Mrs Kendall asked if you might repeat the experience on a later occasion. Is that right?'

'Yes.'

'Yes. And you replied that you didn't think that would be a good idea.'

'Yes.'

'Why was that?'

'Why was what?'

'A few minutes previously you had thought intercourse a good idea, hadn't you?'

'Yes. I ... I thought ...'

'Why did you change your mind?'

'I didn't. I ... I thought it would be just the once. But ... she got all clingy ... as if ... you know ... like it meant something. More than it was. And it wasn't. It didn't. Not to me.'

'Yes. And you had a girlfriend, of course.'

Ouch, thought Kate Kavanagh in the public gallery. She was dying to turn round to look at Sophie, as usual sitting with Jock Armstrong in the row behind her. It must be awful, she thought, for the poor girl, having her boyfriend squirming with embarrassment in the witness box. She looked out of the corner of her eye at Luke. Like everyone else, he was transfixed by the proceedings. This, thought Kate, could be us. And then she looked at David Armstrong again. No, it couldn't, she corrected. Luke isn't like that. Even if David isn't guilty, he's still an arrogant prat.

'Yes,' said David, 'I have a girlfriend.'

'Tell me, Mr Armstrong, did you take precautions of any kind?'

'No. I, er ... She said it would be all right.'

'So, you had unprotected sex?'

'Yes.'

'Why was that?'

David shrugged. 'I didn't have anything with me.'

'That was an enormous risk to take for one brief liaison, wasn't it?'

'I don't know.'

'You gambled your life? For something you had no intention of repeating?'

'In the heat of the moment . . . I didn't think.'

'You didn't think. No. You failed to take any precautions because to do so would have meant releasing your hold on Mrs Kendall, wouldn't it?'

David looked horrified. 'No!'

'Because she was, in fact, actively resisting your advances, wasn't she?'

'No!'

'Mr Armstrong, your account of events on that day is a fiction from start to finish, isn't it?'

'No.'

'I suggest you mistakenly believed Mrs Kendall found you attractive and tried to press your attentions on her. That's right, isn't it?'

'No.'

'But she wasn't interested, was she?'

'She was.'

'She rejected your advances, didn't she?'

'No.'

'You were angry, weren't you?'

It was a brilliant question. Harker was introducing the word anger to the jury just as David himself was betraying signs of that emotion.

But David, just in time, saw her game. He checked the furious invective that was his instinctive reply and, instead, answered in a small, calm voice, 'I didn't rape her.'

'You raped Mrs Kendall in the hall because it would have been difficult getting her up the stairs. Isn't that the truth?'

'No . . .'

'Might she have broken away from you?'

'No.'

'Is that why you didn't go into the bedroom?'

'No. That's not true.'

'Did you choose the hall because, unlike the kitchen or lounge, there was no danger of being overlooked by anyone passing outside?'

David could no longer control his anger – or his distress. 'What? No! No!' he shouted. 'I didn't rape her! Eve, tell them!'

Shockwaves reverberated around the court at David's extraordinary *cri de cœur* to the very woman who was accusing him of rape. Judge Granville, himself rather taken aback, turned sternly to the defendant. 'Mr Armstrong!' he barked.

But David ignored him. 'Tell them!' he pleaded. 'I never did anything to her she didn't want me to. Why have you done this to me? Eve, please! Why?'

The sight of the young man, acutely distressed and on the verge of tears, moved even the heart of the woman juror who, two days previously, had decided he was guilty. Even Kate Kavanagh found herself biting her lip. 'Tell them the truth!' continued David. Then, as the tears started to flow, he buried his head in his hands. 'Oh God! Why are you doing this! Please . . .'

'Mr Armstrong,' said the judge in a slightly less harsh but nonetheless commanding tone, 'unless you can control yourself, I will have you taken down.' Then, as David fought to get a grip on his emotions, Granville turned to the prosecuting counsel. 'Miss Harker?'

Harker nodded in appreciation and continued her questioning. Yet she had, she knew, lost the initiative.

'She asked you to stop, didn't she, Mr Armstrong?'

David's head was still bowed. He shook it vehemently.

'And while you raped her, she wept, didn't she?'

At last David raised his head. He looked at Harker with something approaching hatred. 'No.'

CHAPTER TEN

'Members of the jury,' said Eleanor Harker, 'in a moment His Honour will address you upon the law. I am going to address you upon the facts. His Honour will tell you that in order to convict you must find that, beyond reasonable doubt, David Armstrong raped Eveline Kendall. I am going to suggest that on the facts you have heard here there can be no doubt.' She paused and smiled at the men and women she was addressing. She had led enough cases, cross-examined enough witnesses and summed up to enough juries to know doubt when she saw it: and she noticed it in half the members of this jury. This speech was her last chance.

'You must start,' she continued, 'as did the events leading up to the rape, with the attitude of the two men working in Mrs Kendall's garden. In particular you must start with Gary Porter. He said that Mrs Kendall made it obvious to David Armstrong that she was, in his words, "up for it". He was wrong about that. Remember the examples he gave. Opening jam jars: does that suggest she was "up for it"? Cups of tea. Does that suggest she was "up for it"? Was she "up for it" with Gary Porter as well? What you have, ladies and gentlemen, is a blatant misinterpretation by these two men. Why does the invitation to a drink and a sandwich at lunchtime signify consent to intercourse? Does wearing a skirt mean that Mrs Kendall wanted intercourse? The reality is, it does not. If it did, members of the jury, any woman in the high street on any summer's day would be inviting assault.' She stopped to let her words sink in. It was, she knew, a good and highly emotive point. It hit home with the ladies of the jury. She wasn't so sure, however, about the men.

'It doesn't matter,' she continued, 'that Mrs Kendall said she had a migraine earlier in the day. It doesn't matter that she had been wearing jeans. It doesn't matter whether she phoned into work before or after Gary Porter left. She told you she did not want sex. She was clear about that in a way David Armstrong was not. David Armstrong was not clear about it at all.'

Again Harker paused, this time to look at the notes in front of her. 'One example. You will remember he stated in evidence that he pulled Mrs Kendall's underwear to one side. I read the statement he had made to the police. He had told the police Mrs Kendall had taken off her underwear. Which was the lie? Was he telling the truth to the police? Or was he telling the truth to you? Or was he not telling the truth at all? Mrs Kendall's evidence was corroborated by the injuries to her wrists and the internal injuries. I ask you,' she finished, 'to accept it.'

As Harker sat down, Kate Kavanagh felt like clapping. She had, in the course of the trial, decided that Eleanor Harker was a star. The woman's performance had had such an effect on her that she now began to doubt her decision to study English literature at university. Was it too late, she wondered, to change to law? Then, as soon as Harker sat down, Kate noticed her father rise. Perhaps, she mused, I'll reserve judgement about that until he's finished. She had still not forgiven him for what she saw as his merciless bullying of Eve Kendall.

'Members of the jury, I am going to suggest to you that having heard the evidence you will have a number of not just reasonable, but very strong doubts.' Kavanagh, like Harker, had prepared his summing-up in advance, yet this introduction had been altered while she was making her speech. He too had scrutinized the expressions on the faces of the jurors. 'If so,' he continued, 'there is no doubt that David Armstrong should be acquitted. Mr Armstrong has told you that Mrs Kendall consented to intercourse. But it goes further than that. A lot further. He does not just say she let him have intercourse with her. He says that she positively sought it. She sought it, he emphasized, but he didn't. It is this aspect of the case that gives the lie to Mrs Kendall's version of events. Bear in mind as you consider every detail of the evidence you have heard. Mrs Kendall knew that Mr Armstrong always ate his lunch with Mr Porter at the bottom of the garden. Why then did she ask him if he would like some lunch – in the house – with her?

'There is only one answer to that question. It was because Mr Porter had been called away. You will recall that this was the first day on which Mr Porter had been called away. Mrs Kendall saw her chance to invite Mr Armstrong into the house on his own and she took it. My suggestion to you is that she wanted to get Mr Armstrong into the house because she wanted to have sex with him. All the evidence points to that conclusion.'

Kavanagh paused and nodded towards Eleanor Harker. 'When counsel for the prosecution put it to Mr Porter that Mr Armstrong used to flirt with Mrs Kendall, he told her that it was the other way round.

Mrs Kendall had difficulty remembering whether she telephoned work to say she had a migraine before or after the call that took Mr Porter away.' Here he smiled at his audience. 'I think we can probably help her with that, don't you? The migraine that prevented her from going to work didn't prevent her from doing the garden – in the sunshine. It didn't dissuade her from seeking company for lunch – or from drinking beer. Neither did it prevent her changing her clothes – again after Mr Porter had left – from trousers, appropriate, one might have thought, for working on a flower-bed, to a short skirt.'

Put that way, thought Kate as she listened to her father's argument, it did make Eve Kendall's actions seem rather premeditated.

'And what,' he continued, 'of the shirt? Tied at the waist?' Kavanagh paused, letting the image of a scantily clad woman filter into the jurors' minds. 'Members of the jury, this is not a picture of someone receiving advances from an unwanted admirer. It is a very clear picture of someone making them.'

Then he looked down at his notes once more before continuing. 'It does not stop, however, at advances. Examine the evidence as to what happens once the pair are in the house. Mrs Kendall says that Mr Armstrong ripped her shirt off. You saw the shirt. The button-holes were not ripped. No damage at all. Mrs Kendall told you that Mr Armstrong pulled her through the house – all the way, from the kitchen, through the lounge, into the hall, gripping her by the biceps.' He shook his head. 'No marking at all. And then, members of the jury, Mrs Kendall told you a blatant lie. She told you that Mr Armstrong slapped her face. Only one person slapped Mrs Kendall's face that afternoon. He was reluctant to tell you about it, knowing perhaps that he would be disclosing a truth which was not only painful to him but would do irreparable damage to his wife's evidence. It was Mr Kendall.'

Kavanagh paused again. 'What is to be made of that lie? I would suggest that it is not the only one she told. Everything she did on that day she did because she wanted to. Whatever the reasons, she has been lying ever since. I suggested to you earlier that there could be no doubt that David Armstrong is innocent. I would suggest to you that he must be acquitted.'

As Kavanagh bent to sit down, he turned and caught his daughter's eye. She was glaring at him. Despite herself, she felt, as she had done after Eleanor Harker's speech, like breaking into applause. Her father, she had to concede, had been brilliant. Yet she couldn't forget the image of Eve Kendall in the witness box, dissolving into hysterical tears as she was forced to relive – and in public – the events that had led to this case. Kate was still convinced that David Armstrong was an arrogant prat. Furthermore, she had decided that he was also a smooth bastard – and a liar to boot. She knew he was guilty. Yet as she looked from her father to the jurors, she saw little to match her own certainty. Her father had planted too many seeds of doubt.

All that remained was for Judge Granville to sum up. As was customary, he remained seated at his desk on the raised platform as he addressed the members of the jury. Imperious in his wig, his dark blue robe with its lavender trimming and red sash, he turned slowly to his right.

'Ladies and gentlemen, I am *obliged* to warn you of the danger of convicting on the evidence of the complainant alone. In cases such as these, one must look for some other evidence which would suggest her story is true.' He waved his hand in the air as he illustrated examples of such evidence. 'The demeanour of the accused, a consistency in the evidence, some corroboration. If you are satisfied beyond reasonable doubt that Armstrong had sexual intercourse with Mrs Kendall *without her consent*, then you must return a verdict of guilty. But if there *is* reasonable doubt, then you *must* acquit him. Members of the jury, you will now retire and consider your verdict.'

The court rose and, as all parties in the defence filed into the lobby and as far away as possible from the prosecution and its counsel, an angry Jock Armstrong rushed up to Kavanagh. 'You should have called the lad from the bookshop. Roberts. The one she was having an affair with. He'd have clinched it. I said . . .'

Kavanagh, tense and irritated, turned on him. 'Look, this was considered in consultation, Mr Armstrong. Proper instruction was taken and—'

'But the—'

'And what you ought to realize, Mr Armstrong, is that there's a difference between an affair and a one-night stand. Furthermore, I was not – and am not – satisfied that anything Mr Roberts may have had to say would be of any relevance to this case. Now, if you would excuse me . . .'

Striding off in the direction of the gents' loo, Kavanagh silently cursed Jock Armstrong. The pugnacious little man would never forgive him if his son lost the case. Shutting the door behind him, Kavanagh fished in his pocket for a cigarette. He was supposed to have given up, but he reckoned that the combination of Jock Armstrong and a jury that could go either way counted as an extremely stressful moment. Furthermore, this wasn't the first time that Jock had reprimanded him for not calling Roberts, and only now, too late, Kavanagh was beginning to think that maybe, just maybe . . .

The jury took for ever to reach a decision. Twice they reconvened and when, finally, they reached a verdict it was not unanimous. But it was enough. They found David Armstrong not guilty. The cheers and the uproar that followed the announcement by the foreman of the jury were instantaneous – and very loud. David slumped in the dock; Eve collapsed into uncontrollable sobs. Jock and Sophie roared with delight, and Kate and Luke exchanged a silent but telling look. Behind them, and unnoticed by anyone else, the girl on her own left as quietly as she had arrived.

They went to a wine bar to celebrate. Jeremy Aldermarten, Peter Foxcott and the new pupil, Alex Wilson, joined Kavanagh and Julia Piper to drink a toast to their success, and to River Court Chambers.

So, after she had commiserated with her clients, did Eleanor Harker. The Kendalls would no doubt have been shocked that their barrister was consorting with the enemy, but to everyone in the legal profession such behaviour is perfectly normal. The case was over: before it they had been friends; now they were friends again.

'I thought,' said Eleanor as she and James grabbed a booth while the others ordered at the bar, 'that I had him on the ropes at one point.' She grinned. 'I was counting on you calling Christopher Roberts, the great lover. Then I'd have had you caught and bowled.'

'Why?'

'Because, my dear, Christopher Roberts is as gay as your hat.'

Kavanagh was completely taken aback. 'But I thought . . .'

Eleanor shook her head. 'There was no affair. Eve was helping him get over the loss of his mother. Hubby got hold of the wrong end of the stick and began his own little escapade with Miss Typefast by way of a payback.'

Kavanagh looked both relieved and amused. Before he could reply, Eleanor rose and, with a muttered 'Back in a mo',' left the booth.

Immediately, a young woman slipped into her place. Kavanagh looked at her and smiled apologetically. 'I'm afraid that seat's . . .'

'I was in court,' said the girl by way of explanation. Then she smiled rather strangely at him. 'I just had to say, you were brilliant. But for you . . .'

'Are you a friend of David's?'

'He raped me. Does that count?'

Kavanagh sprang back in his seat as if he had been hit. For perhaps the first time in his life, he was utterly lost for words.

The girl, speaking without emotion but with great deliberation, leaned towards him. 'That, Mr Kavanagh, is the man you defended. Eve Kendall wasn't the first. And he'll do it again. He's like his father. Arrogant. Selfish. They take what they want. You say no, they take it just the same.'

'Why,' said Kavanagh carefully, 'should I believe you?' Even as he said the words, he knew they were wasted. This girl was speaking the truth.

'Why should I lie? I thought he might go down for this one but, you see, you were so brilliant.'

'You should have spoken out earlier.'

The girl snorted derisively. 'And have someone like you tear me apart in court? No. One rape was enough.'

'If what you say is true, your silence protected him. Why?'

The girl shrugged. 'I'm at Cambridge. I worked very hard to get there. He raped me, but I won't let him ruin the rest of my life.'

Kavanagh, desperate not to let her go, furiously trying to think of some way to make her tell her story, asked her what her name was.

But she was already on her feet. Instead of answering, she smiled sweetly. 'Was that your daughter I saw with you in court? About university age, isn't she?' And then she was gone.

Trudging wearily back to chambers, Kavanagh was surprised to find his office door open and the light on. Tom, he mused. It must be Tom Buckley delivering a brief.

But it wasn't Tom. Standing at the window, and holding a framed photograph of Kate that had been on the sill, was David Armstrong. Hearing Kavanagh's tread, he turned round and smiled. 'I hope you don't mind. There wasn't a chance to thank you properly at court. All the hullabaloo.'

Kavanagh didn't return the smile. His mind was on the photograph in David's hand. 'Would you put that back, please?'

David looked at the picture. 'Pretty girl,' he said. Then he put it back in its rightful place.

Kavanagh stayed in the doorway. 'I just met someone,' he said. 'A girl. She was in court. A cloaky-shawl sort of person. And a hat.' He looked closely at David. 'Said she knew you. From university.'

'Oh yes. What was her name?' David, buoyed up by the events of the afternoon, was being open, friendly, interested.

'She wouldn't say. Fair-haired.' Kavanagh raised his arm. 'About so high, blue eyes. Your age.'

Horrified comprehension dawned on David. Too late, he tried to disguise his reaction. 'Sorry,' he said, suddenly avoiding Kavanagh's eye. 'Doesn't mean anything to me.'

'No. I didn't think it would.' Kavanagh stared at the young man. I know, his expression said. And you know that I know.

David was suddenly desperate to get out of the room. He held out his hand. 'Well. Thanks again.'

Instead of extending his own hand, Kavanagh held the door open. 'Yes,' he said. 'Goodbye.'

'You had to defend him.' Lizzie handed her husband a large whisky. He looked as if he desperately needed it. 'If not you,' she added, 'then someone else. And don't forget, it was down to Harker to prove the case, Jim. She didn't. You would have. You've done it before. You should prosecute more.'

Kavanagh shook his head. 'Not really me.'

'No.' Lizzie put her arm round her husband. 'You're a true romantic. You look for the best in people. Not your fault if you can't always find it.'

CHAPTER ELEVEN

The Collenshaw Park Estate had been the brainchild of a 1960s town planner who, as was the fashion at the time, had decided that people – especially poor people – would enjoy living in tower-blocks built so close to each other that the covered walkways connecting them were all but superfluous.

The people who were obliged to live on the estate had a different version of enjoyment. And thirty-odd years after the estate had been built, it was considered – both by them and the new breed of town-planners – an urban hell. Rising unemployment, increased dissatisfaction with life and mounting crime statistics had rendered Collenshaw Park one of Sunderland's most dangerous places to live. The police, who relished patrolling its streets about as much as the inhabitants enjoyed walking them, seemed powerless to prevent burglaries, car thefts, joy-riding and worse.

When the patrol car manned by police constables Ray West and Peter Hill was rammed by two twelve-year-old joy-riders, another statistic was added to the benighted reputation of Collenshaw Park. Peter Hill died from multiple injuries exactly three hours after impact. Ray West was luckier: he sustained multiple fractures to his left leg which, while not endangering his life, boded ill for his career. Sure enough, as soon as he came out of hospital, he was, to the 'deep regret' of his superiors, invalided out of the Force. Opinions varied as to the effect the accident had had on him: many people thought they detected a bitterness that, a year later, showed no signs of abating. Yet everyone was agreed on one thing: the organization he had set up subsequent to his enforced retirement had benefited the entire estate.

Ray's brainchild, the Collenshaw Park Pals Community Defence Association – or, in short, the Pals – was, as far as Ray was concerned, an extension of the Neighbourhood Watch Scheme. But as far as others were concerned, it was a vigilante group that took the law into its own hands. Ray and a few friends armed themselves with mobile phones and CB radios and, in their own vehicles, patrolled the streets at night. The local police, initially worried, changed their minds when, after six months, the activities of Ray and his friends had directly contributed to a significant lowering of reported crimes in the area. They did, nevertheless, keep a close watch on their ex-colleague: Ray had always been known for his short fuse, and while the Pals had sworn never to use violence or even intimidation, they were still a maverick organization that, strictly speaking, should not be allowed to exist.

It was partly due to the reaction of the community at large that the police turned a blind eye to the Pals. Most people welcomed their presence on the streets at night: most people, that is, except Ryan Jarvis.

Ryan was the sort of young man who was liked by both his own and the opposite sex. Women liked him because he was fun, charming and sexy. Men liked him because he was 'one of the boys', a great drinker and a good laugh. His mother, Jackie, doted on him. His father didn't: he had done a disappearing act when Ryan was less than a year old and had never been heard from again. That event had left the feisty Jackie with the unenviable task of bringing up her high-spirited boy on her own. She had taken all sorts of jobs – any job – in order to support herself and her son. Ryan, as he grew up, became aware of the sacrifices and the hard work that defined his mother's life, and he determined to do something to make things easier for her. And the easiest way, he discovered when barely into his teens, was to steal things. Because of his charm and happy-go-lucky attitude to life, most people trusted him and found him impossible to dislike. Now that he was in his early twenties, people still found it difficult to dislike him – but some did distrust him. He had, two years previously, been arrested for stealing cars, had voluntarily agreed to do a custodial rehabilitation course and, according to his mother, was now a reformed character. She certainly believed what she said. Nobody knew Ryan better than she, and Jackie knew – as she had always known – that there was a great deal of good in the boy.

Jackie smiled at her son from her position behind the bar of the Packhorse pub. Of all the jobs she had done, this was probably the most pleasant: it was sociable, not too hard, and she had the added bonus of sometimes seeing Ryan while she was at work. Tonight, however, it looked as though she wasn't going to be seeing much of him. He was in strutting peacock mode, laughing and chatting to a group of young girls. As she pulled a pint for Stan Wrigley – the most regular of her regulars – she looked again towards Ryan and frowned. He was paying particular attention to one of the girls in the group – and that girl was Lisa Parks. Jackie had nothing against Lisa, but she did disapprove of her boyfriend: Ray West. She hated what she saw as Ray 'lording it' over everyone else, and she was secretly afraid that, should Ryan revert to his old ways, Ray might catch him – Ray, or one of his vigilante colleagues. And Ray's closest colleague was Don Parks, Lisa's father.

Jackie frowned again as Ryan left Lisa and came up to the bar. 'I'm just going to walk Lisa home, Mum,' he said with an easy smile. 'Shouldn't be on her own. Muggers 'n' that.'

'Oh aye, that'll be right.' Jackie gave Ryan the dubious benefit of her most tight-lipped smile. No stranger to his mother's disapproval, Ryan grinned and left her with a hurried, 'See you later.'

Ryan caught up with Lisa at the door. 'How come Charles Bronson isn't collecting you tonight?'

Lisa hated it when he referred to Ray like that. She was in love with Ray. At least she was sure she was in love with Ray. And she really wasn't sure that she liked Ryan. He was, she knew, a bad 'un. Still, he was a laugh – and he had a nicer body than Ray.

'He's working,' she said of her beloved.

'Look, don't get me wrong, I'm not trying to pull you,' said Ryan untruthfully. He looked at her as they stepped out into the rain. 'Unless . . . that is . . . you want me to.'

They walked most of the way in silence. Only when they turned into the street where Lisa lived with her widowed father did Ryan make another tentative move.

'You were always the best-looking girl in class, you know, Lees.'

'And you were always the biggest liar.'

Ryan threw back his head and laughed. 'I'm serious. You ever ditch the Terminator, gimme a call.'

Lisa fished for her front-door key as they reached

her house. This time she trusted herself to speak, but not to look back at Ryan. 'You never know,' she said. Still she didn't dare look up at Ryan. She knew, she could *feel* what was about to happen. Ryan's face was so close to hers that she felt the warmth of his breath.

When, a second later, his lips sought hers, she made no attempt to resist.

'You're early, pet,' said Don Parks as, ten minutes later, Lisa walked through the hall and into her father's den. The room, festooned with police posters and crime information pamphlets, was also filled with the crackle from the CB radio that her father was manning. 'Girls not coming in for coffee?'

Lisa shook her head. 'I left them at the Packhorse.'

Don frowned. 'You didn't walk all this way back by yourself?'

'Ryan walked me back.'

'Ryan who?'

'Ryan Jarvis.'

Don's indulgent expression gave way to a look of horror – and rage. 'You want shakin', you do!' he yelled. 'Have you no sense?'

'He's all right!'

That only served to enrage Don further. He stood up and glared at his daughter. 'All right? *All right?* An' I suppose they locked him up for being "all right", did they? Listen to me, Lisa-Marie Parks, I don't want you seeing that . . . that criminal again! Understand?'

He needn't have worried. Half an hour later Ryan Jarvis was on his way to hospital, critically injured. He had been run over by a car; a car belonging to Ray West.

CHAPTER TWELVE

'Basically, Mr Foxcott, the son's a courgette.' Tom Buckley, the inevitable cigarette in one hand, was in mid-conversation as James Kavanagh entered the room. 'Mum wants to go after the driver of the car for attempted.' Buckley shrugged. 'Her own solicitor's of the opinion she hasn't a cat in hell's.'

Foxcott looked at his senior clerk. Tom, as usual, was letting it be known that he knew best. 'What've you told them?'

'I've said there's a problem with dates. Which there is. You're going to be tied up on your nice little fraud at Guildford. To be honest, I'd peg Sunderland as a bit of a lost cause.'

Kavanagh, intrigued, approached the two other men. Buckley turned as he heard his tread. 'Yes, Mr Kavanagh, what can I do for you?'

Kavanagh had heard only enough to be mildly intrigued. A case somewhere in Sunderland: a mother whose son had been badly injured – and a probably futile attempt to sue the driver of the car. If Buckley was advising Foxcott not to take the case, it obviously meant there would be no money in it. Tom Buckley, like everyone else involved in the Bar, was a realist. High ideals were all very well – but they didn't pay the bills. Yet Kavanagh, who at least tried to hold on to his principles while serving the best interests of his clients, had been severely shaken by the David Armstrong case. He, one of the country's top QCs, had successfully defended a known rapist. Jock Armstrong had had the funds to pay for expensive lawyers and to hire private investigators, and his efforts had paid off. If ever the expression 'one law for the rich, one law for the poor' were applicable, it was to the Armstrong case. But in the dark, private moments of the night when Kavanagh had lain awake, he had admitted to himself that there was more to it: there was the undeniable fact that he, like every other barrister, took the cases his clerk gave him, and that was that. Lizzie had been right when she'd said that if her husband had not defended Armstrong, then someone else would have.

It would have been a professional disaster – or at the very least laughable – if Kavanagh had admitted to the conclusion he had drawn from that experience: he wanted to atone for what he privately saw as his own crime – he wanted to do some *good*. What he had overheard of Tom's conversation with Foxcott seemed to suggest that this might be his chance.

He was careful, however, to give a light-hearted answer to Buckley's question. 'Bit of a lost cause, eh, Tom? Don't often hear you saying that.'

But it was Peter Foxcott who replied. Holding both hands in the air in a gesture of dismissal, he turned to his colleague. 'No, Jim, Tom's absolutely right. This one's a real stinker – thank God I'm professionally committed elsewhere.' Then he looked thoughtful for a moment and, to nobody in particular, added, 'Shame, in a way. It would be good for River Court's reputation to be seen to take on something like this.'

That was Kavanagh's cue. 'Oh? Tell me more.'

Tom, quick as a flash, turned to Kavanagh. 'It's a prosecution, sir. Not your style.' Experienced barristers, especially criminal ones, rarely prosecuted *and* defended. One tended to make one's reputation in one or the other, not both. The tactics employed in court by defending and prosecuting counsel were entirely different: the latter went hell-for-leather to produce witnesses and construct a watertight case, while the former, often using stalling tactics, picked holes in the evidence and argued endlessly – sometimes with the judge before the jury was called – about points of law and what was admissible in court.

But Kavanagh had decided that he ought to do more prosecutions. A decision partly arrived at by his burning desire to see David Armstrong behind bars, it was also due to a more recent event: a week ago, the Kavanaghs had been burgled. Lizzie, strangely, had been fairly calm about the whole affair. Her husband had not: he erupted into a towering rage and swore that he would not rest until he saw the culprits in the dock. A most un-barristerlike reaction.

'I do,' said Kavanagh stiffly, 'know how to conduct a prosecution, Tom.'

'Yes, sir, but . . .'

'It's a private prosecution, Jim,' said Foxcott, still looking thoughtful.

'Even better for River Court's reputation, then. A chance to show the Crown Prosecution Service what's what. Who,' continued Kavanagh, 'is the client?'

'A single mother from a council estate in Sunderland, sir. Can't imagine there's much in the way of spondulies.' Tom Buckley shrugged. 'Hopeless cause as well.'

'Tell me about it,' said Kavanagh, intrigued.

Tom, against his will, told him what he knew. A woman called Jackie Jarvis, he explained, was trying to accuse some sort of self-styled vigilante of the attempted murder of her son Ryan. The case, he insisted, was a no-hoper on several counts. First, the son was in a coma on a life-support machine and therefore could not give his own version of events. Second, the accused, one Ray West, had not been alone in the car when, according to him, Ryan Jarvis had leapt out in front of him. He had another vigilante with him who supported his claim that the whole thing had been a terrible – and unavoidable – accident. And third, there was, according to Jackie Jarvis's solicitor, no obvious reason why West should have wanted to kill Jarvis anyway.

'So why,' asked Kavanagh, 'is this woman persisting?'

Tom Buckley snorted. 'Intuition or something. She claims she just knows.'

Kate, remembered Kavanagh, had 'just known' of David Armstrong's guilt.

'Does she know just how expensive litigation is?'

Tom looked at the papers in his hand. 'Nick Carnforth – her solicitor – says he warned her. She didn't care. Said she'll sell her house if she has to.' He looked mutinously at Kavanagh. 'Don't even think about it,' the expression said.

Kavanagh ignored the look. 'I'd like to meet this woman,' he said.

Nick Carnforth and Jackie Jarvis travelled down from Sunderland three days later. Kavanagh, seated behind his elegant walnut desk, looked at the anxious woman opposite him. She had, he thought, a powerful face. While it spoke of a life of hard, relentless work, it also portrayed a great deal of spirit and determination. The eyes, in particular, were revealing. When she looked at Kavanagh, Jackie Jarvis's eyes told him that she was right, and that she knew that he knew she was right.

He found it extremely unnerving – and heartbreaking. It was his duty to inform her of her position within the law.

'As things stand, Mrs Jarvis, you don't have a case.'

'You brought us all the way down here to tell us that? He was trying to kill Ryan. He ran him down.'

'That West ran your son down isn't disputed. But what would be the devil to prove is that he meant to – and that his intent in so doing was to kill your son.'

'But . . .'

'Given the findings of the Accident Investigation Unit, the police would be hard pushed to make "without due care" stick, let alone—'

But Jackie had heard enough. 'The police!' She leaned forward in her chair. 'Well, they're not going to do anything, are they? He was one of them, that Ray West. What about what Wrigley had to say?'

Stan Wrigley was Jackie's only shred of hope. An elderly man who lived on the road where the accident had taken place, he had apparently seen everything while he was letting his cat out for the night. And according to him, it had been no accident.

'Mr Wrigley's account is uncorroborated. Mr West's account of events is corroborated by his passenger . . .'

Jackie glared at him. 'So they'll believe them who's got an interest in it not going ahead, but ignore what a man saw who's nothing to do with it?'

'I do sympathize, but . . .'

'I don't want your sympathy, Mr Kavanagh.' Jackie sat bolt upright and looked him in the eye. 'I want you to take the case. I want you to stand up and speak for someone as can't. Ryan's in a coma. They say there's probably brain damage.'

Kavanagh had to admire the woman. She didn't,

indeed, want sympathy. She wanted justice. But it was, he reckoned, a tragedy that she was so misguided.

'Mrs Jarvis, at the end of the day, if that's what you want then the barristers' code of conduct says I am bound to accept. But my *view* is that you do not have sufficient evidence to proceed – and I must strongly advise you against doing so.'

Jackie looked thoughtful for a moment. 'What if I got you more evidence?'

Persistent, thought Kavanagh, was not the word. 'If it was persuasive enough, then, yes, we might have a chance. Otherwise . . .'

'Otherwise Ray West as good as kills my son and gets away with it?'

Jackie Jarvis went back to Sunderland and back to her job behind the bar at the Packhorse. Everything she did, she did mechanically and out of habit. Her mind was elsewhere: part of it was with Ryan as he lay, covered with tubes and wires, in his hospital bed; the other part was occupied with thinking of how to get the extra evidence she would need to give herself a fighting chance in her case against Ray West.

The day after her meeting with Kavanagh, lost in contemplation as she wiped the counter in front of her, she was startled out of her reverie by a voice at the far end of the bar.

'Two pints of lager. And a Dubonnet and lemonade, please.'

Jackie, wordlessly, reached for the pint glasses below the pumps. Her face set, she pulled the first pint and approached the customer. He, she was glad to see, had his back to her for a moment: he was looking round and smiling at his companions – at his girlfriend Lisa

119

Parks and her father Don. Jackie gave him his pint. She lifted it with a deft flick of the wrist and threw the entire contents of the glass over his head.

Ray, stunned, turned round in horrified surprise. Then, for the first time, Jackie spoke to him. 'You come in here?' she screamed. 'You . . . I don't know how you can show your face!' Everyone in the bar, hearing her words, immediately fell silent.

'I can't stay out for ever!' Ray yelled back. 'I just want a drink, all right? I don't want any trouble. It's done with.' He looked Jackie in the eye. 'All right?'

Jackie, ready to launch into another impassioned salvo, was interrupted by Frank, the Packhorse's landlord. 'Hey, hey, hey!' he shouted as he came charging in from behind the bar. 'What's going on here?'

'Sling him out, Frank,' ordered Jackie.

Ray West now turned on him. 'Mad! She's bloody mad, man!' He raised a hand to indicate his soaking head and the shirt that was now clinging to him. 'Look what she's done!'

Frank took in the situation in two seconds flat. He felt sorry for Jackie: he had been immensely fond of Ryan. But he also had a business to run. To Jackie's fury, he pulled another pint for Ray. That, and the drinks he got for Lisa and Don, were on the house. Jackie, too furious to trust herself to speak, stormed out of the bar and into the back yard.

Malcolm Gibson, the most regular of regulars at the Packhorse, witnessed the entire affair from his favourite position at the end of the bar. No one, as usual, paid him much attention. And no one noticed his sudden change of expression as he watched Jackie's departure. His customary vacant stare gave way to a look of resolute determination and, leaving his half-finished pint on the bar, he followed Jackie into the yard. He found

120

her there, pacing up and down amid the empty crates and beer kegs, smoking furiously in an attempt to calm herself down. 'I . . .' he paused, seeing the tears that were welling in her eyes. 'You all right?' Jackie didn't reply. 'I was just . . . I wanted to say . . . I was sorry. About Ryan. I liked him. He bought us a drink . . . a few times. I . . . I liked him.' Malcolm shrugged resignedly. 'He shouldn't have done it. West. He shouldn't have . . .'

'Oh,' said Jackie with a derisive snort. 'Him? He's a hero, he is. It was an accident, Malcolm. Haven't you heard?'

Malcolm hesitated, seemingly fighting against some inner compulsion. Then he gave way to it. 'Wasn't an accident. Not going up on the pavement. I . . .' Then, with great conviction, he added, 'Wasn't no accident.'

'What?'

Already, Malcolm seemed to regret his outburst. 'Nothing.'

'What d'you mean, Malcolm? "It wasn't an accident"?'

Malcolm took a deep breath. 'He done it on purpose. He went up on to the pavement after him. On purpose.'

'The pavement? No one's said that before.' Jackie paused and looked Malcolm straight in the eye. 'How do you know?'

'I was there.'

CHAPTER THIRTEEN

Jeremy Aldermarten was glad – very glad – that he had had the foresight to take on Alex Wilson as his pupil. Really, he thought, she was shaping up very nicely. And she was remarkably bright. Really very bright. Considering. A pity, therefore, that she had just recently made such a mess of this tin-pot case in a Magistrates' Court. For a pupil to be given a trial of her own – no matter how small – was quite an honour.

As they sat in the wine bar, Alex was close to tears. Jeremy poured the dregs of the bottle into her glass and moved closer.

'I didn't blind them with science,' said Alex. 'I didn't argue with the boys in blue. But I lost – horribly.'

'Don't take it to heart, Alex. Long as you gave it your best shot . . .'

'I don't know if I can do it,' she moaned. 'I really don't. Another day like today and . . .'

Jeremy moved even closer and put a comforting arm round her shoulders. 'Oh . . . there. There. Alex, Alex, we can't have you down in the dumps. Listen, why don't I get another bottle and you can tell me all about it, hmm?'

'No. No, really, I mustn't.'

'Nonsense.' Jeremy was adamant. 'You're a big grown-up girl. And for big grown-up girls there's no such thing as mustn't.' Only when he had slipped off his seat and woven off in the direction of the bar did a frown cross Alex's features. Was she misreading the situation? Was he just being avuncular – or were there other, less pleasant undertones to his solicitous attitude? Then, lost in misery, she drained her glass. Perhaps another bottle would be a good idea after all. Drowning sorrows and all that. And what she was most sorry about was that Tom Buckley had given her the case in the first place. He *must* have known it was far more complicated than it had first appeared. Alex shook her head. The last thing she needed – positively the last thing any barrister needed – was to be on the wrong side of the senior clerk. Yet she couldn't figure out where she had gone wrong with him.

Alex would have been somewhat mollified to know that she hadn't gone wrong anywhere. Tom Buckley liked her very much. He found her good fun and intelligent, and he hoped that she would be taken on for a tenancy at River Court. And he certainly hadn't meant to humiliate her by giving her an unwinnable case for her first trial. The fault of this afternoon's débâcle, Alex would have been glad to know, lay with Tom, not with her. On the morning he had given her the papers for the trial he had had a thundering hangover. He had arrived late for work, and the bad mood induced by incalculable amounts of alcohol and very little sleep had worsened when Kavanagh had come up to him to declare that he would accept the Jarvis *v.* West case. Tom had been furious. 'We're not Oxfam, sir,' was the mildest reply he could think of.

Kavanagh had smiled. 'For England, Harry and St George.'

Tom glowered at him. 'In other words, for bugger all.'

'Of which you're on for five per cent.' Kavanagh had been uncharacteristically sharp. 'All right?'

Tom, feeling mutinous, had slunk out of the office. Kavanagh, being a QC and with a superb reputation, didn't need to keep on the right side of Tom all the time. He was too important. Still, there were other ways for Tom to get back at him for what he saw as an unwise decision. Retreating to his own office, Tom looked at his book of cases – as yet unallocated within River Court – coming up for trial. He soon found what he was looking for: a family law case. Kavanagh hated doing family; he performed best in front of a jury. And this was a real corker. A mother challenging the custody order of her child; the father kidnapping the child and then giving himself up in a blaze of publicity after which he went on to accuse the stepfather of child abuse. Juicy, thought Tom. And at least he could defend his decision to Kavanagh on the grounds that, while this was a private prosecution, it was not – unlike the case of the dismal woman from Sunderland – going to pay peanuts. There was, Tom was glad to see, a lot of money in this one.

With a wicked smile, Tom then phoned the instructing solicitor on the case to inform her that Mr Kavanagh, QC, would be representing her client. Only afterwards did he realize that he had neglected to allocate a small, as yet unread Magistrates' Court case. Julia Piper, initially, had been scheduled to take it, but at the last moment a more important trial had run over and she had been unable to fit it in. It had been Alex Wilson's misfortune that she had chosen that moment to come into Tom's office.

By the time Jeremy came back from the bar with another bottle of wine, Alex had worked herself up into a further frenzy of misery. She knew, however, that it wouldn't do to complain about Tom Buckley. Instead, she went back to describing the actual events that had led to her humiliation in the court that day. 'They made me feel this big—'

'You don't,' interrupted Jeremy pompously, 'want to be frightened by the Mags. Middle-class morons to a man. Pity,' he added, 'I wasn't there to protect you . . .'

'*Protect* me?' Warning bells started clanging in Alex's mind.

'Yes. You're my pupil. Of course I feel protective towards you . . . I have to take you under my wing . . . teach you things . . .' He trailed off, more intent now on the progress of his hand which, to Alex's horror, he had placed on her stockinged knee. Then he started moving his fingers in a circular, caressing movement.

'Jeremy . . .'

But Jeremy wasn't listening. He was looking, in slight awe, at the chocolate-brown leg up which his hand was now progressing. 'You've got such beautiful skin . . .'

'Jeremy!'

Startled, he looked up. 'What? What is it? What're you doing?'

Alex, flustered, angry, ashamed and slightly drunk, started fishing for her bag. 'Look. I've got to go. This is too much. I simply can't handle this.'

But Jeremy, genuinely surprised, didn't seem to know what she was talking about. 'What . . . what . . . what on earth have I . . .?'

But he was talking to thin air.

Jeremy Aldermarten wasn't the only member of River Court Chambers to have trouble with women that night. James Kavanagh, at home in Wimbledon, was startled by Lizzie's reaction to his going to Sunderland on the Jarvis case.

'But you already know you're going to lose?'

'Yes.'

'Then why? It's not as if you've got something to prove.'

'Because,' James said with a far-away expression, 'her son's in a coma. Because she hired me . . .' He shrugged. 'Because she wouldn't take no for an answer.'

'But you, on the other hand, can say no to your family. You can say, "No, I won't be here for you. No, I won't be able to support Matt. No . . ." '

'Lizzie . . . !'

'It's not good enough, Jim. Matt's got problems at school and we're both so busy that we hardly even knew!'

'Then why don't you . . . ?'

'Stay at home?' Lizzie glared at him. 'Are you intimating that my career's less important than yours? That it doesn't matter because you're the one . . .'

'No!'

They stood facing each other in mounting antagonism. Neither of them was prepared to admit what they both knew: that they had not been paying enough attention to Matt, of late. The boy, so his headmaster had informed them, was causing trouble at school; he was being inattentive and insolent and was neglecting his studies. The headmaster had asked if there were problems at home, perhaps? Jim had been horrified. Problems at home were things that happened to his clients – not to his own family. But he knew, deep down, that the private hell he and Lizzie had just come through must have affected Matt as well.

Even worse, as far as his parents were concerned, was the fact that neither James nor Lizzie had been there to see their son's recent success. Matt's great passion, matched only by his great talent, lay in swimming – and he had recently qualified to represent his club in the 200 metres freestyle. He had been thrilled to bits – and bitterly disappointed by the absence of his parents.

Kate, who was still so involved with Luke that she barely noticed anyone else, had surprised them both with an unprecedented critical outburst: she had accused her mother of 'thinking more of other people's blasted kids' than of her own. It had, inevitably, been a fund-raising meeting that had prevented Lizzie from seeing Matt's race. Kavanagh, equally inevitably, had been in conference. And here he was planning to be away in Sunderland for several days on a completely unwinnable case.

Kavanagh took a deep breath. 'Look, it's done now. I *have* to go. But I'll be back to see Matt in the final. I promise.'

Lizzie too calmed down. They were, she had to concede, equally to blame. 'So will I. No matter what comes up at work, I'll be there. It means so much to Matt.'

'And Matt means so much to me.' Suddenly Kavanagh grinned and looked towards the corner of the room; at the new hi-fi, TV and video replaced only the day before after their burglary.

'He's the only one who knows how to work the new video, after all.'

CHAPTER FOURTEEN

Raymond Philip West pleaded not guilty when the court clerk in Sunderland read out the accusation of the attempted murder of Ryan Jarvis, contrary to Section One of the Criminal Attempts Act of 1981.

Jackie Jarvis, sitting in the public gallery, pursed her lips and looked over at the man who was going to prove him a liar. Unlike the defence counsel, Kavanagh had no junior. Jackie's solicitor, Nick Carnforth, sat behind him, and behind the solicitor sat a callow youth who Jackie had been told was a court clerk seconded to their cause. The defence counsel comprised a barrister called Clive Pendle, a junior behind him, and their solicitor at the rear.

Jackie had been immensely pleased with herself when she had been able to tell Kavanagh that she had found another witness in Malcolm Gibson. Nick Carnforth had been less ecstatic – Gibson had 'a bit of previous', was a drunk and extremely unreliable to boot. That unreliability was underlined by the fact that he had not come forward in the first place to declare himself a witness. Kavanagh was extremely uneasy about him – Carnforth explained that Gibson, given his background, was reluctant to get involved with the police. Kavanagh had told Jackie that, even if Gibson did come to court, his evidence still would not go to prove beyond reasonable doubt that West had intended to kill Ryan. Their chances of winning were, he said, still negligible.

Jackie had looked him straight in the eye and said that despite everything, those were better odds than West had given her son. Ryan was unlikely ever to recover.

Kavanagh had felt humbled.

And now the first witness was in the box and, in response to Kavanagh's careful questioning, was explaining what he had seen on the night of the incident. Stanley Wrigley, thought Jackie, was a star. She listened with rapt attention as he told the court how he had been letting the cat out and, while standing in his front garden, had seen Ray West deliberately run down Ryan Jarvis. He was adamant that West actually speeded up in order to get Ryan. He was also, to the amazement of the entire court, adamant that West had been alone in the car. That last statement caused much whispering in the public gallery: West's entire defence rested on the assumption – unquestioned until now – that his passenger would corroborate his version of events. And that passenger would later be giving evidence.

Jackie, who had never before seen barristers in action, was impressed by Kavanagh's questioning of Wrigley. Surely, she thought, the 'enemy', now poised to cross-examine him, couldn't possibly pick holes in his argument?

Clive Pendle stood up, inclined his head towards Judge Garton, and then turned to Wrigley.

'Mr Wrigley, in your estimation, how far were you from the exact scene of the collision?'

The old man thought for a moment. 'Thirty odd yards, mebbe.'

'Thirty odd yards. Maybe. Mmm. If we called evidence showing that a proper measurement of the distance had demonstrated it was in fact eighty-seven yards, you would accept that, would you?'

Wrigley shuffled uneasily in the witness box. 'I . . . er . . . yes, I suppose.' Then, with more confidence, he added, 'But I know what I saw.'

'You know what you saw. Very well. Now, you say the car was going fast when it came into contact with Mr Jarvis? Is that right?'

'Aye. When he put his foot down he must've hit him around fiftyish.'

'Really. What does fiftyish look like?'

Wrigley bridled at the impudence of the question. 'I know what fast is.'

'Is that an opinion based on your own personal driving experience?'

'Er . . . no.'

'It's not? But you *do* drive a car?' Clive Pendle was enjoying himself.

'Er . . . no.'

'I see. Have you *ever* driven a car?'

'No.'

'Then *how* did you arrive at the figure of fifty miles an hour?' If Pendle's intention was to prove this witness was an imbecile, he was well on the way to succeeding.

'It was . . . well, I was guessing.'

'Yes. Well, you've also said, in response to my learned friend's earlier question, that the car was accelerating when it hit Mr Jarvis. Was *that* a guess?'

'No.' Wrigley was disparaging. 'Any bugger can tell whether a car's going faster or slower. The engine gets louder, dun't it?'

'Louder. Yes. A moment ago prosecuting counsel asked how you could tell the car you heard before you let your cat out was the same car you saw when you opened your door. Can you recall your reply?'

'Not offhand, no.'

'All right.' Pendle leaned forward to look at the notes he had taken during Kavanagh's examination of the witness. 'Let me help you. Counsel asked you, "How were you able to tell it was getting nearer?" To which you replied, "Well, from the noise." ' Pendle looked back up at Wrigley. 'Do you remember saying that?'

'Yes.'

'Yes. Now, what you've just described as acceleration could simply be the same effect, couldn't it?'

But Wrigley was lost. 'Eh? What effect?'

'Well, with the vehicle coming closer to you, the engine would have sounded louder, wouldn't it?'

Too late, Wrigley saw the trap. 'I . . . yes. Yes, I s'ppose it would've done.'

'So, the car wasn't necessarily going faster at all, was it?'

'No.'

'No. And if the car wasn't going faster, Mr West wasn't accelerating, was he, Mr Wrigley?'

'No. But . . . he was going fast.'

'Mr Wrigley, I have here the report of the police Accident Investigation Unit. If I told you their findings – which are not in any way in dispute – were that Mr West's car was travelling at a maximum – a *maximum* – of twenty-eight miles per hour, would that surprise you?'

Wrigley indeed looked surprised. 'Yes. Yes it would.'

'Mr Wrigley, when you read the oath you wore glasses. That's right, isn't it?'

'Yes.'

'Were you wearing them when you witnessed the incident you described?'

'No.'

'No. I see. Now, you've said that after the incident, Mr West got out of his car and went across to where Mr Jarvis was lying. What did you do?'

'I came out to the gate after him, after West, like. I thought he was going to run off.'

'And did he make any effort at all to do that? To run off?'

'No.'

'No. What did he do, Mr Wrigley?'

Wrigley's reply was given with great reluctance. 'He told me to go in and call for an ambulance.'

Clive Pendle fixed the jury with a meaningful stare. Then, with something akin to pity, he turned back to the hapless Wrigley. 'I see. He told you to call an *ambulance*. Not the action of a guilty man, surely.'

From there on, Kavanagh's case deteriorated with alarming speed. The next two witnesses were traffic policemen who had, they said, arrived at the scene approximately ten minutes after the accident – shortly before the ambulance. All that Kavanagh could get out of them of any use was the fact that, because of the heavy rain earlier in the evening, neither man was able to ascertain whether Ray West applied the brakes before or after the collision.

Clive Pendle's cross-examination of the traffic policemen ended by driving yet more nails into the coffin that the prosecution's case had become. Sergeant Redbridge, who had been both a friend and a colleague of West's from his days in the Force, made a remark which, while totally out of order, nevertheless made an impression on the jury. In response to Pendle's question about West's specialist skills, Redbridge replied that he had been an Area Car Driver, and as such had an extremely high standard of driving. 'I know,' he finished, 'that if there was any way he could've avoided hitting Mr Jarvis, he would've done so.'

Judge Garton was furious – and on to Redbridge like a ton of bricks. 'No, no, no.' Then, turning to the jury, he told them to disregard the sergeant's remarks. 'He was not in the vehicle in question and is indulging in nothing more than wild surmise.' Then he fixed Redbridge with a withering look. 'Really, Sergeant, you should have known better.'

But the damage had been done, and Kavanagh knew it. So strong did West's case look that Kavanagh was expecting Pendle shortly to submit to the judge, in private, that there was in fact no case to answer. And if things continued this disastrously, it was likely that Judge Garton would agree and dismiss the case. Kavanagh's only hope was Malcolm Gibson, the witness who had approached Jackie after she had decided to bring the prosecution. He, like Stanley Wrigley before him, was going to testify that Ray West was the only man in the car when it had hit Ryan Jarvis.

Yet even that was a slim hope. Gibson was even more unreliable than Wrigley and he was, in addition, an alcoholic. It would take the most extraordinary jury in the world to believe his evidence against that of two traffic policemen – both of whom had sworn on oath that a distressed Ray West, when they had arrived at the scene of the accident, was standing with his passenger beside Jarvis's prone body. And they had both confirmed that the passenger was his closest colleague in the Collenshaw Park Pals Community Defence Association – Don Parks.

Lisa Parks, because she was going to be called as a witness at some point in the case, was not allowed into the public gallery. Yet she had heard enough from Ray's cronies, packed into the gallery beside the press, to know that Jackie Jarvis was going to lose her case – and with it all her money. She had already, to all intents and purposes, lost her only son.

The more she heard about what was going on inside the court, the more Lisa was troubled by her conscience. But she couldn't, she just *couldn't*, tell the court what she knew. What would be the point? Ryan would never recover; her father would never forgive her – and how could she possibly stand up in court and say that her boyfriend was a liar, that her father could not have been in Ray's car because he had been, at the exact time of the accident, at home talking to Lisa herself? It wasn't that Ray was a murderer: Lisa couldn't go out with a murderer. It had been an accident, just like they said. A horrible, tragic accident. And anyway, it really had nothing to do with her.

Yet she found it impossible to dissociate herself from Ryan. Every day since he had been in hospital, she had made surreptitious visits to his bedside, each time bringing flowers with her. Every day she looked at his prone body; and every day she touched the cold lips, and felt a corrosive regret. It was unfortunate that on this particular day, after the court session, she should bump into Jackie Jarvis.

'I'm sorry,' she mumbled in horrified embarrassment. 'I didn't think . . .'

Jackie, equally horrified, stared at the girl with

unconcealed dislike. 'I wondered who was bringing him flowers.' Her voice, thought Lisa, was icy. Almost scary. 'You come every day?'

Lisa nodded.

'What for?'

'To . . . to see him.'

Jackie looked at her. 'I know you come "to see him". What I want to know is – why?'

But Lisa couldn't tell her why.

Jackie stared into her eyes, scrutinizing her soul: searching for the truth. 'I don't know how you people sleep,' she said after a moment. 'You? You let Ray West put his hands on you? You lie on your back for him?'

'No,' lied Lisa. Each of Jackie's words was a deadly knife piercing the very core of her being.

'Have him inside you?' taunted Jackie.

Lisa couldn't bear it. Suddenly she burst into great heaving sobs. 'Stop! Please!'

But Jackie carried on, now thrusting her face close to Lisa's. 'A murderer. And you think bringing flowers makes it all all right? Get out,' she barked. 'Get out before I have you thrown out.'

Lisa, the tears streaming down her face, fled out of the ward, out of the hospital, and out into the wet, unwelcoming night.

By the time the court adjourned for lunch the next day, Kavanagh's case had disintegrated even further. And, ironically, the person most to blame for that was the man who was supposed to be his star witness – Malcolm Gibson. It wasn't Malcolm's fault that he performed so badly in court. He was ill-at-ease, scared – and in pain. At the same time as Lisa had fled St Edmund's Hospital the night before, Malcolm, ambling along a deserted street, had been ambushed by the very people who were supposed to be protecting the community – the Pals.

Keith, the leader of this particular group, had stepped forward out of the shadows and accused Malcolm of 'rocking the boat', of 'making trouble for a friend'.

Malcolm was taken completely by surprise. 'I . . . I . . . don't know what you're talking about.'

Keith punched him in the gut in order to jog his memory. 'Go to court against Ray West,' he threatened the winded man, 'and we'll kill you. All right? Got it, Malcolm?'

Just in case Malcolm didn't get it, Keith and the other two Pals knocked him to the ground and gave him several hefty kicks to the stomach and chest.

It was therefore a tribute both to Malcolm's bravery and to his loyalty to Jackie and Ryan Jarvis that he went to court the next day. He responded well to Kavanagh's questions; he gave a wholly believable account of the events he had witnessed and he stated, with complete conviction, that there was only one man in the car when it had hit the man he later realized was Ryan.

After that, Clive Pendle tore him apart. It wasn't very difficult. It took Pendle five minutes to establish that Malcolm had first met Ray West when the latter was still a policeman; when he was, in fact, the traffic policeman who had arrested Malcolm for drunken driving – an event that led to Malcolm losing his licence, his job as a sales rep and, ultimately, his wife and his house.

Having established Malcolm as a no-good drunk with a long-standing grudge against Ray West, Pendle didn't have to work very hard to convince the jury that he was also a liar. Why, he asked, had Malcolm waited so long before declaring himself as a witness? Malcolm replied that he was scared of the 'larruping' he'd get from 'West's goons' if they got to hear about it. As arguments went, it wasn't entirely convincing, and Pendle continued his relentless quest to rubbish everything Malcolm said. So incensed, so angry and so incoherent did Malcolm become that, to the great surprise of the entire court, he ripped off his shirt to show the jury the bruises he had sustained at the hands of 'West's goons' the previous night. The jury, to a man, was unimpressed. Judge Garton, aghast at such behaviour in his courtroom, had Malcolm forcibly removed from the witness box. Kavanagh, appalled, didn't dare look at Jackie Jarvis. He had no more witnesses to call. He now had no chance of winning the case.

CHAPTER FIFTEEN

Halfway through his questioning of Ray West, Clive Pendle stole a glance at the jury to try to gauge their reaction to him. He was slightly put out to discover that all the jurors were looking extremely bored. So, he then noticed, was Kavanagh. And Judge Garton, he saw with a mixture of horror and amusement, was fighting to stay awake. Perhaps, he thought, he'd pursued this particular line of questioning for long enough. Ever since West had taken the oath, Pendle's questions had been limited to West's past career as a policeman, to his current occupation as organizer of the Pals, and to the impact of the latter on the crime statistics of the Collenshaw Park Estate. By now, Pendle realized, the court had got the message: West was a star and the Pals were the best thing that had ever happened to the estate. It was time to move on to the night in question.

'Mr West, could you explain to the court what you were doing immediately prior to the accident?'

West smiled confidently. 'I was conducting my usual patrol,' he said, 'when a report came over the radio that there had been a break-in on the estate. A young man had been spotted running from the scene. I went round there, spoke to the victim, made sure she was all right and waited until the police turned up.'

'Then what did you do?' Pendle was relieved to note that the jury had perked up.

'I resumed my patrol – keeping one eye out for anyone as matched the description – clothing and so on – that I'd got.'

'What happened then?'

'I drove around for about another half-hour until I saw Ryan.'

'How did you know it was Ryan Jarvis?'

West allowed himself to look slightly disapproving. 'I knew Ryan from around the estate and from when I was in the police. He's a lad who's been in trouble a lot.' He paused to let the jury savour his words. 'So, I approached him, said I wanted a word, and he ran off. I then arranged to pick up Mr Parks, which I did, and we drove round looking for Ryan until we found him.'

'And when you found him?'

'We saw him running into Mancroft Road – so we followed him. He was running down the pavement behind the row of parked cars and then . . . and then he suddenly ran out into the road, right in front of us.' West looked pained at the memory. 'I slammed on the brakes but . . . well, it was too late. I hit the lad.'

'So you hit Ryan – then what happened?'

'I'd hit the brakes that hard, Don had been thrown forward, like, and was slumped in his seat. I'd caught my head on the wheel – so I got out and I was dazed, obviously, and shocked – and then I came across to Ryan . . . and . . . and then Don came across from the car and then the police arrived.'

The jury, listening with rapt attention, could forgive him his incoherence. The man was obviously distressed as he recalled the events of that night.

'How would you explain,' continued Pendle, 'the

evidence of Mr Gibson who claims he saw your car mount the pavement in pursuit of Mr Jarvis?'

West shrugged. 'I can't explain.' Then he bowed his head in sorrow. 'I'd do anything to turn the clock back, believe me.'

Kavanagh adopted a rather less sympathetic tone in his cross-examination. 'Mr West, wouldn't it have made more sense to remain in pursuit of Mr Jarvis, rather than to go off and fetch your colleague Mr Parks?'

'I didn't feel confident I could tackle him on my own. I wanted some back-up.'

'Surely Mr Parks could have notified the police as to your location, while you kept Ryan Jarvis in view?'

West shrugged. 'That would've been one way.'

'So,' persisted Kavanagh, 'why didn't you do that?'

'We always act in twos in the Pals.' West fixed Kavanagh with a challenging look. 'Then there's a couple of us to give evidence.'

'Mmm. Breaking off the pursuit to fetch Mr Parks could have meant losing Jarvis altogether. That's right, isn't it?'

'Well, that's a risk we have to take.' West turned with a half-smile to the jury. 'We don't win 'em all, you know.'

Some of the jurors returned the smile – but without much conviction. They looked attentive to what West was saying – but they weren't warming to him.

'It's for that reason you didn't break off the pursuit, isn't it?'

'Mr Kavanagh,' protested West, 'I did just what I told you.'

'You were determined to catch Ryan Jarvis by whatever means, isn't that right?'

'No, sir. Not by whatever means. No.'

'And so you pursued him into Mancroft Road, only you still couldn't get to him because for a while he was shielded from the road by parked cars, wasn't he?'

'I wasn't trying to "get to him". I was trying to talk to him.'

'Because he answered to the description of the man who had committed the burglary?'

'Yes.'

'So you were angry that he was running from you, and hitting him was the only way to stop him, wasn't it?'

'No, sir.'

'And when he ran out, you had your chance.'

'No, sir.'

'You deliberately ran him down. Isn't that the truth?'

'No, sir.'

Kavanagh paused for a moment. To the court, it looked like a studied move; a brief hiatus before he pounced on West with a new and more effective line of attack. At least, that's what Kavanagh hoped it looked like. The reality was different; he was making no headway whatsoever. He had not even made a dent in West's armour. But on the point of sitting down, he decided to play his trump card. He turned back to the defendant.

'Mr West, you did some first aid in the force, didn't you?'

'Oh yes.'

'Yes.' Kavanagh looked at his notes for a moment. 'In court yesterday Dr Atkins, who examined Ryan Jarvis on his arrival in hospital, said that it was in the ten minutes between the accident and the arrival of the ambulance that Mr Jarvis sustained the injuries that led to his present condition . . . '

'I don't . . . ?'

'After the accident Mr Jarvis's airway became obstructed by his tongue.' Again Kavanagh looked to his notes. 'In Dr Atkins's words, "Oxygen could not reach his brain and it began to die." Dr Atkins then went on to say that if someone at the scene had been able to clear the obstruction in the first minute or so, there would have been every chance that Mr Jarvis would have made a full and complete recovery.'

Kavanagh then looked West straight in the eye. 'Mr West, why didn't you attempt to clear Ryan Jarvis's airway?'

All eyes in the court were now on West. Why indeed? they seemed to be asking. West looked distinctly uncomfortable.

'Sir,' he said with apparent regret, 'you may be right. I probably should have, but I'd just been the driver in a major road accident. I was in no state to make any diagnosis of anything.'

Kavanagh had given it his best – but to no avail. He didn't dare look at Jackie Jarvis. After the adjournment for lunch, Lisa Parks, followed by her father Don, would be called to the witness box. And as they were witnesses for the defence, it was hardly likely that Kavanagh, prosecuting, would make any headway with them either.

Pendle's examination of Lisa Parks was brief and left little room for misinterpretation. He wanted to keep it as short as possible: Lisa, for some reason, was an extremely reluctant and highly nervous witness. Yet the jury, he noticed as he questioned her, were looking at her with sympathy. She was young and was obviously finding the whole business highly distressing. It wasn't every day one's boyfriend was accused of murder.

'I left the pub,' she was saying, 'at about quarter to ten, and I was indoors by ten.'

'What happened when you got home?'

'Well, my dad was on the radio, like, and a message came over from Ray.'

'And what was Mr West's message?'

'He said he was chasing the burglar and he wanted help.'

'And what happened then?'

'My dad went off to join Ray.'

'Thank you, Miss Parks.'

Lisa looked even more nervous when Kavanagh rose to cross-examine her. Kavanagh wasn't surprised. Over lunch, Jackie Jarvis had told him something extremely interesting about Lisa Parks.

'Miss Parks,' he asked without preamble, 'you left the pub with Ryan Jarvis, didn't you?'

Lisa avoided his eye. 'We left at the same time.'

'Why was that?'

Lisa shrugged. 'He'd offered to walk me back.'

'And *did* Ryan walk you home?' Silence from Lisa. 'Miss Parks?'

'No.'

'Why not?'

'I just didn't think I should let him. He's . . . he had a bad reputation.'

'I see. Was that the only reason you didn't want him to walk you home?'

'How d'you mean?'

'Well – you already had a boyfriend, didn't you?'

'Yeah.'

'Who is your boyfriend, Miss Parks?'

'Ray. Mr West.'

'Yes. And Mr West didn't like Ryan Jarvis, did he?'

'Well . . . he didn't *not* like him.'

143

Kavanagh sighed. 'Oh, come now, Miss Parks, he thought Ryan was a troublemaker, didn't he?'

'Yes, but . . .'

'He disliked him intensely. That's the truth, isn't it?'

'Well . . . yeah, but not enough to do anything like what he's here for.'

'So there was some dislike, then?'

Lisa shrugged. 'A bit.'

'A bit. So you knew Mr West wouldn't like you walking home with Ryan?'

'Yes.'

'So you left Ryan at the pub? Is that right?'

'Yeah. I don't know where he went. I went home.'

'And shortly after you arrived home you heard Mr West on the radio telling your father that he was chasing a burglar. Is that right?'

'Yes.'

'Did he identify the person he was chasing by name?'

'No.'

Kavanagh looked over to the jury. They were transfixed. For the first time in this case, some of them were beginning to think that something was not quite right. 'He didn't say,' continued Kavanagh, ' "I'm chasing a burglar. It's Ryan Jarvis"?'

'No.'

'Neither you nor your father knew who Mr West was chasing?'

'No. We only found out later.'

Kavanagh was on to her like lightning. 'Found out what?'

'That it was Ryan.'

'What do you mean when you say "later"?'

'After the accident.'

'How did you find out?'

144

Lisa wiped a bead of perspiration off her forehead. 'My dad said when he got home.'

'I see. Who else was there when you were told?'

'No one. Just me.'

'But you said "we", Miss Parks. You said, "We only found out later." '

'Er, sorry. I meant me.' It was now patently obvious to the members of the jury that Kavanagh was on to something. Lisa, equally obviously, was not having a good time.

'I suggest,' said Kavanagh quickly, 'that your father was with you when Mr West radiod through that he'd knocked Ryan down. That's why you said "we", isn't it?'

'No.'

'Your father didn't leave the house until after the accident, did he?'

'No . . . he left when Ray said he was chasing a burglar.'

Now Kavanagh picked up the piece of paper in front of him.

'Mr West first saw Ryan in Kershaw Street, didn't he?'

'Yes.'

'Yes. That's very close to Bloemfontein Road, where the burglary took place, isn't it?'

'Uh . . . yes.' Lisa was further unnerved by this different line of questioning. 'It's the next road up. That,' she added, suddenly inspired, 'was why Mr West was suspicious of Ryan.'

But Kavanagh wasn't impressed. 'Miss Parks, the street on which you live runs parallel to Bloemfontein, doesn't it?'

'Yes.'

'So, when Mr West found Ryan Jarvis he was only

two streets away from your house. Is that right, Miss Parks?'

'Er . . . yes.'

'Yes. In that case, he could just as easily have been walking back from your house, couldn't he?'

'I s'ppose.'

'He needn't have been walking back from Bloemfontein at all, need he?'

'No.'

'No.' Kavanagh leaned forward. 'Ryan walked you back home that night, didn't he?'

'No. I've told you.'

Again Kavanagh changed tack. After a fleeting and reassuring look at Jackie Jarvis, he turned back to the witness. 'Miss Parks, as I understand, you have been visiting Ryan in hospital. On a fairly regular basis.' Lisa's mouth opened in a silent 'o'. That was one question she had certainly not expected. 'Miss Parks?' urged Kavanagh.

Lisa shrugged. 'Yeah . . . well, I've been once or twice.'

'It's more than that, isn't it?'

'A few times. Maybe.'

'Does Mr West know you have been visiting Ryan?'

'No.'

'No. You thought it best to keep that from him, didn't you?'

'With things as they are . . .'

'Yes.' Kavanagh nodded. Then he rounded on her once more. 'With things as they are, why should you regularly visit Ryan?'

'I don't know . . . I just . . .' Lisa's voice rose to a wail and then, desperately trying to get a grip on her emotions, she lowered her voice and looked sullenly at Kavanagh. 'I don't know.'

146

'You're visiting Ryan Jarvis because he's on your conscience, isn't he?'

'No!'

'Because, if Ryan Jarvis hadn't walked you home that night, he wouldn't have been on Kershaw Road, would he?'

Lisa, confused, angry and upset, could hardly keep up with the battery of questions being fired at her. The jury could, however. They were riveted.

'He didn't—' tried Lisa before being interrupted by yet another question.

'And if he hadn't been on Kershaw Road, Mr West wouldn't have seen him, would he?'

'I don't know.'

Kavanagh, realizing the girl was about to break, was merciless. 'If he hadn't walked you home, he would not now be lying in a coma in a hospital ward, being kept alive by machines. That's the truth, isn't it, Miss Parks? Mr West ran Ryan over because he was angry that Ryan had walked you home. That's right, isn't it?'

'No.'

'He was jealous, wasn't he?'

'No!' wailed Lisa. 'He couldn't. He never saw . . .' In a desperate attempt to stop herself, she put a hand to her mouth.

But it was too late. Kavanagh was on to her in a flash. 'He never saw Ryan walking you home?'

'No.' Lisa hung her head in misery.

'So, *did* Ryan walk you home?'

'Yes,' whispered the hapless girl.

'I'm sorry, I don't think the jury quite heard that.'

'Yes.'

Kavanagh allowed himself the smallest trace of a smile. Some of the jury looked at him in admiration.

'Mr West,' continued Kavanagh, 'would've been

angry if he had found out that Ryan had walked you home, wouldn't he?'

'Er . . . yes.'

'And your father? How did he feel about Ryan walking you home?'

'He said he didn't want me seeing him again.'

That was what Kavanagh had been waiting for. Involuntarily, his knuckles whitened as they gripped the bench in front of him. 'So, he must have said that before Ryan was run over?'

'Yeah. Er, no . . . no . . .'

'There'd be little point, Miss Parks, in his telling you he didn't want you to see Ryan again *after* Ryan had been knocked down, would there?'

'No. I s'ppose not.'

'No. So he said that to you before he set out to meet Mr West. Is that right?'

Lisa, too confused to see where the question was leading, brightened up. She could answer that one with conviction.

'Yes. He said that when I got home, yeah.'

'Then, when your father left, he knew that Ryan had been with you in the pub that evening. That's right, isn't it?'

'Yes. Sure.'

'Yes. And if he knew that, then he also knew that Ryan couldn't have committed the burglary. Isn't that right?'

Lisa's brief moment of relaxation was over. She had dug herself into yet another trap. 'Yes,' she said reluctantly, 'I guess.'

'Then what you are saying, Miss Parks, is that your father pursued a man he knew to be innocent of any crime?'

'No!'

'A pursuit that led ultimately to Ryan Jarvis being run over.'

'No! He didn't know the burglar they were chasing was Ryan.'

'But if he didn't know who he was chasing, he wouldn't have been much help in the hunt, would he?'

'I don't think Ray told him it was Ryan.'

Kavanagh frowned. 'But he knew Ryan by sight, didn't he?'

'Yes, but . . .'

'Then, if he was in the car with Mr West, he would have seen Ryan and recognized him, wouldn't he?'

'No! He didn't know it was Ryan.'

Kavanagh pounced on that one. 'Your father didn't know that Mr West was chasing Ryan Jarvis?'

'Yes.' Lisa, thoroughly bewildered by the speed of this interrogation, was beginning to tie herself in knots. 'Er, no . . .'

'How could he not know – if he was in the car with Mr West?'

'Because,' wailed Lisa, 'he wasn't—' suddenly she stopped and looked at Kavanagh in utter horror.

'He wasn't what?' Kavanagh's voice was now ominously quiet.

Lisa lowered her hand and bent her head as the tears began to flow. Tears of frustration, of guilt and of shame. 'He wasn't there. In the car.'

Suddenly all was pandemonium in the public gallery. West's supporters erupted in fury at Lisa's admission. They began to hurl abuse at the weeping girl, and Judge Garton, furious himself at such unseemly behaviour, had to shout for silence.

Then Kavanagh continued his questioning. This

time he addressed Lisa more in sorrow than in anger. 'So Mr West was alone in the car?'

Lisa nodded miserably. 'Yes. Dad didn't know anything about it being Ryan . . . not until after.'

'Until after he was knocked down?'

'Yeah.'

'I see. How did you find out?'

There was no point, thought Lisa, in keeping anything back now. 'Ray radio'd through – asked Dad to go and meet him immediately. I'm sorry. I'm sorry,' she added to no one in particular. 'I'm really sorry.'

'So,' continued Kavanagh, 'your father was at home with you when Mr West ran Ryan Jarvis down? Is that right?'

'Yes.'

'And you and your father have since been covering for Mr West?'

Lisa looked at him in desperation. 'No – not covering. Just . . . well, it was still an accident, wasn't it? Ray said it was, but no one'd believe him if he was by himself.' She raised her hands in a gesture of futility. 'What could we do? We were just trying to help.'

Kavanagh looked up at the witness. 'You were just *trying to help*?'

But this witness was more belligerent than the last. Don Parks was going to go down fighting. He held his head up and glared at Kavanagh. 'Yeah.'

'So, you lied for Mr West.'

'Yes. I lied for him. And I'd do the same again. Ray's a good bloke. One of us. You can't have a man like that go to jail.' He paused, oblivious to the expression of horror on many of the spectators' faces – and on

150

all of the jury's. Then he looked derisively at Kavanagh. 'You? Huh. You don't know what the estate was like before Ray started the Pals—'

But Kavanagh had heard enough about the Pals. 'So the pair of you stood over Ryan as he was fighting for his life and discussed how you were going to deceive the police? Is that right?'

'Deceive the police? And I suppose your lot never do that, do they? Your bloody bail bandits and . . . and . . . the law', he continued, almost inarticulate with rage, 'is all for them, isn't it? On their side.'

'But Ryan hadn't done anything, had he?'

'He had in the past. And he'd got away with it.'

'So Mr West decided to appoint himself judge, jury and executioner. Is that right?'

Don Parks, almost unbelievably, held his head high in a gesture of defiance. At the back of the court, Ray West lowered his in misery. 'He did what he had to,' said Don. 'What any man'd do. Otherwise they're laughing at you. Ryan's not laughing now, is he?'

Kavanagh felt physically sick. Even Judge Garton, he noted, had gone slightly green around the gills. 'Are you saying that Mr West ran Ryan down deliberately?'

Don Parks nodded. 'That's what he said. It's how you deal with scum like Jarvis. And you show me anyone here as wouldn't do the same.'

Kavanagh lapsed into stunned silence. And only when Parks saw the expressions on the faces of the jurors did he realize the full, horrific implications of appointing oneself judge, jury and executioner.

CHAPTER SIXTEEN

Jeremy Aldermarten, once more ensconced in his favourite wine bar, leaned conspiratorially towards Peter Foxcott. 'It's a very difficult situation, Peter. You see, this chap – a lecturer at LSE – he's, well, it appears that he's overstepped the mark with one of his students.'

'Oh? Caught with his fingers in the honey pot—'

Jeremy, horrified, interrupted him. 'No. No. No. Nothing quite so bad as that. You see, I . . . that is to say, *he* . . . he thought there was, um, something on offer and he's . . .'

'Misread the water?'

'Exactly.' Jeremy beamed at Peter and then took a deep slug of wine. 'He's done nothing overt, you see, but . . . well, she seems to have got hold of the wrong end of the stick. You know how these things happen?'

Peter knew. He also knew exactly who 'these things' were happening to. Sometimes he really did wonder about Jeremy. Who was it, he thought: Julia Piper? Alex Wilson? Surely not the latter – Jeremy had made his feelings about her abundantly clear. Yet Julia was also unlikely: she would have told Jeremy, in no uncertain terms, what to do with stray parts of his anatomy.

Trying to disguise the weariness he felt, he looked

across the table. 'So – what does the girl say? Is she trying to make things difficult for him?'

'It's my understanding that they haven't actually discussed the incident. Yet.'

'Mmm.' Peter thought for a moment. If Jeremy was actively seeking his advice, it had to mean that he hadn't done anything too awful. Best, he decided, to nip it in the bud. The last thing he wanted was for River Court to be awash with accusations of sexual harassment. The Bar had a bad enough reputation for sexism in the first place. 'Well, my advice would be to grasp the nettle. This ... this student wants good grades, I take it. If I were him, I'd apologize, make it clear that he's no interest in making things unpleasant, and tell her to forget the whole thing.'

Jeremy beamed again. Good old Peter. He always had the right answers.

'And,' added Peter with a particularly penetrating look, 'I'd tell him to have the good sense not to do anything so bloody juvenile and witless again. Wouldn't you?'

'Whatever it is I did, or that you *thought* I did, I apologize unreservedly. I can only assume you misread the situation. I assure you my intentions were strictly honourable.'

Alex looked at Jeremy in amazement. He was standing ramrod-straight, and eyeing her as though she was a miscreant schoolgirl. What she really wanted to do was hit him. 'Jeremy,' she said, 'you put your hand up my skirt.'

'Inadvertently.'

Alex nearly laughed. 'How can you inadvertently put your hand up someone's skirt?'

'Easily. Easily. By accident. It's the sort of thing that used to happen all the time at school.'

Alex didn't care to ask where Jeremy had gone to school. She folded her arms in front of her and stared at him. 'An accident?'

'Yes.' Jeremy, warming to his theme, explained his version of events. 'I put my hand on your leg in a fatherly and comforting sort of a way, because you were upset, but . . . but your skirt had ridden a fraction up your, up your . . . and I, er, was a bit wide of the mark.' He grinned in, as he would have put it, 'a hopeful sort of way'.

But Alex was having none of it. 'No, Jeremy, that isn't what happened, and you know it. I was upset after losing that case and you tried to take advantage. I'm meant to be able to trust you. You're my pupil-master, for God's sake!'

Jeremy seemed genuinely surprised by her outburst. He also entirely missed her point. He looked at her with a pained, puzzled expression. 'Yes. But I've apologized.'

'So?'

Jeremy then played his trump card. This was one case he certainly wasn't going to lose. 'Well, I mean, play the game, Alex. Let's just keep this in perspective. Yes? At the moment you are on the bottommost rung of your chosen profession . . .' He left the sentence unfinished, the threat unspoken. Then he smiled again. 'But, of course, it's your choice, isn't it?'

Alex, open-mouthed, just stared at him as he turned and left the room. Never, she thought, *never* had she been subjected to blackmail like that. I need, she thought, a strong drink. Then she looked at her watch: it was ten o'clock in the morning. That made her even more annoyed. Then she brightened; the next best thing to a strong drink was a strong friend.

Storming into Julia's room without knocking, she didn't even pause to say hello before launching into an impassioned invective against Jeremy and his sexual misconduct. Julia, once she had got over her initial surprise, listened carefully. As she heard the tale, she felt upset for Alex, furious at Jeremy; furious, in fact, at the entire male species. But she was also a realist, and she knew that Alex was in a no-win situation.

'Let me see if I've got this straight,' she said when Alex had calmed down. 'Your pupillage is nearly up. Buckley's got a down on you 'cause you cock up a case, and last, but by no means least, Mr Touchy-Feely of River Court puts his hand up your dress?'

'Yes.' Alex gestured helplessly. 'What am I going to do about it?'

'You're going to stop snivelling, pull yourself up by the bootstraps and start behaving like a barrister.'

Alex looked stunned. 'Oh. You ... you think you can help?'

Julia grinned and clenched her hand in a victory salute. 'There isn't a male-dominated edifice yet built in England can hold Julia Piper!'

For the first time that morning, Alex laughed. Then Julia stood up and punched the air in a gesture of defiance. 'We fight on! We fight to win!'

Alex giggled. Julia, she mused, was an absolute brick. But as Alex left the room, the absolute brick allowed a deep frown to cross her features. She knew she had done the right thing; she knew that there would be no point in even hinting to Alex that she could do anything about Jeremy's little 'accident'. Still, there were other ways of making sure that he would behave himself from now on. Picking up her phone, she dialled Peter Foxcott's extension.

Ten minutes later Julia, Jeremy and Peter were sitting in Peter's office, discussing the Magistrates' Court case Alex had lost so disastrously.

'There's no way,' Julia was saying, 'that Alex should've been passed that brief. If Buckley hadn't clocked in with the mother and father of all hangovers, he'd have realized.' She looked from Peter to Jeremy. 'The case was unwinnable.'

'That's a matter of opinion, surely,' said Jeremy in his most pompous manner.

'Yes. *My* opinion. It was my case originally, don't forget.' Then she turned back to Peter Foxcott. 'Alex was dropped right in the bloody deep end, Peter. It really won't do. If River Court didn't have such a reputation for fairness and equality, I'd say someone had gone out of their way to damage her prospects.'

Peter looked horrified. 'But why? Who on earth would do such a thing?'

'There are those,' replied Julia with a pointed look at Jeremy, 'who would rather see fewer women coming into chambers.'

Jeremy bridled. 'I hope that remark wasn't directed at me. I'm all for seeing more of women in chambers.'

'You're all for seeing more of women full stop.'

Oh, thought Jeremy. So she knows. This little chat, following so quickly on the heels of his other 'little chat' with Alex, is no coincidence.

'So what do you propose we do?' asked Peter.

'It's not for me to propose anything. I merely bring it to your notice in the certain knowledge that, as Head of Chambers, you'll ensure that when Alex's pupillage

156

comes to an end, the possibility of her tenancy here will be judged purely on merit.'

Peter and Jeremy exchanged a brief, chastened look. Julia noted it and suppressed a smile.

CHAPTER SEVENTEEN

'What did he get?'

'Eight years.'

'Is that all?' Lizzie looked up in amazement. From what James had told her about the Sunderland trial, she would have expected Ray West to go down for longer. He sounded like a particularly nasty piece of work.

'We couldn't get him for attempted,' said Kavanagh as he sipped his whisky. 'The sentence was for GBH.'

'Huh.' Lizzie was unimpressed. 'Grievous Bodily Harm. Is that what they call it when you're condemned to spend the rest of your days on a life-support machine? Seeing nothing, hearing nothing. Feeling nothing. What sort of a life is that?'

'It isn't. Not now, anyway.'

'What d'you mean?'

Jim looked at his wife who, with her customary efficiency, was simultaneously reading a recipe book, cooking and talking to him – all with rapt attention. 'His mother asked the doctors to switch off the life-support machine. She told me she'd do it.' He paused and took another sip of his drink. 'But only after she'd seen justice done.'

'She must have had great faith in you.'

Kavanagh shook his head. 'Not in me. In herself.

She *knew* what had happened. She knew if she pushed hard enough, she'd get to the bottom of it.'

Lizzie, slightly amused, looked across the kitchen at her self-effacing husband. 'She also knew where to go to get the barrister who would succeed where all others fail.'

Kavanagh, pleased at the note of pride in her voice, allowed himself a smile. 'Well . . .' Then he checked himself and frowned. 'I just wish Jock Armstrong hadn't known the same thing.'

'One day,' said Lizzie with conviction, 'those Armstrongs will get their come-uppance. Just you wait.' Then she shrugged and went to open the oven door. 'And anyway, as you say, you can't win 'em all.'

'*Do* I say that?' Kavanagh didn't think he was prone to making such trite remarks.

'You said it to Matt.' Lizzie, wincing under the weight of the huge casserole dish, deposited it with a grateful sigh on the table.

'Oh. So I did. Poor old Matt. Still, he did bloody well coming second. Mmm. Smells delicious.' Then he peered closely into the pan. 'Feeding the five hundred, are we?'

'No. Just us. And Luke.'

'Ah. That explains it. I suppose he does need more than the rest of us. Nourishment for that tortured artistic soul and all that.'

'Jim! Please . . .'

'Well really, having Luke around is like having the Russian army camped out in the fridge.'

'You're exaggerating because you don't like him.'

'What makes you say that?'

'Because,' said Lizzie, 'you wouldn't like any boy who went out with your beloved daughter.' Then, drop-

159

ping her jocular tone, she looked Kavanagh in the eye. 'The only problem is, Jim, she's not a baby any more.'

But further discussion of Luke and Kate was interrupted by the noisy arrival of Matt. 'Hi!' He smiled briefly at both his parents and then, scenting food, made a bee-line for the casserole and dipped a finger into its delicious and piping hot contents. 'Ow!'

'Serves you right,' said his father. 'What happened to your manners, young man?'

'They were drilled out of me at school.'

Kavanagh could believe that. This, he thought as he looked at his son, was the boy who had almost been banned from taking part in the swimming competition for writing 'Mr Norriss is a wanker' on the school wall. Mr Norris, who taught English and spelled his name with only one 's', was understandably less than amused. He was also successful in preventing Matt from taking part in the competition – until the intervention of Lizzie. Kavanagh, as she rather too pointedly told him, had been away in Sunderland. With the tenacity of a lioness fighting for her cub, Lizzie had pleaded with the school to let Matt take part. It would be ludicrous, she had claimed, to prevent her son from doing something that meant a great deal to him and – potentially – to the school, just because of a minor misdemeanour. Surely there were other, more fitting ways to punish Matt? The headmaster, who was rather scared of Mrs Kavanagh in full flood, had quickly capitulated.

Matt had been delighted: both because he could take part and because his mother had been firmly and unequivocally on his side. He had been even more delighted when his father had hot-footed it straight from Sunderland to the swimming-pool to see him competing. He had been rather less pleased when he came second. Still, and as his father had said, you can't win 'em all.

It was all the more unfortunate, thought Kavanagh, that tonight's cosy family meal was to include Luke. It wasn't, he reasoned, that he didn't *like* Luke. Well, it was only partly because he didn't like Luke. It was mainly because, as Lizzie had astutely remarked, he hated the fact that Luke was taking Kate away from him.

But dinner, despite Kavanagh's reservations about both Luke's presence and his appetite, turned out to be an interesting affair. This was mainly due to Matt, Kate and Luke's prurient interest in Kavanagh's next case. The day after his return from Sunderland, he had gone straight into conference about the forthcoming complicated child custody battle that Tom Buckley had assigned to him – but before that one came to court, there was another, less complex but rather more sensational case to try.

It concerned one Debbie Drake, a woman who earned her living in a manner of great interest to the teenagers round the dinner table. Even Lizzie, although she pretended to be above the whole thing, was riveted by the affairs of Debbie Drake.

Debbie, who had grown up in London's East End, had determined at a young age not to follow in her parents' footsteps. While both were extremely hard-working, their efforts – as a Billingsgate Market porter and an office cleaner – reaped little reward. Money, throughout Debbie's childhood, was in consistently short supply, and while her parents had learned to accept the situation, Debbie had not. During her childhood, there was little she could do to alter the situation, but once she hit her teens, she was presented with an opportunity for change. As a little girl, she had often been told by adults that she was bright and angelic. As a bigger girl, she was told by a different sort of adult that she was sexy. It didn't take Debbie too long to realize what they meant, and at sixteen she had become sufficiently street-wise to know that her future lay not in the dingy backstreets of Plaistow but in the altogether brighter thoroughfares of Soho. Her parents, solid working-class people with a strict sense of morals, had nothing against their daughter's wish to establish herself in the job market as soon as possible, but they did wonder why she had to choose Soho as the place to begin her career as a waitress. Yet they kept their doubts to themselves, and as a gesture of goodwill, they gave Debbie enough money to buy her first uniform.

Debbie didn't need very much money for the uniform: her first job was as a topless waitress in a 'private club'. With her pretty face, her generous physical attributes, her easy smile and her quick wit, she was an instant success. The manager of the club was so impressed by her that within a month she was promoted. Six months after that, Debbie had learnt enough about her trade to branch out on her own.

Fifteen years later, Debbie had become an extremely successful businesswoman with a small but thriving empire embracing clubs, magazines, videos and a highly successful mail-order business. Her activities interested a great number of people from all walks of life, including, inevitably, the police. And now, because of a raid on her premises three months ago leading to a prosecution headed by Kavanagh, those activities were proving of great interest to the Kavanagh family.

Kavanagh, perhaps because he had drunk rather more wine at dinner than was advisable, found himself telling his children and Luke more about Debbie than he should have. Still, he thought, it was all fairly harmless, and there was nothing about Debbie's activities that would shock or revolt anyone.

'So what,' asked Kate at one point, 'is her defence?'

Kavanagh grinned at his daughter. 'She claims that the videos in question are "art".'

'And are they?'

'That, my dear, is up to the jury to decide.'

'D'you think,' said Kavanagh as he and Lizzie withdrew to the sitting-room after dinner, 'that I told the kids too much?'

'About what? Debbie?'

'Mmm.'

Lizzie looked at her husband with the beginnings of a slight frown. 'No. No. I think you're right not to shelter them from things.' Then she paused and added, 'Anyway, sex is . . . well, it's a fact of life, isn't it?'

'It most certainly is.' Kavanagh, smiling, turned to Lizzie and was surprised to see that she was looking both serious and thoughtful. 'Is anything wrong?' he added.

'No. Not as far as I'm concerned. It's just that . . . well,' Lizzie shifted uncomfortably on the sofa, 'I want you to stay very calm, Jim.'

'Eh?'

'Kate's asked if Luke can stay the night with her.' Dammit, thought Lizzie, that didn't come out right.

Kavanagh looked as if he was in shock. Then his face clouded over. 'No chance. No way.' As he spoke the words, he reached for the telephone beside him.

'What are you doing?'

'I'm calling a mini-cab.'

'Jim . . .' With quiet deliberation, Lizzie leaned over and took the telephone from her husband. 'We have to face the inevitable sooner or later, you know.'

'Maybe. But not in my house and not now.' He looked thunderous. 'She's still at school.'

Lizzie sighed. 'Okay, so she's still at school. But she *is* seventeen and at least she's being up-front about it.'

Hearing her words, Kavanagh too sighed. This, he thought, is all my fault. Bloody Debbie Drake. He turned to his wife. 'And so am I. I'm sorry, Lizzie, it's not on.'

Lizzie didn't reply. Taking her silence for disagreement, he carried on in less forceful tones. 'Is she really serious about this Luke?'

'For now, yes.'

'Mmm.' Again an uneasy silence filled the room. 'Am I really being so unreasonable, Lizzie?'

Lizzie shrugged. 'No. Just doing what you think is right.' Kavanagh, with a mixture of guilt and wistfulness, stared straight ahead. 'I never even had a chance to tell her the facts of life.'

Lizzie couldn't help grinning as she noted his troubled tone. She leaned closer to him and put an arm round his shoulders. 'I did it.'

'When?'

'When you were off prosecuting a juicy fraud in Cheltenham.'

CHAPTER EIGHTEEN

Debbie Drake was no stranger to appearing in court. The jury, of course, didn't know that, and Kavanagh, as prosecution counsel, was not allowed to draw their attention to the fact. As with any other trial, references to previous prosecutions or convictions were strictly off-limits. Yet the very nature of this case was enough to indicate to most of the court that the law and Debbie Drake's chosen career were uneasy bedfellows.

The detective inspector who had obtained a warrant to search Debbie's business premises had already informed the court, under examination from Kavanagh, that the address in question was the registered trading address of Drake Productions Ltd., Drake Home Video, and DMD International. Those companies, claimed Detective Inspector Bryce, dealt with the production, distribution and mail order of adult films 'of a particularly explicit kind'.

During his questioning of Bryce, Kavanagh noted the expressions on the faces of the jurors. Without exception, they eyed Debbie Drake, sitting at the back of the court, with almost indecent interest. On advice from her solicitor, Debbie was wearing a demure navy blue suit and an expression of innocence tinged with outrage.

It was the second witness, a professor of art named

Hilary Dixon, who informed the jury that Miss Drake was not a pornographer nor even a mere artist but a pioneer in the exploration of the role of female sexuality. Professor Dixon took herself so seriously that the jurors were inclined to do so as well. Chris Barnard, counsel for the defence, was pleased with the effect she was creating. When asked for her opinion of Deborah Drake's work, the professor became both excited and deeply earnest.

'I think it's fascinating,' she said. 'Deborah Drake is making a very strong statement about male and female sexuality. You see, straight pornography is about the objectification and ultimately the degradation of women. Drake's work uses pornographic imagery to explore ideas of female empowerment.' In a rare pause for breath, Professor Dixon smiled encouragingly at the jury. Half of them looked bemused: the other half, highly amused. 'In my view,' she continued, 'her work contains a valuable critique of gender roles.'

Barnard, po-faced, addressed her once more. 'What is the effect of this critique?'

'It means that the text becomes far more than merely pornographic. It becomes a comment and criticism on conventional perceptions of obscenity.'

'The material in question is uncommonly graphic?'

'Oh yes.' Professor Dixon, becoming even more animated, leaned forward in the witness box. 'But the *explicitness* – or obscenity, if we must use that word – is absolutely vital to the overall analysis.'

'Thank you, Professor Dixon.'

Kavanagh, adopting a highly sceptical expression, stood up to begin his cross-examination. 'Professor Dixon, isn't it true that the typical customer for these films would have little or no awareness of the finer qualities you detect in them?'

If the professor detected the underlying sarcasm behind the question, she chose to ignore it. After a thoughtful pause, she answered, again with great sincerity, 'I don't know what you mean by typical. But I think anyone looking for straight pornography would be in for a pretty uncomfortable time. They're certainly not a titillating experience.'

'But are you seriously telling us that these films are art?'

'I believe that her video work is exploring an important dialectic.' Nodding to herself, she then shot Kavanagh a slightly reproving look. 'There's a very strong aesthetic at work here.'

'Forgive me, Professor, but was that yes or no?'

In the public gallery, crammed with pressmen, there was a wave of muted laughter.

'There is a serious artistic intent . . .'

But Kavanagh had had enough of the professor. In a sweeping gesture, he raised one of the offending videos for all to see.

'Is this, or is it not, art?'

'Yes. I think it is.'

'Thank you, Professor.' The fact that the defence had obviously scored a point with Professor Dixon didn't worry Kavanagh unduly. The jury, of course, had already seen the videos in question and Kavanagh was convinced that the likelihood of their sharing Dixon's view was minimal. It was a case he was certain of winning, and for that reason he had requested that Alex Wilson act as his junior. He had heard all about her ignominious defeat in the Magistrates' Court – not to mention her 'comforting' at the hands of Jeremy Aldermarten – and felt that this case would lift her spirits. He sat down and, smiling, turned to her.

'Where on earth d'you think they dredged her up from?'

As Debbie Drake was led to the witness box to be sworn in, she reminded Alex of Mandy Rice-Davies, or at least as she had been portrayed in the film, *Scandal*. While hardly a girl any more, Debbie had the same swagger, the same confident sexuality – and, it soon became clear, the same intention of flirting with the entire courtroom. It was a lethal and highly attractive combination.

Chris Barnard stood up, smiled at his client and asked her how she would describe her occupation.

Debbie didn't hesitate for a second. 'I'm a film-maker and performance artist.'

'And how did you come to your present position?'

'Well, I was stripping in pubs before I left school. I worked in clubs and sex shows, and then I acted in hard-core films.'

At that, the jury looked slightly stunned. From her tone, Debbie might have been telling them how she had worked her way up to become a village post-mistress.

'And what,' asked Barnard, 'did you think of that?'

'I didn't.' Again Debbie replied without hesitation – and with disarming honesty. 'I needed the money.'

'Is that still your attitude?'

'No. Oh no. I left all that behind when I began thinking about the real relationship between women and male pornography. The work I've done since then is totally different.'

'How so?'

Debbie adopted Professor Dixon's tone for her reply. 'As a woman artist, I want to provoke, to make people think . . .' She stopped and looked crossly at the public gallery and the source of the muffled laughter. 'What I'm really trying to explore is the relationship between pornography and society's attitudes to female sexuality in general.' Artistically, she waved a hand in the air. 'Sex is a wonderful field for an artist. There are still so many taboos operating in our society.' Then she paused and smiled all around her. With a coquettish little shrug, she continued, 'Well, that's why I'm standing here now, I suppose.'

If ever a speech was calculated to appeal to a jury, thought Alex Wilson, it was that one. Debbie was so friendly, so honest and so engaging that they couldn't help but warm to her. And as Barnard's examination continued, so Debbie warmed even further to her theme. Alex, frowning behind Kavanagh as he finally stood to begin his cross-examination, began to doubt the certain victory which Kavanagh had promised.

'You're something of an industry, aren't you, Miss Drake? Magazines, videos, live shows. It's a prodigious output.'

'Thank you.' Debbie beamed with pleasure. 'I was brought up to work hard.' Again, there was muffled laughter from the public gallery.

Kavanagh ignored it. 'You must have performed in, what, scores of films?'

Debbie shrugged. 'I don't keep count. Something like that. Not so many these days.'

'Why is that?'

'I really always wanted to direct.'

At that, the quiet amusement of the public gallery gave way to outright laughter. Judge Baxter, elderly and imposing on his dais, silenced it with one furious look.

'Your films,' continued Kavanagh, 'involve repeated

acts of sexual intercourse in every conceivable form and combination, don't they?'

Debbie smiled sweetly. 'I do my best.'

This time gales of laughter emanated from the corner of the court. Judge Baxter, whose frowns had been deepening at each of Debbie's answers, leaned forward and looked down towards her. 'This is not the moment for levity, Miss Drake.'

Debbie, though still smiling, bowed her head in acknowledgement. Chris Barnard had been insistent that the one thing she mustn't do was antagonize the judge. 'Baxter,' he had said, 'is a crusty old goat who's probably never even heard of sex. Keep him sweet.' Debbie, however, knew more than her barrister did about crusty old goats who claimed to disapprove of sex. Even so, she couldn't resist playing to the gallery.

'It's just a parade,' continued Kavanagh when the uproar had subsided, 'of men and women rutting like farmyard animals, isn't it?'

'I don't accept that description. They are having sex. It's a perfectly normal human activity. Everybody does it.' Again the flirtatious smile. 'Probably even you, Mr Kavanagh.'

Above her, Judge Baxter went purple. 'You must treat learned counsel with more respect, Miss Drake,' he stammered.

Kavanagh smiled and nodded his acknowledgement to the irate judge. 'I'm obliged, Your Honour, not to say touched by Miss Drake's faith in me.' Then he turned to Debbie again, noting, for the first time, the steel behind her display of girlish innocence. 'My point, Miss Drake, is that the feminist manifesto you claim is behind your work is merely a smokescreen to legitimize what are nothing more than dirty movies of a particularly nasty kind. You and your audience know that.'

'I don't agree with you.'

'Very well. Let us turn to the issue of your audience, Miss Drake. How does the average member of the public gain access to these films?'

'By mail order and through adult shops.'

'Adult shops. That's a curious place to find a work of art, isn't it?'

'I want my work,' said Debbie with passion, 'to be seen by people who wouldn't normally go near a gallery, or a theatre or whatever. I'm not interested in preaching to the converted.'

Kavanagh was unimpressed. 'I put it to you, Miss Drake, that the real reason you make these films is for financial gain.'

'No.'

'Your clientele knows what it wants and that is pornography – and that is what you provide. The artistic rationale is nothing more than a cynical ruse, isn't it?'

'That's not true,' challenged Debbie. 'It's serious work with a serious purpose.' She did indeed look serious, but Kavanagh, and Alex behind him, detected a hint of desperation in her voice.

As there were no further questions from either counsel, and no further witnesses to be called, Debbie was led away from the witness box, and Judge Baxter, heartily relieved to see the back of her, invited Kavanagh to sum up for the prosecution.

'Ladies and gentlemen of the jury,' he said as he stood up, armed with a photocopy of a statute, 'the law allows that an obscene article may be published if it is for the public good, and, if I may quote, "in the interests of drama, opera, ballet, literature or learning, or any other art form".'

Pausing, he turned and handed the paper to Alex and then addressed the jury once more. 'Where, we might well ask, does the work of Deborah Drake fit into this definition? Is it opera? I think not. Ballet? I concede there is much athleticism on display but not, I think, of the kind we would understand as dance.' In response to the wide grins from the members of the jury, he allowed himself a small smile. 'Is it drama then? Sadly, we search in vain for even the crudest of narratives. Literature, I think we may discount, and as for learning, well, anything we may have learnt from seeing these films we may fervently and rapidly wish to forget.'

As Kavanagh sat down, Chris Barnard rose to sum up for the defence and cast a withering look in Kavanagh's direction.

'Ladies and gentlemen of the jury, as you well know art is not so easily categorized as m'learned friend mockingly suggests. During this trial, you have heard expert witnesses testify that Deborah Drake has a valid artistic statement to make. In a free society it is imperative that Deborah Drake should be able to pursue her genuine artistic concerns without fear of prosecution. You may find her work shocking, but art sometimes has a duty to confront and provoke, and the public good can be served by powerful and disturbing imagery in its proper context.'

But it was obvious that his heart just wasn't in it.

'What do you think? Am I going to fall flat on my face?'

Alex Wilson, sitting opposite Kavanagh in the pub, reflected for a moment before answering. She cast her mind back to the videos in question, then immediately dismissed them from her mind. The videos, she remembered, weren't the point: the point was, who had made

172

the better case? 'Well,' she said non-committally, 'the jury didn't seem very shockable.'

'No, still, can't always tell.' Then Kavanagh grinned. 'Good value, wasn't she?'

Alex looked up from her drink in surprise. 'I thought you disapproved?'

'Oh no, I rather warmed to her actually.'

'Oh. It didn't show. But I suppose that's the trick, isn't it?' Then, twirling her glass in her hands, she added, 'I just think the prosecution should never have been brought in the first place.'

'Why? Because it's weak?'

'No. It's just that we're surrounded by soft porn images. Page three; dirty magazines.' She shrugged. 'But when a woman actually tries to say something about it, the law comes down on her like a ton of bricks.'

Kavanagh, while sympathetic to the theory, couldn't help being sceptical. 'I wouldn't be too impressed by Debbie's late conversion to feminism, Alex. She's got a list of previous as long as her arm.'

'Hmm.' Alex supposed she shouldn't be surprised. 'What do you think she'll get if she's found guilty?'

Kavanagh waved a hand. 'Oh, a fine, or a bit of suspended. Not much more than a slap on the wrist, anyway.'

Debbie Drake was indeed found guilty. She looked, thought Alex as she watched the woman in the dock, disappointed rather than surprised. And then Judge Baxter turned to her. Alex had never heard a more venomous tone.

'Deborah Drake, you are a thoroughly corrupt and cynical woman who has – rightly in my view – been found guilty of a very serious crime.' He paused to let the words sink in and then, with even more vituperation, continued his invective.

'Standards of decency are under siege in every area of public life and it is my duty to protect civilized society from the barbarians at the gate. You will go to prison for one year.'

Alex was not the only person in court to gasp at the severity of both the words and the sentence. Kavanagh, she noted, caught his breath; even several members of the jury looked shocked – and Debbie Drake herself looked as if she had been hit. After a moment's stunned silence, she opened her mouth to protest – yet found herself incapable of speaking.

Judge Baxter, however, was not. He fixed the court ushers with a steely glint. 'Take her down,' he barked.

The shell-shocked Debbie finally found her voice. 'But I never hurt anyone!' she wailed. The cheerful, cocky confidence was gone – now she looked frightened and diminished, and no match for the grim policewoman who took her by the arm and, none too gently, ushered her out of the dock.

Even Kavanagh, the victor, took no pleasure in his victory.

CHAPTER NINETEEN

'So you see,' said Jeremy Aldermarten, 'it's as safe a seat as one is likely to find these days.' He smiled contentedly at Peter Foxcott. 'They've returned a Tory every election for the past forty years.'

But will they, thought Peter, return *you*? He hoped his expression didn't betray that thought: he hoped he was looking delighted.

He was, in fact, extremely surprised. Jeremy, as far as he could remember, had never expressed any interest – let alone any personal ambition – in the world of politics. And now here he was telling his Head of Chambers that he had just been short-listed as a potential Conservative MP for the blue-blooded Home Counties constituency of Brigham. He realized that some further form of congratulation was required by the expectant Jeremy. 'So the chosen one . . .'

' . . . is on his way to the House.' Jeremy beamed. 'Quite.'

'Well, I must say . . . well, congratulations, Jeremy. It's a wonderful opportunity. Although we'd be sorry to lose your services, however briefly.'

Jeremy tried, and failed, to look modest. 'Not that briefly, I hope. One does, you see, have ambitions . . .'

'Quite. Quite. I've no doubt you're destined for high office.'

'Thank you, Peter. Still, better negotiate the first

fence before thinking about Beecher's Brook. I haven't, of course, actually been nominated yet. It's between me and one other chap who I gather isn't quite . . .' he leaned forward and gave Peter a knowing look, ' . . . who isn't quite *the thing*, if you know what I mean.'

Peter, who knew Jeremy was a roaring snob, realized exactly what he meant. 'Oh, I wouldn't worry about it, then. I'm quite sure you've got it in the bag.'

Jeremy's smile suggested that he too was sure. Yet before he could reply, he started guiltily at the sound of a voice, clearly audible through the open door of Peter's room. It was Alex Wilson's voice.

'It wasn't exactly a slap on the wrist, was it?' she was saying.

Jeremy, who was now rather terrified of Alex, hoped she was not referring to the unfortunate 'incident' between the two of them. Peter, he knew, would be horrified if he found out.

Peter, however, on hearing Alex's voice, was now striding to the door. 'Come in, come in,' he said jovially. 'Ah, Jim. Good. Come in, both of you, and hear Jeremy's news.'

Realizing that Alex must have been talking to Jim about the trial from which they had just returned, Jeremy relaxed. Preening himself and adopting what he hoped was a sympathetic, sincere, *politician*'s tone, he turned to Alex and Jim as they walked into the room.

Like Peter before them, they were taken completely by surprise; not so much by the fact of Jeremy putting himself forward as a Conservative candidate but by why he had kept quiet about it until now. Most unlike Jeremy, thought Kavanagh. Alex, for her part, was delighted: she hoped it meant she would see the back of her pupil-master.

'How', asked Peter after they had congratulated Jeremy on his new venture, 'did it go with the . . . er . . . you know, Crown versus Drake?' Peter, like every other male member of River Court, had been extremely interested in the Debbie Drake case. Somehow, all the men had managed to find themselves in Kavanagh's room when he had been watching the 'artistic' videos.

'We won,' replied Kavanagh, 'although I must say I was surprised that she went down for a year.'

'A year? Good God! Who was presiding?'

'Baxter.'

'Ah. That explains it. Awful man. Sexist old fossil.'

Alex looked at Peter in surprise. She had not heard her Head of Chambers speak in that tone before.

'I was just telling Alex,' Kavanagh continued, 'that I'd expected her to get a fine and a slap on the wrist.' He shook his head. 'A year really seems a bit much.'

But Peter was fast losing interest in Debbie Drake. 'Well, all one can do is put forward the best argument. It's nobody's fault if the judge got out of bed on the wrong side.'

Again Alex was surprised – this time not so much by Peter's words as by their implication. So much of what went on in court was arbitrary and had, in effect, little to do with justice. It was at times like this that Alex doubted the worth of her chosen profession. But at least, she thought, it was better than politics.

'I'm off down to Brigham, then,' Jeremy was saying. 'See the committee and all that. Just a formality, really.'

The others looked at him with varying degrees of doubt as, with a spring in his step, he walked out of the room. It was Kavanagh who broke the silence. 'And I', he said with considerably less relish, 'am off to discuss this ghastly child custody business with Julia.'

*

It was, indeed, a fairly ghastly business. The Duggans had once, Kavanagh supposed, been a happy family. Now they were divided, acrimonious – and very much in the public eye.

Nine months before, Michael Duggan, a successful businessman in his late thirties, had hit the headlines when he kidnapped his son Peter. Scenting a scandal and the 'sexy' subject of child custody, the press had gone after him with a vengeance. The more persistent reporters managed to unearth a great deal about the background to the kidnapping and had inundated the public with the sensational 'facts'.

Kavanagh, on the other hand, knew all the facts – and none of them were sensational. They were just sad. Following the irretrievable breakdown of his parents' marriage, eight-year-old Peter Duggan remained in the care of his doting father while his mother Samantha, busy with her new boyfriend, saw him only occasionally. But after two years, and much to Michael Duggan's surprise and horror, Samantha successfully applied for a residence order for her son. Now remarried to her boyfriend Terry Fisher, she reckoned it was time to be a full-time mother again.

Michael, however, thought otherwise. He felt that his former wife was deliberately sabotaging his relationship with his son, of whom he now saw increasingly less. Furthermore, he was convinced that Peter was deeply unhappy in his new home and hated his stepfather. Prevented by the courts from doing anything about it, Michael resorted to desperate tactics and abducted his son in the middle of a school sports session.

It was a stupid as well as a desperate move: he hadn't planned where to go, what to do. After three days of a camping 'holiday' with Peter, he gave himself up. The media, annoyed because they been unable to find him, made the most of his subsequent spell in custody – and of his trial before the Family Division. The judge, citing the fact that Michael had exposed his son to 'great emotional trauma and a very real physical danger', sentenced him to six months' imprisonment.

Kavanagh knew all about the case because, by an accident of fate and a mix-up in timetables, he had conducted Michael Duggan's defence. Family law was not his area and he had only taken on the case because the original defence counsel was double-booked and, anyway, the hearing would only last one day. What he hadn't known – what he couldn't have known – was that Michael Duggan was so obsessed with getting custody of his son that he was prepared to fight in court for a cross-application for residence.

Nor could Kavanagh have known that Duggan – against his solicitor's advice – wanted Kavanagh to represent him again. Normally, Tom Buckley would have made sure someone else took the case: but Tom hadn't been feeling normal the day the brief came through. He had been in a vile mood with Kavanagh for taking on the Sunderland case.

Kavanagh had been furious. 'I don't like family stuff,' he had snapped. 'No adrenaline. Give me a jury any day.'

'Don't worry, Mr Kavanagh,' Tom had teased. 'I'll make sure you get a smart junior to look after you.'

Kavanagh, ignoring the implication that he needed a guiding hand, had asked for Julia Piper. 'It ought', he said, 'to be right up her street.'

Julia hadn't thanked him for that. She didn't much like family law either: she hated having to witness the hurt that people who had once loved each other started flinging around; she perceived as false the notion that cases such as this were 'for the good of the children'.

In her experience the children always suffered more than the adults. Both she and Kavanagh had warned Duggan's solicitor Judy Simmons that the cross-application didn't stand a chance.

And then Michael Duggan, still serving his prison sentence, had dropped his bombshell. They *would* stand a chance, he claimed. A very good chance. He didn't want custody of his son for selfish reasons – quite the opposite. He wanted Peter because the boy was suffering at the hands of Terry Fisher. He was being sexually abused by the man.

As Kavanagh walked to Julia Piper's room at River Court, he reflected on the awful allegations. It made him feel rather guilty about his attitude to Kate. All she wanted was her parents' approval for her to sleep with a perfectly normal boy with whom she claimed she was in love. And he had refused. Perhaps, he reflected, he *was* too Victorian. Perhaps he ought to talk to Kate.

'Well,' he said as he entered Julia's office and, in response to her wave of the hand, sat down opposite her. 'What's the score?'

'Fifteen–love – to them.'

'Oh?'

''Fraid so.' Julia looked at her colleague and shrugged. 'The Local Authority Social Services have dropped their investigation into Terry Fisher. They say the allegations are unfounded. And the Court Welfare Officer appears to be firmly on their side.'

'Oh.'

'And an eminent psychiatrist has examined the boy and is in agreement that there's no evidence.'

'Ah.'

Julia raised an eyebrow. 'Are you going to be this monosyllabic in court?'

Kavanagh laughed. Other QCs might well have reprimanded a junior for being 'disrespectful', but Kavanagh, for all the clout he carried, wasn't into power games and rank-pulling. As far as he was concerned, he and Julia were equals.

'No,' he said, 'I was just wondering what our best line of defence will be. The home situation?'

'Mmm.' Julia nodded in agreement. 'The boy is obviously less than ecstatic about his stepfather. He's increasingly withdrawn and since Samantha was granted custody the problems at school have increased.'

'You can imagine what the judge will say to that.'

Again Julia nodded. 'Mmm. Trouble in adjusting. But he *will* say that contact with the father should be maintained.'

'But the father's not interested, is he? He wants custody or nothing.' Kavanagh stopped, lost in thought. 'How long have we got?'

'A week.'

'Mmm. Well, let's see what we can come up with at the next con. Judy Simmons appears to think we've got a chance – she seems to believe everything he says.'

'She would.'

'Not all solicitors believe their clients, Julia.'

'Not all solicitors are having affairs with their clients.'

'*What?* She's not?'

'She is.'

'Oh God.'

For a moment Julia looked wistful. 'Not that I entirely blame her. He is rather attractive. There's something very gentle behind all that passion.'

'You sound as if you've fallen under his spell as well.'

Suddenly Julia looked directly into Kavanagh's eyes.

'Oh, I dare say I might have gone for him in different circumstances. He's rather my type – older, very bright, confident but still vulnerable.' She shrugged. 'Still a bit rough round the edges.'

But Kavanagh had developed a pressing need to rummage through his notes. 'Sorry?' he asked vaguely. 'What were you saying?'

Julia smiled. 'Oh, nothing. It doesn't matter.'

She was still smiling when he left the room. She had no feelings for Kavanagh beyond great affection and deep respect – the same feelings she had for his wife. She had just wanted to test his reaction to flattery. It was, she had noted with approval, a great deal better than Jeremy's. If she'd made that speech to him, he would have thrust an engagement ring in her face. Poor old Jeremy, she thought as she went back to work. I wonder how he's getting on.

Jeremy was getting on as well as could be expected. No, he thought, better than expected. Seated at the opposite end of the table from the committee members of the Brigham constituency party, he was rather enjoying himself. He had, he reckoned, charmed Patricia Runcorn, the chairman, and impressed the agent, Roy Heston. And the other committee members, sitting in a row beneath the rather bad portrait of a benign-looking Harold Macmillan, were looking favourably at him.

'Of course,' he said with authority, 'there's a lot to be said for EU membership.' Then he paused. 'But, then again, sovereignty is a vital issue as well.'

'Would you say,' repeated Patricia Runcorn, 'that you were pro- or anti-Europe, then?'

'I would say I'm a firm supporter of the Government line, while remaining constructively critical, of course.'

'Ah.' Runcorn looked baffled. 'I see.'

'You're a legal chap,' said Heston. 'What about law and order?'

At least Jeremy felt at home on that one. 'I think we have to pursue a very vigorous agenda of reform in the criminal justice system.' Then he paused and added, 'While proceeding with caution and due respect for tradition, naturally.'

Heston's clipped vowels scythed through the air as he barked out his next question. 'What about hanging?'

Aldermarten looked slightly alarmed. 'I . . . I have a very open mind on the subject.'

'Something like eighty per cent of the population are in favour. What would you say to that?'

Aldermarten, given a free rein, would say that was complete rubbish. Instead, he smiled and said that everyone should be mindful of the wishes of the majority.

'Would you plan', asked Patricia Runcorn after a moment, 'to live in the constituency?'

'I think that's entirely possible.'

'Mmm . . . yes. We do prefer a local man.' Then, after looking round to see if there were any more questions, she brought the meeting to a close. Aldermarten, scrupulously polite, made a point of shaking everyone's hand and telling them how much he was looking forward to seeing them again. Runcorn, hearing this, turned to him with a warm smile. 'Oh, but you will, you will. At our little soirée. I do hope you can make it. The other candidates will be there.'

'I'd be honoured, Mrs Runcorn.'

'Marvellous. Oh, and do bring Mrs Aldermarten.'

Jeremy suddenly looked stricken. 'I'm . . . er . . . well, I'm not married.'

'Not married?' Patricia Runcorn looked appalled – and her implication was clear. Not married equated not human.

'No.' Jeremy was quick to recover. 'Not married. Engaged.'

'Splendid! Splendid!' Patricia Runcorn replied, thawing the atmosphere as quickly as she had chilled it. She beamed at Aldermarten, her eyes ablaze with visions of a smart wedding for which she would do the flowers. 'You *must* bring the intended. We'd be delighted to meet her.'

Jeremy's smile was slightly more forced. 'Yes,' he said. 'Of course.'

CHAPTER TWENTY

Kavanagh and Julia Piper had not wasted their week. They had both worked extremely hard on preparing their presentation and, in addition, had come up with some extremely useful information that they hoped they could use to paint a rather interesting picture of the supposedly harmonious marriage of Samantha and Terry Fisher. Yet, as they sat in the Crown Court watching Nayana Singh, counsel for Samantha, they had to concede that the woman's case for keeping custody of her son was looking stronger by the minute. Furthermore, the judge, the Hon. Mr Justice Griffin, was well known in family circles as a proponent of the theory that children were usually better off with their mothers. And certainly, the kidnapping episode had not disposed him favourably towards the father.

' . . . and after the kidnapping,' Singh was saying to the judge as she concluded her argument, 'Peter was held for three days before the father gave himself up to the authorities. Against this background of impulsive, irrational and harmful behaviour by Mr Duggan, the mother is applying for an order terminating further contact.'

The mother was then called to the witness box. An attractive woman in her late thirties, Samantha, not surprisingly, was looking slightly haggard. Her appearance, noted Julia Piper, was not helped by the fact that she dressed rather younger than her age. This, Judy Simmons had explained with great disapproval, was because her new husband was several years younger than herself.

'Mrs Fisher,' said her counsel, 'you say that Mr Duggan's behaviour towards you was often aggressive when he collected Peter for his regular contact. Could you clarify what you mean by that?'

Samantha could. 'Michael would always accuse me of making Peter deliberately late,' she said. 'Or he would say that he wasn't properly dressed.' She grimaced in distaste. 'He always found *something* wrong.'

'And was there any truth in what he said?'

'I don't think so, no.'

'You also say that he would shout at you on these occasions. What did he shout?'

'He said that I was sabotaging his relationship with Peter. He called me all kinds of names.'

'Was Peter present?'

Samantha, evidently upset, paused before answering. 'Sometimes, yes.'

'And what was his reaction?'

'It really upset him. He used to be an outgoing, friendly boy but he went more and more into himself. It got so bad that on the days before Michael's visits he'd make himself ill.'

'You state,' continued Singh after letting the judge digest that information, 'that Peter's behaviour has deteriorated further since the kidnap by his father. Can you expand on that?'

'He's a very bright boy but he's lost interest in school. He's withdrawn and prone to tantrums.' Samantha was clearly becoming upset as she recalled how her son had changed. 'At times he's almost uncontrollable.'

'Why do you think that is?'

'I'm sure it's partly because of the abuse inquiry. But I also think he's terrified that something like the kidnap might happen again.' Samantha paused and looked across the court at her former husband. Her face betrayed not hatred, but an awed disbelief. 'He won't go out on his own any more, even to the corner shop.'

Again Singh paused in her questioning. Julia felt rather than heard Judy Simmons comforting Michael Duggan behind her. It really didn't help, she mused, that they were having an affair. She hoped to God the opposition didn't know about it.

When Singh continued, it was on a different tack. 'How would you characterize Peter's relationship with his stepfather?'

'They get on very well.'

'What is your reaction to the allegation of sexual abuse made by Michael Duggan against your husband?'

This time Samantha did eye Michael Duggan with undisguised and intense dislike. 'It's total rubbish. If it wasn't so revolting it would be laughable. Terry,' she added not without pride, 'is a normal, healthy man.'

'And what is your feeling about the recent Local Authority inquiry into these allegations?'

'To begin with,' replied Samantha, 'I was outraged. But . . . but now I'm glad we had to go through it. I feel we've been totally vindicated. It's made us stronger as a family.'

So where, thought Julia, is the display of family solidarity? Peter Duggan, naturally, was not in court – and wouldn't be during the hearing. If the judge felt it necessary to talk to the boy, he would talk to him alone and in a private room. But surely Terry Fisher, the loving husband who had just been vindicated, ought to be here to support his wife?

'Mrs Fisher,' asked Singh, 'why are you applying for this order now?'

'Because I'm terrified of what Michael might do next. I can't risk having Peter damaged any more than he is already. I have to protect him.'

'Do you have any other motive for taking such a drastic step?'

'No.' Samantha was adamant. 'Peter's security and safety are the only things that matter to me.'

'Thank you.'

As Singh sat down, Kavanagh scribbled a quick note on the pad in front of him, and, inclining his head towards the judge, rose to his feet.

'Mrs Fisher, it wasn't until you petitioned for divorce that Mr Duggan knew you would be applying for a residence order. How long had you been living with Terry Fisher by this point?'

Samantha looked at him in surprise. This, her expression implied, was all in the past. 'Em . . . nearly two years.'

At this Judge Griffin, evidently in accord with Samantha, leaned forward and addressed Kavanagh. 'This is all ancient history, isn't it, Mr Kavanagh? The circumstances of the divorce were covered pretty comprehensively at the original hearing.'

But Kavanagh was not to be deflected. 'My contention, my Lord, is that subsequent events put the facts in a new light.'

Griffin shrugged his agreement. 'Oh very well. If you're convinced it's relevant.'

'Yes, my Lord.' Then he turned again to the witness box. 'What took you so long, Mrs Fisher?'

'I couldn't give him a proper home until then.'

'So it was always your intention that Peter should live with you and Terry Fisher?'

'Yes.'

'Why, then, when you left your husband, did you tell him the exact opposite?'

Samantha shrugged. The gesture made her appear defensive, helpless. 'I didn't plan it that way. I just didn't want to hurt him. It was easier to let things slide.'

'Easier in all sorts of ways.' Kavanagh looked at Samantha without sympathy. 'Terry Fisher was younger than you, had a more carefree lifestyle and little experience of children. Surely it was easier to keep Peter out of the way while you concentrated on your relationship with him?'

'No! It wasn't like that.'

'Very well. Let's move on.' In other words, mused Julia, let's come back to that later. Both she and Kavanagh knew that Samantha Fisher was hiding something.

'It's the case, isn't it,' he continued, 'that Peter missed his contact with his father on two consecutive occasions, only a few weeks before the kidnapping incident. Why was that?'

'It's like I said in my statement. The first time he had a cold and the second he said he had a headache and felt sick. I kept him in bed.'

'When did Peter's father find out that Peter wouldn't be able to see him?'

'When he arrived to pick him up.'

'You couldn't have telephoned to save him a needless journey?'

'It was too late,' pleaded Samantha. 'He'd already left.'

'Both times?'

'Yes.'

'Mmm. On the second occasion, Peter subsequently spoke to his father on the phone and told him he did want to see him after all?'

'Yes.' Samantha nodded. 'That's true.'

'And he said something else, didn't he? Something you have omitted from your statement.'

For the first time Samantha tried to avoid both his glance and his question.

'Mrs Fisher?' prompted the judge.

But it was Kavanagh who replied to his own question. 'He told Mr Duggan that he wasn't ill, that you had deliberately kept him in, and that he would prefer to be living with him, didn't he?'

'Yes . . . but . . . but we'd had a row. He was being childish. He was ill earlier in the day, got better, then got upset because he'd had to miss Michael's visit.'

To Julia's intense annoyance, Judge Griffin leaned forward and, in a kindly manner, informed Samantha that it was just the sort of thing children did when they were angry, wasn't it? Kavanagh stole a quick glance at Julia: she returned a discreet grimace of dismay. So that, they were both thinking, is the way the land lies. Neither of them was too surprised, but the blatant intervention on behalf of the mother was, they felt, a bit much.

'Is it not actually the case,' continued Kavanagh, 'that Peter has repeated his desire to live with his father on numerous occasions?'

'But he doesn't know what he's saying . . .'

'It's a simple enough question, Mrs Fisher. Yes or no?'

'Yes.' Samantha's voice was a mere whisper.

Kavanagh now picked up a file from the desk in front of him. 'I have here the report from Mrs Winston, the Court Welfare Officer. Mrs Winston notes a distance and lack of warmth between Terry Fisher and Peter, doesn't she?'

'Only since the abuse investigation. I think Terry's

frightened to go anywhere near him in case they say he's been messing about.'

'So before the inquiry, everything was fine?'

'Yes. It was.'

'Mrs Fisher, you blame Mr Duggan for the deterioration in Peter's health and behaviour. Is it not in fact the case that the source of his unhappiness is closer to home?'

Samantha glared at him. 'If you mean Terry, the answer is no.'

Kavanagh nodded in the direction of Nayana Singh. 'You suggested to m'learned friend that Peter was traumatized by the kidnap. But Peter's behavioural problems began long before that, and persisted even when his father was in prison.'

'The fear,' replied Samantha, 'doesn't go away just because his father does.' Judge Griffin, Julia again noted with disapproval, looked as if he agreed with the remark.

'There is no physical closeness', persisted Kavanagh as he put down the welfare officer's report, 'between Terry Fisher and your son. Peter is clinging and possessive of your company. He wants to be with his father. Surely the facts tell their own story.' He paused. 'Peter is being abused by your husband, isn't he?'

Samantha held her head high. 'No. He is not.'

'You say that with complete certainty?'

'Yes.'

'But you don't deny that Peter is a deeply disturbed young boy?'

'I've *told* you why that is . . .'

'Over five weeks away from school ill in the past six months. Regular truancy. Anti-social behaviour. Fighting.' Kavanagh paused for effect and noted that the judge, for the first time, was frowning slightly. 'None of this, Mrs Fisher, has anything to do with Peter's home life?'

'I don't think it does, no.'

'It's all down to his father's baleful influence?'

'Yes.'

'He hardly ever sees the boy, yet it is all his fault.'

Kavanagh let the court mull over that one before continuing. 'What was Peter's school record like before he came to live with you and Mr Fisher?'

Samantha looked a trifle wary, Julia thought, as she replied, 'It was very good.'

'I would suggest it was outstanding. How many days did he miss from school in the two years he lived with his father after you left the marital home?'

'I . . . I don't really know . . .'

'Let me help you,' said Kavanagh kindly. 'It was none. Not one.' It was a kindness Samantha could have done without. Her silence and hostile glare indicated that much.

'You claim that the relationship between Terry and Peter is basically a good one,' Kavanagh continued. 'How does that manifest itself?'

'I don't know what you mean.'

'Well, do they play football together?'

'Terry isn't really a sportsman,' explained Samantha.

'Perhaps they go to the cinema then?'

'No . . . not often.'

'What do they do, then?'

Samantha was looking decidedly doubtful. 'They . . . well, they talk . . .'

'Just talk. Does Peter actually *do* anything at all in Terry's company?'

'I've told you. They get on all right.'

Kavanagh looked anything but convinced. 'Mrs Fisher,' he said with emphasis, 'I put it to you that when Peter is with his father he is contented, healthy and hard-working. Put him in the same house as Terry Fisher and the situation is the exact reverse. Do you still insist this is a good relationship?'

'Yes.'

'Thank you, Mrs Fisher.' With that, Kavanagh sat down, but not before he noted something new on the face of Judge Griffin – an element of doubt.

Nayana Singh, betraying not the slightest sign of consternation that her opponent had just mauled her client, stood up to address the judge once more. 'No re-examination, my Lord. With reference to the matter we were discussing earlier, I can now confirm that Mr Fisher is detained on business. With your leave he will give his evidence in the morning.'

'Very well, Mrs Singh.'

So, thought Julia as she gathered up her papers, tomorrow we'll see the man for whom Samantha left her husband – and, initially, her son.

On the way back to River Court, Julia and Kavanagh talked of their chances of winning. The judge, they agreed, was firmly biased towards Samantha Fisher; a situation, Kavanagh assured Julia, that had every chance of changing. A lot depended on the two men – on Michael Duggan and Terry Fisher. And, of course, there was the little matter of questioning Samantha once more on something that appeared to have slipped her mind.

Feeling more confident, yet weighed down with the work she needed to do by the following day, Julia went into her room and, anxious for a little privacy, shut the door behind her.

The privacy didn't last long. After ten minutes, Jeremy Aldermarten sidled in. His unfathomable expression, Julia knew of old, meant only one thing: trouble.

'Ah, Julia.'

'No need to sound so surprised, Jeremy. This is, after all, my office.'

'Yes. Yes. Quite.'

Torn between amusement and irritation, Julia told him to spit it out.

He did – to Julia's complete and utter astonishment. She was so taken aback by his suggestion that it was a full thirty seconds before she could reply. 'You are completely off your head,' she said. Then she looked at him again. He was, she realized, deadly serious. 'I am not', she added, 'going to pose as your fiancée.'

'Oh, come on, Julia. We can break up the minute the selection process is finished. Once I'm in, there's not much they can do about it.' He smiled in encouragement. 'It'll be a piece of cake.'

'We don't even support the same side, Jeremy.'

Sensing weakness, Jeremy invited himself to sit down. 'I wouldn't ask unless it was important. 'You know what the Tories are like – it's all family values. I'll never get the nomination if they know I'm single.'

'You must be mad. Supposing they find out?'

Jeremy spread his hands in front of him. 'Why should they? Look, Julia, I'm asking you because I knew you'd take it in the right spirit. In the circles I move in, the women are definitely the marrying kind, and I don't want to give them any ideas.' Then, with a grimace of distaste, he added, 'Or their mothers.' After another pause, he told her there would be a bottle of bubbly in it for her. Vintage.

Julia had had better offers. Still, she thought, in Jeremy's parlance he had just bestowed a compliment upon her – and the whole idea *was* beginning to appeal to the wild streak in her.

'A case,' she replied. 'Dom Perignon. And that's just a down-payment.'

'Oh, God.' Jeremy ran a weary hand across his brow. He might have known Julia wouldn't come cheap. 'Oh . . . all right then.'

But Julia hadn't finished. 'And no kissing or hand-holding.'

'Agreed.' Jeremy had given up on that idea long ago, anyway.

'Mmm.' Julia tapped her lips with her pencil. 'I'll think about it.'

Jeremy knew victory when he saw it. Getting to his feet, he flashed her a grateful smile. 'You're a brick, Julia. I'll be in your debt for ever.'

Julia grinned. 'I know. That's exactly what makes the idea so attractive.'

Relationships were very much on Kavanagh's mind as he drove home that night. Michael Duggan's battle with his estranged wife was upsetting him more than he cared to admit. He had noticed the acrimonious looks that passed between them, the sharp intakes of breath as Samantha made, or responded to, an accusation. And the worst of it was that he reckoned neither Samantha nor Michael was, in their current situation, a suitable parent for Peter.

Samantha, he knew, was a troubled woman: Michael was almost worse – he was a man so obsessed by his

195

son that he could not see the possible harm he might be doing to him. Charming, personable and attractive, he was obviously well-balanced and successful when it came to business. But, with the mention of his son, he became a completely different, almost irrational person.

While Kavanagh warmed to neither his client nor Samantha, he was, at least, convinced of one thing: Peter Duggan was a happier boy when he was with his father. Michael was by no means the perfect parent, but certainly better than Samantha. Still, Kavanagh mused as he let himself into the house, there probably wasn't such a thing as a perfect parent.

He hardly noticed Lizzie, sitting reading on the sofa, as he went into the sitting-room and strode purposefully to the far end.

'It's a long time since you dived at the drinks cabinet as though your life depended on it,' said Lizzie drily.

Kavanagh, whisky decanter in hand, turned and gave her a weary smile. 'It's that kind of brief.'

'Bad?'

Kavanagh sighed and took a contemplative sip of his drink. 'All that rage and hatred,' he mused, 'pouring from people who must have loved each other once. You catch yourself thinking, "There but for the grace of God . . ." I mean, what if it had happened to us, Lizzie?'

'But it *didn't* happen, did it?'

Kavanagh, however, did not appear to have heard her. 'Are we so sure we would have been any different? Would we have ended up tearing each other apart over the kids if some Miles Petersham or other had come along earlier?'

Seeing that her husband was deeply troubled, Lizzie sought to reassure him. Heaven knows, she thought, he ought to know by now that I'm here to stay. Rising from the sofa, she went up to him and folded her arms around his shoulders. 'It wouldn't have mattered who had come along. I wouldn't have been interested.' Then, half-serious and half-teasing, she looked him in the eye. 'And I bloody well hope you feel the same way.'

Kavanagh, realizing that he had been unfair, pulled her against him and hugged her tightly. Then, in a gentler tone, he broached the other subject that had been playing on his mind. 'Look, I've been thinking about Kate.'

Lizzie grinned. 'Don't tell me – you've booked her into a nunnery?'

'Good God! Am I really that bad?'

Lizzie thought for a moment before replying. 'The fact is, Jim, if they're going to do it – which they are, whether we like it or not – I'd rather it was here, where I can keep an eye on them, than down some seedy lovers' lane with a maniac lurking in the bushes.'

Kavanagh had to agree that she had a point.

Two minutes later he knocked gently – and apprehensively – on Kate's bedroom door. The atmosphere between him and his daughter had been more than a little frosty of late. Kate, who saw everything in black and white, had decided her father was an unreasonable, draconian monster totally out of step with the times, and had made no bones about letting him know that.

This time, Kavanagh had the element of surprise in his favour: Kate looked rather put out to be found sprawling inelegantly on her bed reading an old copy of *Cosmopolitan*.

'Is this a good moment?'

Kate, knowing a lecture was on the cards, looked warily at her father. He took her silence for assent and perched on the edge of her bed. 'Look,' he said with a rueful smile, 'about this Luke. How serious are you about him?'

Kate, for the first time in ages, met his gaze. 'I really like him, Dad.'

'You're both very young.'

This time it was Kate who smiled. 'I could have been married for nearly two years.'

'True. Look, I've always thought ... I've always known you were very sensible ...'

Kate, seeing his embarrassment, interrupted. 'I know all about safe sex and everything. You don't have to worry about that.'

'Oh.' Now Kavanagh was completely nonplussed. 'Well, I won't then.' I must, he thought, remember that she's no longer a little girl. 'What about Luke's parents? What do they think?'

'Oh, they're really cool about it.'

'Yes. I thought they might be.' If they had produced Luke, he supposed they must be pretty cool. 'Well, your mother and I have been talking and we think you're old enough to know your own mind. If you really want Luke to stay over ... once in a while ... we're not going to object.' He forced a grin. 'Well, not much, anyway.'

Kate's grin wasn't forced. Springing up from her prone position, she leaned towards her father and gave him a smacking kiss on the cheek. 'Thanks, Dad. Really, thanks.'

Kavanagh, delighted that the air had been cleared, but still riddled with mixed feelings about this acknowledgement of adulthood, stood up and walked to the door. As he opened it, he turned back to his daughter and added, 'Strictly weekends, though. School work comes first. Deal?'

Kate, who knew how much this conversation had cost her father, nodded her assent.

Families, thought James as he trudged downstairs. Who would have them?

CHAPTER TWENTY-ONE

By lunchtime the next day Judge Griffin was looking worried. Yesterday's near-certainty that Samantha Fisher was the injured party had disappeared and in its place was the one feeling that his Lordship hated most – doubt. The morning's activities in Number Three Court of the Knightsbridge Crown Court had seen to that.

Michael Duggan had been the first witness to appear. Under questioning from Kavanagh, he made it clear that his ex-wife, jealous of his relationship with their son, was deliberately trying to sabotage that relationship. He also, at first reluctantly, repeated to the court the dreadful conversation he had had with Peter when the latter had told him that Terry Fisher, his stepfather, was touching him 'down there'. He said he had been so shocked by the story that his initial reaction had been to get angry with Peter, to accuse him of telling fibs. Yet Peter, so he said, stuck to his story.

Nayana Singh's cross-examination concentrated at first on why Michael had waited so long before reporting the alleged abuse. Michael said that he had not wanted to report it, that he had wanted to spare his son – until Samantha's application to sever all contact made him realize that he had no choice.

Singh, clearly unimpressed, reminded Michael that Peter had never once mentioned the abuse, even under examination by sympathetic and trained professionals. She went on to accuse Michael of fabricating the entire story in a misguided effort to get Peter back, to take revenge on his adulterous wife and on Terry Fisher, the man he admitted to disliking intensely.

The next witness was one Dr Steven Grindlay, the child psychiatrist who had examined Peter. Without much preamble, Singh led him to the admission that it was 'a strong possibility' that the father's aggressive and demanding behaviour had compounded the natural trauma of separation and had led to Peter's disturbed behaviour. Kavanagh, cross-examining, tried to pour scorn on that one, but only succeeded in getting Grindlay to concede that Terry Fisher and the home environment were 'part of the problem'.

The next witness, the Court Welfare Officer currently overseeing Peter, refused even to go that far. Despite Kavanagh's prompting, Elaine Winston stuck to her guns, claiming that Peter's main problem was that he was 'taking responsibility for his father's unhappiness' and that there was 'nothing of great significance' wrong with his relationship with Terry Fisher.

All three witnesses served to incline the judge further in the mother's direction, and were not the cause of his deep concern. It had been his meeting with Peter himself, in a private room beside the court, that had sown the seed of his unease. As was normal in such cases, the only witness to the meeting was the Court Welfare Officer.

Judge Griffin, a father and a grandfather several times over, was renowned for his sympathetic, delicate handling of children. Peter had warmed to him instantly and, after a few minutes testing the ground, had started to talk about his relationship with all three adults involved. When asked who he would like to live with, he replied without hesitation: his dad. He was equally quick and even more vehement in his response when asked how he felt about Terry Fisher. He hated him.

With great delicacy, Griffin then asked Peter if he remembered telling his father about 'a nasty thing Terry did to him'. It was only then that the boy became evasive. He suddenly refused to meet the judge's eye, shifted uncomfortably in his chair, and didn't answer. Griffin, to his credit, didn't push the matter. He didn't want Elaine Winston to be able to accuse him of putting words into the boy's mouth and, much more importantly, he didn't want to upset Peter further. Instead, he reverted to the question of why Peter hated Terry. Raising his troubled little face to the judge, and with his bottom lip quivering, Peter replied that it was because Terry made his mother cry. Often.

It was not, then, only Julia Piper who was looking forward to the appearance of Terry Fisher in the witness box. Judge Griffin, as the man was sworn in, found himself examining him with a highly critical eye. Terry was a rather different kettle of fish from Michael Duggan. Younger and brasher, he was, he supposed, attractive in a rather obvious sort of way. He also looked as if the last place in the world he wanted to be was in this courtroom.

Julia, watching Nayana Singh rise to question Terry, was thinking along the same lines as the judge – except she went one step further. She decided, even before Terry had opened his mouth, that he was an arrogant, chauvinistic bastard and a bully. It was just as well, she reflected, that she wasn't a judge.

'What was your reaction,' asked Singh, 'when told of the abuse allegations, Mr Fisher?'

'I felt sick. It's a load of . . . well, it's totally false. I'm the real victim here.'

Stupid bastard, thought Julia. Selfish shit.

Singh, also alarmed by Terry's reaction, ploughed hastily on. 'How would you characterize your life as a family man, Mr Fisher?'

'Very happy. All I ever wanted was for Sam and me to be together.'

Julia was heartily glad that Terry wasn't their witness. He certainly wasn't making Singh's task easy. Singh, thoroughly unimpressed, glared at Terry, silently willing him to complete the sentence.

Eventually, he caught on. 'With Peter, of course.'

But the damage had been done. Nothing in Singh's subsequent questioning could alter the less than favourable impression Terry had made on the judge; no matter how hard Singh tried to create the impression of a happy family, it was evident that Terry's interest in that family did not extend much beyond his wife.

Kavanagh, in his cross-examination, went straight for the jugular. 'Were you often alone with Peter, Mr Fisher?'

'Of course. From time to time.'

'Did you ever enter the room when he was having a bath?'

'I might have done.'

'Why?'

'I dunno.' Terry shrugged irritably. 'To wash or to shave or something. I can't spend all day waiting for him to come out, can I?'

'Did you ever wash or dry him?'

Terry looked genuinely revolted by that prospect. 'No way. He's a big lad.'

'Did you ever touch him when he was naked?'

'No!'

'Are you fond of children, Mr Fisher?'

Terry looked guarded. 'Not in the way you're after.'

'It was a general question.'

Relaxing somewhat, Terry shrugged again. 'Yeah. Kids are OK.'

'Then I expect you were eager to meet Samantha Duggan's son once you began your affair with her?'

'Well . . . yes . . .'

'How eager?'

'Well, I was keen.' He looked hopefully at Kavanagh. 'You know.'

'I'm afraid I don't. Actually, it was very nearly two years after you met Samantha before you saw Peter Duggan. That doesn't sound very keen at all.'

'It was difficult. There was a lot of anger and hard words. It was easier for Sam to visit on her own.'

Kavanagh adopted a polite, innocent look. 'Purely as a matter of interest, when did you first find out that Samantha had a young son?'

'I . . . I don't remember.'

'Was it five minutes after you met? A week? Six months? Roughly when was it, Mr Fisher?'

'I don't know.' Terry looked at Kavanagh with intense dislike. 'Months, I suppose. It just never came up.'

'Months? That's rather extraordinary, isn't it? The woman with whom you were having a passionate affair didn't mention she had a son?'

'It wasn't deliberate like that . . .'

But Kavanagh had the bit by the teeth and wasn't going to let go. 'You don't actually like children at all, do you, Mr Fisher? The reason Samantha concealed

Peter's existence from you was that she was terrified you would reject her if you knew about him?'

'I might have said something,' conceded Terry, 'about not liking kids – early on. It was just pub talk.'

'She only told you about him when she felt sure enough of your affection?'

Terry, now looking distinctly fed up, gave in. 'I suppose so. That was her problem.'

You *bastard*, thought Julia.

'Let's look', continued Kavanagh with a tinge of sarcasm, 'at a more recent instance of this warm relationship you have with Peter. On March the second of this year, Peter wasn't collected from school after a special museum trip. Why was that?'

'March? I can't remember.'

'I would have thought you might, Mr Fisher. By all accounts there was something of a row between you and the teacher involved when you didn't turn up.'

'Oh, right, I've got you. I remember. Well, I couldn't be everywhere at once, could I? I mean, I had to pick Sam up first from . . .' Suddenly Terry checked himself. So fixated was he on remembering the situation that he had almost fallen into the trap.

Kavanagh, however, was determined to sink him. 'From where?' he prompted.

Terry, again, gave in. 'From . . . from the clinic.'

'The clinic, Mr Fisher? What clinic?'

'Sam . . . er . . . she was having woman's problems. You know . . .' Floundering in deep water, he looked around helplessly.

'I'm afraid I don't know, Mr Fisher.'

'It's personal.'

At that, Kavanagh looked towards Judge Griffin.

Nodding slightly, Griffin then turned towards Terry. 'Answer the question, please, Mr Fisher.'

Terry did answer – but not before casting an agonized, helpless look at Samantha. 'She had an abortion,' he said.

If Terry and Samantha looked stricken at the revelation, their barrister looked completely astounded. Turning to Samantha, her appalled expression said it all: 'Why didn't you *tell* me?' Samantha herself was too distressed even to speak.

It was Kavanagh, turning to address the judge, who broke the silence. 'In the circumstances, your Lordship may wish to hear again from Samantha Fisher.'

His Lordship, now regretting his previous benevolent attitude towards Samantha, agreed with alacrity. This, he thought, was one of the few and upsetting occasions when his work interfered with his personal credo: Griffin was a staunch, even fervent Catholic. Abortion was absolutely anathema to him.

'Why did you have a termination, Mrs Fisher?' Julia Piper felt rather sorry for Nayana Singh as she asked the question. The poor woman, floundering in the dark, was having to think on her feet.

'I'm nearly forty,' replied Samantha. 'There's a lot of risks with late babies.'

A good answer, and spoken with conviction, thought Julia. And Singh decided to end her examination there. 'Of course there are.'

Smiling encouragingly at her client, she sat down.

Kavanagh was on his feet in a flash. Using the same relentless tactics that had so upset his daughter when he had cross-examined Eve Kendall, he launched straight into the offensive. 'Did you want to keep this baby, Mrs Fisher?'

Samantha had to bite her bottom lip before replying. 'I . . . I might have liked a baby with Terry.'

'He didn't want a child, did he?'

'He was worried about me . . .'

'Is it not actually the case that Terry, who you knew had no liking for children, who resented your son Peter, insisted you have an abortion?'

'It wasn't like that. It was a mutual decision.'

I'll bet, thought Julia, who was now feeling more than a little sorry for the distressed Samantha.

'You are devoted to Terry, aren't you?' persisted Kavanagh. 'You would do anything for him?'

'Is that wrong? He's my husband. I love him.'

'Love him so much that you would not only have an abortion you didn't want, but even conceal the existence of the son you did have in case he rejected you?'

'You make it all sound planned and calculated,' wailed Samantha. 'I always intended that we should be together again as a family.'

'Perhaps. But a family where Peter's needs emphatically take second place to your husband's.' Kavanagh paused and looked down at the file in front of him. 'It's true, isn't it, Mrs Fisher, that when the abuse investigation began you were advised that it would be in your interest for Fisher to leave home temporarily?'

'Yes.'

'But he didn't, did he?'

'It was unfair. Terry hadn't done anything wrong.'

But that cut no ice with Kavanagh. 'So it was more important to you not to be separated from him than to protect the best interests of your son?'

Samantha now began to lose her composure. 'I

wouldn't allow any of Michael's rubbish to pollute our home,' she spat.

'Isn't this just another example of your husband's interests coming before your son's?'

Samantha, provoked beyond endurance, lost it completely. 'It was nothing but lies!' she screamed. 'Peter had no idea what he was saying. I never believed him for a second . . .'

Suddenly, in mid-flow, she stopped – but too late to retract the beginnings of her awful confession. She stared in horror at Kavanagh as the impact of her words flowed around the courtroom, creating a taut, electric atmosphere.

'Peter?' goaded Kavanagh. 'You said you didn't believe *Peter*, Mrs Fisher?'

'Michael,' whispered Samantha. 'I meant Michael.'

'I don't think you did, did you? Did Peter say something to you about Terry Fisher?'

Samantha didn't reply. Exposed, vulnerable and ashamed, she looked down at her feet.

'You must answer, Mrs Fisher,' prompted Judge Griffin.

'Yes,' she whispered.

'What did he say?' asked Kavanagh.

Samantha raised her head. She stared, glassy-eyed, at her interrogator and replied in a wooden voice, 'He said that Terry had touched his private parts.'

'And this was before Mr Duggan reported the allegation?'

'Yes.'

'What did you do?'

Samantha just shook her head.

'What did you do, Mrs Fisher?'

'Nothing. It wasn't true.'

'You did nothing?'

'No.'

'You didn't say a word to anybody?'

'No.'

'Not to the social workers?'

'No.'

'The psychiatrist?'

'No.' Samantha flinched at every question, trying to ward off the blows raining down on her.

'The boy's father?'

'No.'

'Did you tell Terry Fisher what your son said?'

'Yes.'

'What was his reaction?'

'He was very angry.'

'He denied it?'

'Of course!' shouted Samantha. 'It wasn't true.'

'What did he say exactly?'

Samantha, looking pained, took a deep breath before replying in heavy, reluctant tones, 'That either I backed him or I'd never see him again.'

'So you told Peter to keep quiet?'

Kavanagh had broken Samantha. She fumbled in her pocket for a handkerchief and dabbed ineffectually at the tears that had begun to flow. 'It was better that way,' she sniffed. 'If it wasn't true, what was the point of stirring everything up?'

But by now, no one in the court, not her husband nor even her legal team, eyed Samantha with any sympathy. And Kavanagh's next attack was blistering.

'The truth is, Mrs Fisher, that you couldn't bring yourself to admit that the man you adored, whom you needed above anyone, might be capable of such a thing.' He paused. 'So you rejected a cry for help from your own son.'

*

209

Kavanagh took no pride in his demolition of Samantha Fisher. He didn't think her evil – just misguided and hopelessly in love with the wrong person. Yet there was no denying that, by her admission, she was guilty of betraying her son; of neglecting his interests. There was no way, thought Kavanagh as he waited for the judge to make his decision, that Samantha would be granted custody.

He looked covertly at Michael Duggan. There was a fierce pulse beating in the man's neck; his hands were clenched in front of him and his whole demeanour betrayed an agonized tension. Kavanagh shook his head. If only he thought that Michael was a suitable father. But he didn't: he thought that Michael was a man so dangerously obsessed that he would go to any lengths to get his hands on his son.

Judge Griffin looked on in sorrow at the court as he began to speak. It was abundantly clear that he too was extremely unhappy about this case.

'This is a difficult case and one that gives me a great deal of concern. However, having considered the situation in a fresh light, the fact that Peter Duggan lived with his father for two years after his parents separated – in what appears to have been a satisfactory arrangement – weighs heavily with me.'

He paused and looked at Michael Duggan. Then he transferred his gaze to Samantha. 'I am also persuaded that on the balance of probability there is something gravely wrong with Peter's present family circumstances. Therefore, I am going to grant Mr Duggan's application for residence.'

It was a strange party that filed out of the court. A jubilant, elated Michael Duggan led the way, with an equally joyful Judy Simmons at his side. Kavanagh and Julia followed close behind them; the latter had just congratulated the former, yet his mood was far from triumphant. He felt the whole proceedings had been hurtful, unpleasant and a deeply bitter experience. As far as he was concerned, there were no winners; just a confused eleven-year-old boy who was about to become even more bewildered.

Samantha, white-faced and in shock, had to be supported by Terry as they brought up the rear. Not a word passed between the couple: Terry was as pale as his wife, yet something in his bearing suggested that he was white with anger.

In the lobby, Michael turned to Kavanagh. 'There are no words,' he said with sincerity, 'for what I feel. Thank you.'

Kavanagh merely nodded in acknowledgement. There was something terribly wrong about all this, he thought. He couldn't put his finger on it, but there was definitely *something*.

Then he saw the boy.

So did Michael. At first he couldn't believe his eyes. There, standing before him, was his son. 'Peter? What on earth are you doing here?'

Peter, obviously nervous and over-awed at his surroundings, looked wide-eyed at his father. 'I ran away from school.' Then, smiling shyly at both parents, he added, 'Are we going home now, Dad?'

No longer was Michael the triumphant, proud victor. Suddenly he looked panic-stricken. He walked quickly towards Peter and took his hand. 'Yes, Peter, just like I said.'

'All of us?'

All the adults in the lobby looked startled at the boy's words. 'Not straightaway,' said Michael, trying desperately to lead Peter away. 'You're coming home with me now.'

But Peter, with the sharp antennae of the young, had already sensed that something was amiss. Suddenly afraid, he backed away from his father. 'What about Mum?'

'I'll explain everything later,' said Michael quickly.

'When? When is she coming?'

Samantha, visibly in agony, tried to hold back the tears as she addressed her son with a brave smile. 'You have to go with Daddy now, darling.'

Peter, confused and angry, stared at his father. 'You promised. You promised we'd be together again.'

Michael was now seriously alarmed. He did his best to keep his voice level as he approached his son once more. 'Come on, Peter, I told you I'll explain everything . . .'

'You promised!'

'Peter . . .'

'You promised me if I said all those things about Terry, Mum would come home again!'

Never, Julia recalled later, had she experienced such an awful moment. Never had she seen so many adults struck dumb by the agonized words of a child. Samantha, collapsing against her husband, put a hand to her mouth to stifle the moan that escaped her lips. But it was her ex-husband who broke the silence.

'Shut up!' he shouted. 'For Christ's sake, Peter, you'll ruin everything!'

'You lied to me!' screamed his son.

Michael turned in desperation to address the others. 'He doesn't know what he's saying!'

But it was quite evident that Peter knew exactly what he was saying. He stared at his father in horrified disbelief. 'You said that I could make everything better,' he sobbed.

At that, Samantha rushed forward to try to comfort her son. But Peter, sensing dissent in the adult world, not knowing who to trust in that world, shrank back against the wall like a frightened animal. Collapsing to the floor, he stared at his father with pure hatred as the tears streamed down his cheeks. 'You lied to me,' he repeated. 'You lied to me.'

Michael looked wildly at Judy, at Samantha, at Terry. All he saw was disbelief and horror. Then he turned to Kavanagh. 'I had the right,' he said. 'He's my son.'

CHAPTER TWENTY-TWO

'Odd,' said Jeremy Aldermarten, 'that a child of that age could sustain a lie like that for so long.'

'Mmm.' Julia looked out of the car window as they sped through Wiltshire. She was glad to be out in the country after yesterday's events. Yet the image of Peter slumped against the wall would, she knew, stay with her for a long time. 'Well, the hostility towards Terry Fisher was real enough, you see. Duggan just built on that. He coached Peter very effectively.'

'What a thoroughly unpleasant man – letting his son believe he could bring the parents together. Poor little boy.'

Julia looked at Jeremy in surprise. Was this, she thought, the new Jeremy? The caring, thoughtful, compassionate Jeremy? Jeremy the politician. Was this the Jeremy she was going to be exposed to all evening, at this dismal-sounding 'soirée'? Still, she mused, it would make a pleasant change. 'I know, the poor chap desperately wanted to believe what his father had told him. There had been so much anger and unhappiness; he thought it was up to him to put things right.'

Jeremy sat silent at the wheel before replying. 'And what about the father? What do you think'll happen to him?'

'Dunno. Jim reckons he could be looking at two years inside for perjuring himself.'

'And the solicitor woman? Judy Simmons. She still standing by him?'

I might have known, thought Julia, that the subject would get round to sex sooner or later. 'I've no idea, Jeremy. I think she probably will. Poor woman was quite besotted by him. Which reminds me,' she added after a moment's thought, 'I have no intention of playing the little love-bird this evening. There's going to be no dangling from your arm and fawning.'

Jeremy couldn't help grinning. Julia was hardly the dangly fawning type. 'Don't worry,' he said. 'This is strictly business.' Then he looked at Julia in alarm. 'Did you bring a hat?'

'A hat? What on earth for?'

'Well . . . it's a Conservative bash. Don't Conservative women always wear hats?'

'I'm not a Conservative, Jeremy.'

'Jeremy!' Patricia Runcorn shrieked in delight and, print dress billowing behind her, descended on him as if he was a long-lost friend. 'So glad you could make it.' Then she turned to Julia. In the split second of silence that followed, Jeremy held his breath, Patricia Runcorn sized Julia up, and Julia herself smiled her most dazzling smile. 'You must be Jeremy's fiancée?'

Julia extended one elegantly manicured hand. 'Julia Piper.'

Patricia Runcorn beamed. 'Delighted to meet you, my dear. And,' she added after a downward glance, 'what a *divine* dress. If I had legs like yours I'd be into it in an instant.' To Jeremy's utter astonishment, she roared with laughter, winked at him, and ushered the pair of them into the body of the room.

Julia caught Jeremy's eye. She, too, winked.

'Everyone's here,' continued Patricia. 'Thought we'd pitch the candidates into the lion's den, as it were.' Then, after another brief burst of laughter, she turned to Julia. 'So tell me, Miss Piper, when are you going to tie the knot?'

'Oh, we haven't set the date yet.' She smiled sweetly at her 'fiancé'. 'Pressure of work, you know.'

'Do you plan to give up work after your marriage?'

'Certainly not.' Julia looked affronted.

Jeremy, however, sensed danger. He glared at Julia. 'Not to begin with, perhaps, but in the long run . . .'

Patricia, however, ignored him. Squeezing Julia's arm, she leaned closer to her and smiled. 'Don't let him bully you, my dear. My view is, if you've got a good career, you jolly well hang on to it.'

'Oh, I agree,' interjected a desperate Jeremy. 'Absolutely. Of course.'

'Well, do help yourselves to the canapés.' Patricia, evidently, felt that she'd done her bit. 'I'll see you later.'

'Just my luck,' moaned Jeremy as she melted into the throng, 'to find a Tory feminist.'

Julia looked at him. 'Can I give you a tip, Jeremy? Why not try saying what you actually believe, rather than what you think they want to hear? Agreeing with everything makes you look servile. They might,' she added, 'like their candidate to have an independent view.'

Jeremy bestowed upon her his most withering look. 'Forgive me, Julia, but that just shows how much you know about politics.'

Before a furious Julia could think of a suitably crushing reply, they were joined by a stocky, aggressive-looking man.

'Aldermarten?' Jeremy, adopting a disapproving look, nodded at the intruder. 'Green,' the man added as he held out a business card. 'If you're looking for a new car, I'm your man.' Jeremy, horrified, was completely lost for words. He became even more horrified when Green added, 'I'm told that you're the man to beat for the nomination.'

'Oh,' stammered Jeremy, 'I don't know about that.'

'I do. The word is the committee's split down the middle. You or me.'

A car dealer versus a barrister? Jeremy suddenly looked very smug. 'Then may the best man win.'

It took the committee two weeks to make their decision. The best man won.

'They selected the bloody car dealer!' Jeremy's face was the very picture of misery. 'Can you believe it?' He looked up at Julia as she stood at the doorway of his room. 'God, politics is a dirty business.'

'Oh, Jeremy, I'm sorry. Maybe they thought the future wife just wasn't up to snuff.'

Jeremy glared at her. 'It's not funny, Julia. It'll take ages to find another seat like that.' He wrinkled his nose in disgust. 'A car dealer! No wonder the country's going down the pan.'

'Don't be such a snob.' Despite her jocular manner, Julia felt rather sorry for him. She also, did he but know it, had a favour to ask him. 'Come and have a drink. We could both use one – and as it happens, I've got some rather good champagne in my room.'

Jeremy meekly followed her along the corridor and, with a rueful rather than grateful smile, accepted the glass of vintage Veuve Clicquot she thrust into his hand.

'Now, Jeremy.' Julia wasn't going to waste any time in coming to the point. 'About the cricket match.'

'What? Oh . . . yes. Frightful débâcle last year. I'll

never get over being thrashed by a bunch of half-witted oiks. I'll tell you, Julia, if we don't beat Great Chartham this year, questions will be asked.'

'It's only a bit of fun, Jeremy.'

'Fun? What's the point of playing if you're only doing it for fun? It's the winning that counts, Julia, let me tell you.'

Somehow, Julia had known he was going to say that. 'Quite – and that's why I want to talk to you about it.'

'Oh?' Jeremy looked suspiciously at her. 'You're not going to let me down at the last minute, are you? Being scorer is frightfully important, you know.'

Julia took a deep breath. 'Jeremy, I've already tried to tell you: I want to *play*. I mean, for God's sake, you'll have me doing teas next.'

'Actually, I was rather hoping Alex might look after that side of things.' Jeremy looked hopefully at her. 'I don't suppose you'd mention it to her?'

'Do your own dirty work.' Julia pointedly ignored Jeremy's glass as she refilled her own. 'So, what's it to be?'

'You're serious. You actually want to play?'

'Why on earth not?'

'Because . . . because . . .'

'Don't say it, Jeremy. Not if you want to leave this room alive.'

Jeremy said it. 'But, I mean, can you . . . well, *play*?'

Julia took a deep breath. Don't, she told herself. Do not commit murder: not in chambers. 'I can bat a bit,' she said, 'but I'm really a bowler.'

Jeremy was stunned. 'Over-arm?'

Julia nearly bit the rim off her glass. Jeremy, realizing he had overstepped the mark, reached for the champagne bottle and then smiled at his colleague. 'Well, there'll be no special favours, you know. No going soft on the ladies. Great Chartham are viciously competitive.'

'So am I, Jeremy, so am I.'

The annual chambers cricket match against Great Chartham was, in spite of what Jeremy claimed, a 'jolly'. It was one of the few chances River Court had to get together, *en masse*, outwith the legal environment. Great Chartham was a stunningly pretty Cotswolds village, with the requisite green on which the match was played, and the River Court team booked themselves into the village pub for the weekend, drank themselves stupid at night, and generally had a whale of a time. Yet this year, the match wasn't just proving problematic for Julia Piper and Jeremy Aldermarten. It proved, unexpectedly, a bone of contention in the Kavanagh household.

Dinner over, Lizzie and Kavanagh sat over the remains of a bottle of wine in the kitchen. The latter was looking grim. Lizzie's bombshell was, he was sure, going to threaten their new-found family stability.

She had dropped it as soon as Matt, Kate and Luke had departed from the room. 'You remember that European Aid job I went for?'

'Sure.' Kavanagh smiled at her. 'You were too well qualified, or too senior, or something.'

'They've got back in touch.'

Kavanagh looked up in surprise. Lizzie had told him she was positive, for the reasons he had just recounted, that she wouldn't get the job. 'What? For the London job?'

Lizzie twirled her wine glass between her fingers.

'No, that's the odd bit . . . They want to interview me for Chief Executive.'

Kavanagh managed to hide his surprise and looked at his wife, betraying the second emotion that hit him – pride. Lizzie, he kept forgetting, was an extremely capable businesswoman. 'The big cheese,' he said fondly.

'It's a fantastic opportunity. I mean, it's gigantic, Jim.' She looked at him. 'The budget is astronomical.'

Which means, he thought, there's a catch.

Lizzie read his mind. 'It's based at head office in Strasbourg.'

Kavanagh, to his credit, managed to hide his misgivings with a display of enthusiasm. Yet now, after congratulating her, he couldn't help but voice his worries. 'We have to talk about the kids, Lizzie. I know Kate's off to college – but what about Matt?'

'Jim, you know I'd never do anything if I thought Matt would suffer. Anyway, there's no point in discussing this until we know what's happening. It's not as if I've got the job – it's only an interview.'

'But are you going to take the job if they offer it?'

Lizzie, exasperated, stood up and began to pace the room. 'I don't want to think about it now . . . I just feel as though I'm being pulled in too many directions.'

'Well, going off to France isn't going to help with that problem, is it?'

Lizzie stopped in her tracks and stared aghast at her husband. 'Well,' she said icily, 'thanks very much for the support.' Then, as she walked out of the room, she turned and, eyes blazing, added, 'And I'm *extremely* sorry I'm going to miss your cricket match. Still, I'm sure you'll find someone's nice little stay-at-home wife to organize your teas.'

'Lizzie! It was just an observation. I didn't mean it the way it sounded. Lizzie!' But Lizzie had gone.

Kavanagh sat for a moment with his head in his hands. Was the family, he mused, about to disintegrate before his eyes?

When, a minute later, he heard the front door shutting, he thought for one awful moment that Lizzie had walked out. Only when Kate popped her head round the kitchen door did he realize that the departure had been Luke's.

'Luke not staying, then?'

Kate shrugged and smiled. 'Some other night, perhaps.'

Kavanagh stared after her as she went into the hall and up to her room. What, he wondered, had all the fuss been about? Perhaps it had been about establishing the principle rather than doing the deed. Sighing, he walked through to Matt in the sitting-room. The women in his household were constantly surprising or upsetting him. At least Matt was a constant: a constant presence, since the holidays had begun, in front of the television.

Sure enough, Matt was sprawled on the sofa in front of the flickering screen. Kavanagh frowned. Evening television was fine, but he knew Matt spent half the day glued to the box. Enough, he thought, was enough.

'What are you up to next week?' he asked his son.

Predictably, Matt shrugged.

'What about coming to see what your old man does for a living?'

'Boring.'

'You might learn something.'

'Dad . . .!'

'I'm at the Old Bailey, Matt. The Central Criminal Court. Court Number One.' He paused. He didn't approve of the ghoulish attitude people had towards sensational trials – and they didn't come much more sensational than this one. Still, he had to do something to nudge Matt out of his torpor.

Matt displayed a flicker of interest. 'Court Number One? Isn't that where they have all the juicy ones?'

'Well . . . I wouldn't put it that way . . .'

'And you're going to be there? Prosecuting?'

'Defending.'

'Who?'

'Annie Lewis.'

Matt suddenly sat bolt upright. 'Wow! Annie Lewis! Why didn't you tell me? I wouldn't miss it for the world.'

CHAPTER TWENTY-THREE

Annie Lewis sat across the table from her sister Diane. 'How are things back home?' she asked.

Diane shrugged. She hoped Annie couldn't tell how uneasy she felt being here – and how surprised she was at her sister's appearance. Prison, she thought, didn't suit Annie at all. While still undeniably attractive, she no longer looked stunning. The vibrancy, the enjoyment of life that she normally radiated had gone. For the first time, Diane wondered if those qualities had been artificial anyway; if Annie had carefully applied them every day to complement her immaculate make-up, her beautifully styled hair and the designer clothes that formed the exquisite package that was Annie Lewis. On entering the visiting area, Diane had been alarmed to see that the package was definitely looking the worse for wear. Perhaps, given the circumstances, she shouldn't have been surprised.

'All right,' she said in response. 'It doesn't change much.' She smiled at her sister. 'Everyone asks after you.'

Annie laughed her deep, throaty laugh. God, thought Diane, somehow she *still* manages to sound sexy. 'I bet,' said Annie, 'I'm the talk of the town.'

'It didn't have to be like this, Annie. You could've gone up in the world without—'

'You mean,' interrupted Annie irritably, 'if I'd

worked really hard for a couple of GCSEs, I could have ended up packing chickens in the pie factory?'

Diane looked defensive. 'It's a job.'

'I've got a car that cost twenty grand – paid for. My own flat. Nice clothes. I go on holiday to the West Indies . . .'

But Diane didn't want to hear any more about her sister's lifestyle. 'Money's not everything.'

Annie looked towards the child in the crèche in the corner of the room. 'You're happy enough to get what I pay you to look after her.'

Diane followed her gaze. Five-year-old Tracy was playing contentedly with the toys Diane had brought with her. She didn't want to be with the adults. They were looking sad.

'Every penny of that goes on her,' said Diane sharply. 'Kids cost a fortune. But you wouldn't know that, would you?' She stared at her sister. 'I'll tell you what they're saying back home, Annie. They're all saying you did it.'

Annie took a deep breath. 'What do *you* say?'

'I say they're wrong,' replied Diane with conviction. 'I say you might be a lot of things, but you're not a killer.'

Kavanagh, initially, had been annoyed with Tom Buckley.

'You've really got it in for me, haven't you? All I said was that I didn't want a family case again.'

'Well, sir,' Tom had exhaled with a satisfied sigh, 'that's not exactly how I remember it. You said you wanted *anything* but a flaming family. Burglary, assault, GBH, armed robbery – anything criminal.' He paused. 'Even murder.'

'But not *this* murder . . .'

'Murder, sir, is murder.'

'No, it isn't, Tom. Not when one of the country's highest-profile businessmen has been murdered by a high-class tart.'

Tom looked with great disapproval at Kavanagh and made a sound that sounded suspiciously like 'Tut, tut'. '*Allegedly* murdered, sir. You haven't lost yet.'

Kavanagh couldn't help grinning. 'Get out, Tom. Get out before I *allegedly* murder you.'

Two weeks later, however, Kavanagh was feeling less amused about the case. In one of fate's nastier little tricks, he had recently been presented with the news that the counsel for prosecution was none other than Peter Foxcott. Peter had thought it a bit of a hoot that the two colleagues would be up against each other in Court Number One of the Old Bailey. But then, thought Kavanagh, he would. The case for the prosecution was, as far as he knew, an awful lot stronger than his own. They had a witness, so Annie Lewis had told him, who was prepared to testify in court that he had seen her leaving the scene of the crime only minutes after the murder. Annie had no alibi. Furthermore, she was a prostitute. No matter how attractive she was, how smartly dressed or how 'up-market' the expensive elocution lessons three years before had made her sound, she was still a prostitute: and juries tended to have old-fashioned views about that particular profession. And to cap it all, Patrick Hutton, the man she was accused of murdering in one of London's top hotels in the middle of the night, had been, as Kavanagh had said to Tom, extremely high-profile.

A married man in his forties, Patrick Hutton had turned a modest fortune into an enormous one by buying and asset-stripping companies hit by the recession. Such activities normally made people singularly unpopular, but such was Patrick's charisma that everyone (except those whose assets were bought and stripped) seemed to love him. The newspapers also loved him; the charitable activities in which he and his elegant wife involved themselves were high-profile and star-studded, and photographs of the glamorous, charming Huttons, at home or abroad, often graced the gossip columns. At the time of the murder, the tabloids had made their opinions abundantly clear. Patrick Hutton was a rare example, within his exalted orbit, of a happy family man. He was not the sort of man to go around picking up prostitutes. And the coroner's statement that his alcohol levels had been extremely high at the time of his death gave the papers the excuse they needed: the poor man, drunk after a stressful week's business, had been lured upstairs by a scheming minx called Annie Lewis who had then murdered him. Hutton's missing wallet and briefcase supplied the motive: Annie had done it for money.

If there was any consolation for Kavanagh, it was that he actually liked Annie Lewis. She was street-smart, funny, and, he had been surprised to see, possessed a great elegance. But then, he had reminded himself, this was no 'wham-bang under the Arches' type. Annie Lewis was a professional – a businesswoman. She was also, on their first meeting, extremely uncooperative, and had let him know that she thought all barristers were bent. In fact, she had told him that the last barrister she had encountered had worn women's panties and told her to call him 'Mummy'. Jeremy Aldermarten had been fascinated. 'I wonder,' he said afterwards, 'if it's anyone we know?'

But today there was nothing particularly amusing about what Kavanagh was going to tell Annie. Sitting across the table from her the day after her sister had visited, he told her that the Crown Prosecution Service would be prepared to accept a verdict of manslaughter. If, therefore, she pleaded guilty, she would avoid a trial before jury and would probably get only five years.

'Five years?' Annie looked aghast.

'Something like that. With good behaviour and parole.'

'What if I turn it down?'

Kavanagh held her gaze. 'If they find you guilty – life. And that means twelve years at least, probably longer.'

'What do you think I should do?'

'I advise you to think about it, very carefully. Undeniably the prosecution can put together a pretty convincing connection linking you to the murder. All we've got is Hutton's character—'

'But everyone thinks he's a blue-eyed boy!'

'Not, Miss Lewis, when they hear what his colleague's got to say.'

Annie grinned. 'Oh yes, I forget about him.'

'And we've got the disputed timing of when the night manager saw you leave – and the unreliable testimony of the taxi-driver who took you home.' He shrugged and smiled in an attempt to bolster her confidence. 'That's something.' But they both knew it wasn't very much on which to build a defence.

Annie looked into the mid-distance for a moment and then turned back to Kavanagh. 'I'd be crazy not to take the manslaughter plea, wouldn't I?'

Kavanagh just looked at her.

'But the problem is, Mr Kavanagh, I didn't do it.' She looked him straight in the eye. 'I'm innocent.'

Kavanagh wished she hadn't told him that. It wasn't his job to know whether or not she was innocent: all he wanted to do was to *prove* that she was innocent – and that wasn't the same thing. But what really got to him was the way Annie had spoken. For the first time in their many consultations, there was a quiet conviction in her voice.

'In that case,' he said after a moment, 'I couldn't advise you to plead guilty.'

Annie smiled grimly. 'So it's up to you now, Mr Kavanagh.'

'No, it's up to both of us. The impression you make on the jury will be of great importance.'

'You mean you want me to look as though Hutton dying is a deep personal loss?' Annie pursed her lips. 'He was a bastard. Just one more pig at the trough. He had it coming.'

If Kavanagh was surprised by the harshness of her words, he didn't show it. 'Juries try to be fair, Miss Lewis, but they're human, and they are swayed by appearances.'

Suddenly Annie grinned again. 'I could wear my old Girl Guide uniform if you think it'd make a good impression.'

Kavanagh smiled. 'That might be a mistake. We wouldn't want to over-excite the judge.'

Annie looked at him with some surprise – and with genuine warmth. Then her face clouded over again. Her words, this time, were softer – and resigned. 'I'm going to lose, aren't I, Mr Kavanagh?'

'We'll do our best.'

'Thank you for that.'

Kavanagh stood up to take his leave. 'Good luck, Miss Lewis.' He sounded as if he really meant it.

Annie looked up at him. 'It's a long time since I trusted a man, Mr Kavanagh.'

Two days later, Annie's ex-husband, the father of her child, discovered her diaries hidden in her flat. His first instinct was to sell them to the newspapers. His second was to give them to the police as evidence – and then sell them to the newspapers. Money, not justice, was his primary concern, and he reckoned the diaries would be worth more if they were instrumental in Annie's conviction. The police gave them to the CPS. Peter Foxcott was elated. The diaries went back many years – right back to the time when Annie became a prostitute at the age of sixteen. And they contained records of her every action and thought – in particular, her vicious, graphically described fantasies about murdering men.

CHAPTER TWENTY-FOUR

Court Number One of the Central Criminal Court – always referred to by lawyers and laymen alike by its streetname of Old Bailey – was packed to the gunwales with legal teams, policemen, the press and the public. For nearly a century some of the most notorious criminals in Britain had been tried and sentenced within the four dark-pannelled walls of the court – and many of those present were convinced that Annie Lewis was going to join their ranks.

The public gallery, unlike that in most other courts, really was a gallery, giving the spectators a bird's-eye-view of everyone below them – and in particular of Annie Lewis herself. The dock, squarely in the middle of the court, was directly below the gallery and in it, alone yet dignified, sat the woman accused of murdering Patrick Hutton. She stared straight ahead and listened impassively as the court sat and the business of deciding her fate began.

After an impressive opening speech to the jury, Peter Foxcott called his first witness. It was the first time Detective Inspector Wilton had ever been in the hallowed confines of Court Number One of the Old Bailey. It was just as well, he told himself, that that was the only thing he had to be nervous about. Giving his evidence would be no problem. He had been around long enough to know a murderer when he saw one.

And the minute he had seen Annie Lewis he had arrested her. There had been no doubt in his mind – and it hadn't taken his men too long to find the evidence.

'Miss Lewis,' he was saying to Foxcott, 'had in her possession a gold cigarette-lighter which was subsequently identified as the property of the deceased by his wife.'

'And did you discover anything else during your search of Miss Lewis's flat?'

Wilton nodded. 'Yes. One of my officers found a torn and blood-stained dress hidden in the bathroom.'

'Did the defendant offer any explanation for her battered physical appearance or the state of her clothing?'

'She made a statement in which she said that she had met Patrick Hutton at a club the previous night, and had agreed to have sex with him in return for payment. On reaching the hotel there was a violent argument and he attacked her. She claimed,' he continued, emphasizing the last word, 'that she left the hotel at about one in the morning, and returned to her home.'

Foxcott smiled, bowed to the judge, and sat down.

'Detective Inspector Wilton,' said Kavanagh as he rose to his feet, 'were there any other items missing from Mr Hutton's hotel room?'

'Yes. His wallet and briefcase.'

'But you didn't find those in Miss Lewis's flat, did you?'

'No.'

In the gallery, members of the press scribbled frantically on their notepads. They had been told that 'items belonging to Patrick Hutton had been found at Annie Lewis's flat'. The police had, by omission, led them to assume that they meant the missing wallet and briefcase.

'You told m'learned friend,' continued Kavanagh, 'that Miss Lewis's dress was "hidden". Where was it?'

'In the bathroom. At the side of the sink.'

'That wasn't a very good hiding-place, was it?'

Wilton shrugged. 'It was a thorough search.'

'If the dress', persisted Kavanagh, 'had been incriminating evidence, wouldn't you have expected her to burn it, or throw it away the instant she returned from the hotel?'

'It might be that we got there quicker than she expected.'

'But she had all night to destroy such an important piece of evidence if she had a mind to, didn't she?'

Wilton actually sneered. 'You and I have both been in this business long enough not to be surprised at what gets overlooked in these situations, Mr Kavanagh.'

To his great pleasure, Wilton's little lecture was received with appreciative titters from the public gallery. Matt Kavanagh, squeezed between two hefty ladies, couldn't help grinning. It wasn't all that often he saw his father being put down.

Kavanagh, however, remained impassive – and changed the subject. 'It's the case, isn't it, Detective Inspector, that you decided very early on that Anne Lewis was Patrick Hutton's killer?'

'I did. All the evidence pointed to her.'

'You never considered other possibilities, did you?'

There was a look of contempt on Wilton's face as he looked straight at Kavanagh and replied, 'I saw no need whatsoever to look in any other direction.'

As Kavanagh sat down, Foxcott grinned at him. Kavanagh glowered back. He didn't need Peter's smug

232

little grin to make him aware of who had won that round.

Dr Jeffrey Markham, a brisk and enthusiastic Home Office pathologist, was next in the witness stand. After his evidence, and that of police forensic expert Dr Derek Buxton, it was established that the cause of death was a blow to the head with Exhibit 'A' – a heavy lead crystal ash-tray – that death occurred between three and four in the morning, and that there were three sets of fingerprints on the ash-tray in addition to those of Annie Lewis and Patrick Hutton. Kavanagh, by getting Dr Buxton to repeat his statements, made sure the jury understood that there were many sets of unidentified fingerprints throughout the room where the murder had taken place. Buxton, aware of the uncertainties Kavanagh was trying to establish, pointed out that this was hardly surprising. It was, after all, a hotel room.

After the initial buzz in the public gallery that resulted from the revelations about the wallet and brief-case, the court had fallen into a state of, if not exactly boredom, then at least resigned tolerance. The old hands amongst the press corps knew that this was par for the course. Others – Matt Kavanagh included – quickly got bored with the endless questions about forensic evidence, the time of death and blood samples. They wanted excitement. And they got it with the appearance of the next witness.

When Susan Hutton, wife of the deceased, was called on to the stand, there was a general murmur, a clear reawakening of interest – and much craning of necks in order to get a good look at the bereaved widow. Despite the fact that some nine months had passed since her husband's death, Susan looked shell-shocked.

Gone was the radiant complexion and the airy confidence that had so often been commented upon: Susan Hutton was now drawn and haggard – a mere shadow of her former self.

Foxcott, naturally, radiated compassion as he questioned her. He treated her with infinite politeness and gentleness and was more than patient whenever she hesitated with her answers. After five minutes, Foxcott called for Exhibit 'B' to be shown to the witness. 'Do you recognize this object?' he said as a court usher handed it to Susan.

Susan Hutton examined it and took a deep breath before replying. 'Yes. It's the cigarette lighter I gave to my husband on his thirtieth birthday.' Gently, almost in wonder, she stroked her fingers over its base. 'It has his initials engraved on it.'

'Mrs Hutton, did you speak to your husband on the night of September the tenth?'

'Yes, I did.'

'What was his mood?'

At that, Julia Piper, Kavanagh's junior, whispered an admonishment. Peter, she felt, was sailing dangerously close to the wind. But if Foxcott heard, he chose to ignore his junior opponent.

'Exhilarated,' replied Susan. 'He was delighted because he'd pulled off a deal he'd been working on for a long time.'

'And what was the last thing your husband said to you that night?'

'He told me to give Barney – that's our youngest son – a hug for him.'

'Hey,' whispered Julia, 'steady on with the hearsay, Peter.'

Kavanagh, hearing her, turned round and shrugged. 'Let it ride, Julia.' Julia, obliged to obey, nevertheless looked annoyed. She was well aware that Foxcott was establishing a nice scene of cosy, loving domesticity for the benefit of the jury.

Foxcott, pleased with the impression he had created, thanked Susan Hutton and sat down.

Kavanagh rose and bowed briefly to the judge. 'No questions, my Lord.'

'Very well.' Judge Trafford turned to Susan with a smile. 'Thank you very much, Mrs Hutton.'

Susan, however, was not happy. 'But I haven't had a chance to clear Patrick's name!' she wailed.

'Mrs Hutton . . .'

'My husband would never have gone with a prostitute. He loved me. He was a good man. I knew him.' Her voice, lower now, betrayed a hint of desperation. 'I *knew* him.' As she spoke the words, she looked around the court for support. None was forthcoming: the expressions she met portrayed only pity and curiosity. Finally, her gaze came to rest on Annie Lewis. Annie, completely expressionless, stared straight back. Hurt and humiliated, Susan collected herself and stepped out of the witness box with as much dignity as she could muster.

The spectators in the gallery were relieved to discover that the next witness was Gerry Hicks, the taxi-driver who had driven Annie home from the hotel. They would be spared desperate personal pleas from him.

Nervous and highly intimidated by the grandeur of his surroundings, Hicks, in response to Foxcott's questions, managed to identify the woman he drove home as the woman now in the dock, stated that her face had been cut and that there had been blood on her dress, and confirmed that she had entered his cab at about three o'clock in the morning.

Kavanagh, however, was not at all happy with the latter piece of information. 'Do you have a better than average memory, Mr Hicks?'

'Not according to my wife.' Too late, Hicks realized that levity was not appreciated in Court Number One. At a stony glance from Judge Trafford, he turned red, coughed, and revised his answer. 'About average, I'd say.'

'About average. Mr Hicks, when was your last night shift?'

'Monday.'

'Just four days ago. Mr Hicks, could you describe for me each of your fares and the time they got into your cab, please?'

Hicks was thunderstruck. 'What, in order?'

'If you wouldn't mind.'

'Oh. Well . . . there was a foreign girl, Lancaster Gate to the Barbican just gone ten, family of four going up West at about eleven . . .' Hicks was now gazing intently upwards, as if drawing inspiration from the elaborately carved ceiling. 'Then the next was two kids going to some club in Bloomsbury . . . then there was a nurse – that was a long run to Clapham . . .'

'And what time are we at now?'

Hicks blinked. 'About two?'

'Are you asking me or telling me, Mr Hicks?'

Hicks looked distinctly flustered. 'I think it was about two. I can't remember the exact time of every fare.'

'Can't you? You told the police and this court that Miss Lewis was in your cab at three o'clock that morning.'

Hicks shrugged. 'You remember the unusual ones.'

Kavanagh, however, didn't agree. 'We've established that you remember the passengers, Mr Hicks, but it's the times you can't be sure of.'

'I *thought* it was three . . .'

'But you can't say definitely that it was, can you? You can't swear that it wasn't five o'clock?'

'I don't think it was that late . . .'

'And you can't swear that it wasn't one o'clock either, can you, Mr Hicks?'

Floundering completely out of his depth, Hicks gave in. 'No. I can't say for definite that it wasn't.'

'Thank you, Mr Hicks.' As Kavanagh sat down, Julia leaned forward. 'Well,' she whispered, 'at least we're on the scoreboard.'

CHAPTER TWENTY-FIVE

'Look, I'm sorry about the other night.'

Lizzie looked straight ahead at the rain drizzling down the windscreen. 'I know. But that's not the point, is it?' Then she turned and looked at her husband. 'What is it you're really worried about, Jim?'

'I can't help wondering . . . this job. Is it about you, or about us? I know we've had our rough patches, but . . .'

'If I wanted to leave you,' said Lizzie irritably, 'don't you think I'd tell you?'

Kavanagh shrugged and gripped the steering-wheel. 'Some things are hard to say after twenty years.'

Lizzie didn't know what to reply to that. Sighing, she opened her door and hoisted her overnight bag out of the back seat. 'I have to get that plane.'

But Kavanagh was still deep in thought. 'I just keep asking myself – are we strong enough?'

'The question you should be asking yourself, Jim, is – are you?'

Lizzie, as she walked into the terminal building, knew that she was right. She knew that if there were any problems about this job, they were her husband's, not hers. Matt, after his initial surprise at the thought of his mother working in Strasbourg for most of the week, had decided it was a 'cool' idea. Kate, from the word go, had thought it was marvellous, and even Lizzie's mother had greeted the news with enthusiasm – but for rather different reasons.

'I'm thinking', Lizzie had said when she'd gone down to her mother's the previous day, 'of taking a job in Strasbourg.'

Anne Probyn, tending her conservatory plants in between large slugs of a giant gin and tonic, had looked up in approval. 'Oh, you must. French men are divine.'

That hadn't been quite the response Lizzie had been looking for – yet she wasn't surprised. Her mother, still attractive at sixty-three, was obsessed by men. Yet her great misfortune, ironically, had been to marry one – Lizzie's father – when she was still in her teens. 'I should never have married your father,' was her constant refrain. 'I was far too young to bury myself in the country when London seemed to be just stuffed full of handsome young men . . .' Behind the bravado her mother, Lizzie knew, was rather sad and deeply lonely.

'I've got a man,' Lizzie had replied. 'In case you'd forgotten.'

'A husband, yes.' Then, after a pause and another gulp of gin, she had turned, misty-eyed, to her daughter. 'But then, I suppose you don't want to end up with only the garden for company, do you?'

No, thought Lizzie as she checked in for her flight. I don't want to end up like my mother. This marriage, problems or no, is going to keep going. And as far as she was concerned, the only immediate problem was that she and James had, for the first time ever, left Matt alone for the weekend. True, Kate had said she would be 'around', but neither of her parents were under any illusions about just exactly who she would spend the weekend around.

Kavanagh arrived in Great Chartham at the same time as Lizzie's plane touched down in Strasbourg. The rain had stopped half an hour after he had left Heathrow and, as he ate up the miles, the clouds lifted and so, too, did his mood. This weekend, he reminded himself, was all about fun. Family problems could wait – and it wasn't even as though Lizzie had got the job. She was only, he reminded himself, going for an interview. And Annie Lewis could also wait. The last thing he wanted was to discuss her case at the weekend. Anyway, he couldn't: not with Peter, his adversary in court, constantly around.

But he had reckoned without Peter's wicked sense of fun. After both teams had greeted each other, changed and milled about in the sunshine drinking too much Buck's Fizz for elevenses, the game began. Kavanagh and Jeremy opened the batting for River Court, and Peter was umpiring at James's end. The bowler, David Lurie, was also Great Chartham's captain. A handsome and athletic man of around thirty, he was also a mean bowler. Running in towards Kavanagh, he delivered a ball that hurtled down the pitch and then thwacked against James's pads. Peter Foxcott immediately raised his hand in dismissal.

'But that was missing leg stump by a mile!' Kavanagh protested.

Peter shook his head. 'Plainly out.'

'Your eyes', hissed Kavanagh as he trundled off, 'need examining.'

Peter grinned. 'There's no appeal in *this* court, Jim.'

Yet as the morning wore on, Peter came to regret

his rather mean decision. River Court plainly needed all the help they could get. Jeremy didn't last long; Tom Buckley fared slightly better, and Julia, later in the proceedings, managed – to Jeremy's secret glee – only five runs. River Court, to their collective disappointment, closed their innings at 110 all out.

It was, then, a sombre team that went in to field as Great Chartham sent in their first two batsmen. River Court's mood, however, lightened when they managed to get five batsmen out for forty runs. But then David Lurie came in and quickly showed himself to be as proficient at the wicket as he had been lethal with the ball. Julia, fielding at mid-on, found herself paying rather more attention to him than to where he was hitting the ball. He was, she mused, rather her type. Tall, broad-shouldered and ... well, lithe-hipped. He was also blond and tanned and, of course, an excellent sportsman. That, she reminded herself, was why she was watching him with such admiration.

After Lurie had scored thirty runs, sending both ball and fielders flying in all directions, Julia decided she had rather gone off him. Or at least that he needed taking down a peg or two. She looked, for the umpteenth time, towards Jeremy. He ignored her pleading expression. Women, in his experience, just did not – could not – bowl. No matter that River Court had already tried four bowlers without success, he was damned if he was going to let Julia make an even bigger mess of things.

When Lurie hammered the ball for his third six, Julia decided that she'd had enough. Her face set, she strode up to Jeremy. 'Give me that ball.'

Jeremy, harassed, cast her an irritated glance. 'Not now, Julia. This is a crisis.'

'One over. That's all I ask.'

'Oh . . . all right, then.' Handing her the ball with great reluctance, Jeremy also gave her some advice. 'If the first three balls go for six, fake an injury.'

Julia just looked at him. One day, she thought, I really am going to kill this man. Then she turned, marked her run-up, and went in to bowl. She did at least, conceded Jeremy, look as if she knew what she was doing.

Julia knew exactly what she was doing: she had been doing it all her adult life. With infinite grace and extraordinary speed, she sent her first ball fizzing off for a length and watched with a smile of satisfaction as it curved in towards Lurie and, with a satisfying 'smack', removed his off-stump. The entire pitch, spectators included, lapsed into stunned silence – followed by deafening applause. Jeremy, mouth hanging open in disbelief, couldn't believe his eyes.

Julia won the day. She bowled like a demon for the rest of the afternoon, and Great Chartham, thoroughly discomfited after their early confidence, found themselves struggling – and ultimately losing. Yet they, and the by now thoroughly inebriated spectators, cheered as loudly as Julia's team-mates when she was given the honour of leading the team from the field. Even Jeremy clapped until his hands were sore.

Desperate for and deserving of liquid sustenance, both teams headed straight for the pub overlooking the village green. The rivalry was over – now it was time for fun.

'That was a wonderful ball you got me out with,' said David Lurie as he edged towards Julia.

Julia grinned. 'Pure luck,' she lied.

David, disconcertingly, looked straight into her eyes. 'Not at all. It was a fast off-break, wasn't it?'

'Oh, not really. It was pretty straight, but you left a gap between bat and pad.'

'Did I?' David smiled. Really, thought Julia, he *is* rather handsome. 'That was reckless.'

'But you played terribly well. Fantastic, really.' Julia was aware she was speaking too quickly. 'I thought you were going to beat us single-handed.'

'May I,' replied David without taking his eyes off hers, 'buy you a drink?'

Jeremy, beady-eyed, was following this encounter with irritated interest. In the middle of a little group at the other end of the bar, he turned to Kavanagh beside him.

'Incredible,' he said, 'how women always go for the obvious ones. I mean, he's handsome – in his way – but you'd think she might be looking for something a little more meaningful.'

Kavanagh was highly amused. 'Don't tell me the competition's getting to you, Jeremy?'

'No.' For a second Jeremy looked wistful. 'I just sometimes think how nice it must be for you to have someone like Lizzie to go home to. Where is she, anyway?'

Kavanagh shrugged. 'Something came up.'

'Not tempted to chase the barmaid around the cricket pitch while you're off the leash?'

Kavanagh was beginning to wish, fervently, that Jeremy would get lost. 'Too much of an old married man, Jeremy. Not really my thing.'

Jeremy, uncharacteristically envious, sighed heavily. 'In your shoes, I'd probably feel the same way.' Then, evidently deciding that being maudlin didn't suit him, he brightened and looked at Jim with a gleam in his eye. 'As it is, I shall return undaunted to the fray.'

With that, he edged his way through the throng. He

passed straight behind Julia, but she was completely oblivious to all except the tall man standing close to her. 'I've got a complete set of Wisden,' he was saying. 'You might like to have a look later.' The look in his eyes suggested that he wasn't just talking cricket.

'I can't think of anything,' replied Julia as a delightful sensation shuddered through her, 'of anything I'd enjoy more.'

CHAPTER TWENTY-SIX

It was difficult, Julia found to her surprise, to revert to the business of being a barrister. She was heartily glad that she wasn't leading on this case, that, as Kavanagh's junior, she was not required to stand up and ask complicated questions of bewildered witnesses. For on Monday morning Julia herself, for the first time in memory, was feeling bewildered. Never before had she met a man with whom sparks flew so instantly. Never had she encountered anyone quite like David Lurie.

They had, on the Saturday night, rapidly forgotten about the existence of Wisden, the cricketing bible. Late in the evening, oblivious to the knowing looks cast in their direction, they went upstairs to Julia's room in the pub. It seemed fitting, somehow, that the room was grand and old – and contained a huge four-poster bed.

Julia, sitting in full regalia in the middle of the Old Bailey, was lost in the memory of that night. It had been, she recalled with a warm glow, leisurely, beautiful and memorable. And with a rueful grin, she remembered the morning after: waking to the sound of church bells and the caress of the sun on her face through the open window. She remembered how, with her eyes still closed, she had reached out for David; reached out to reassure herself that the night had been real, that his lean, tanned body was indeed sprawled beside hers under the rumpled sheets. She was almost ashamed to recall the acuteness of her disappointment when she realized that she was alone. It was only after a full minute that she had seen the cricket bat at the foot of the bed. With the alacrity of a child reaching for its Christmas stocking, Julia had burrowed down the bed to examine it – and to discover the telephone number written across its blade in a bold, confident hand.

Suddenly she realized that she was grinning like an idiot from ear to ear – and that she was listening to the sad testimony of a man who had been with his best friend Patrick Hutton on the night of the murder. With considerable effort, she reminded herself that she was here, participating in the most sensational murder trial of the year, in a professional capacity. Bringing her mind back to the proceedings, she surreptitiously adjusted her wig, sat bolt upright, and tried to look like a barrister.

Kavanagh, sitting directly in front of Julia, was also finding it difficult to concentrate on what the witness, Mark Randall, was saying in response to Peter Foxcott's questions. Like Julia, his mind kept straying back to the weekend – but for entirely different reasons.

He and Lizzie, by a lucky coincidence, had arrived back at the house at the same time on Sunday. Delighted to see each other, delighted to be home, they had rushed out of the rain and into the house – and then stared in disbelief at the scene before them. They had, yet again, been burgled. The furniture in the sitting-room was all over the place; some of it had been damaged; the carpet was stained with all manner of revolting-looking substances, and the place stank to high heaven. It was only when they noticed that the stereo, the video and the TV were still in place that a seed of doubt was sown. And then, when they saw Matt on his hands and knees, frantically and ineffectually scrubbing the floor, they realized what had happened.

Kavanagh had been apoplectic with rage. Lizzie was so relieved that Matt had not been hurt by rampaging burglars that she couldn't summon up any anger. And Matt was deeply, desperately upset. He hadn't meant it to happen, he said. It was just supposed to be a few friends coming round and it had all got a bit more than he had expected, one of them had been feeling a little unwell and then . . .

And then the recriminations had started. Kavanagh remembered he had said that 'someone should have been there'. That was the cue for Lizzie's temper to flare.

'What you mean is that *I* should have been here.'

'That's ridiculous.'

'Yes, you do. You think it's my fault. Deep down you think the house and the kids are my patch and I should have been here to deal with it.'

Deep down, Kavanagh supposed that was exactly what he had thought. But he couldn't say that to Lizzie. Instead he said what was in the forefront of his mind. 'All right, but let's face it, if you get this job you won't make it back every weekend and I can't exactly drag Matt around Europe every Friday night. And he's obviously not responsible enough to be left on his own.'

For a moment they had just looked at each other. Then, quietly this time, Lizzie spoke. 'You haven't even asked if they offered it to me yet.'

'Did they?'

'Yes, as a matter of fact, they did.'

Kavanagh, to his credit, only hesitated for a moment. Then he went up to his wife and wrapped her in a warm embrace. He remembered how he had patted her on the back and looked over her shoulder and said to himself that it would be all right, that they would, as always, be able to rise above any problems. If Lizzie was happy and fulfilled, he reasoned, it was much more likely that everyone else around her would feel the same way.

Suddenly, and with horror, he started and realized that he was in danger of losing the drift of the examination that was taking place before his eyes. Peter Foxcott had been questioning Mark Randall for five minutes now; what on earth, thought Kavanagh, had Randall said? He had, he knew, been with Patrick Hutton on the night of his death. He had been in the nightclub where Hutton had picked up Annie Lewis. And, once back in the hotel, he had gone straight to his room – the one next to Hutton's – and fallen into a drunken sleep. What else had he said? Kavanagh was sure he hadn't missed anything vital. Still, even that wouldn't be a tragedy; Julia would tell him if he'd missed anything. She, he knew, would never allow herself to daydream in court.

Foxcott, coming to the end of his examination, asked Randall one last question. 'Would you say, Mr Randall, that Mr Hutton's behaviour on the night of September the tenth was atypical?'

Randall didn't hesitate for a second. 'Yes. Mr Hutton was a family man, devoted to his wife and children. But,' he conceded, 'he'd been under a lot of pressure and we'd had a drink or two, and I think that might have affected his judgement.'

'Thank you, Mr Randall.' Foxcott sat down. Perhaps that had been pushing it, he thought. Maybe I shouldn't have tried to re-establish the image of Hutton as a doting husband and father.

Kavanagh got straight to the point. 'Are you experienced with prostitutes, Mr Randall?'

Randall looked horrified. 'Certainly not. I am a happily married man.'

'Was Mr Hutton experienced in that way?'

'Not to my knowledge . . .'

'Yet he met Miss Lewis in the nightclub and made an arrangement with her, took her back to the Caxton International Hotel – all without the least sign of nervousness or uncertainty, did he?'

'He was a very confident man.'

'You said his behaviour on this night was atypical, yet everything in his behaviour showed he was experienced in picking up prostitutes, didn't it?'

Hutton shifted uneasily in the witness box. 'That's your view. It's not mine.'

'Mr Randall, how long had you been staying in a hotel while working on this deal?'

'Since the Friday of the week before.'

'But you weren't staying at the Caxton International all week, were you?'

Bugger, thought Foxcott. I was hoping he wouldn't find that one out.

'No,' replied Randall. 'It was another hotel.'

'Why did you choose to move to the Caxton International for that last night?'

'Well . . . no particular reason.'

'No particular reason. When you arrived at the hotel after leaving the nightclub, did Mr Hutton speak to anybody?'

'Not apart from a brief word with Mr Day, the Duty Manager, no.'

'What did Mr Hutton say to Mr Day?'

Randall shrugged uninterestedly. 'Nothing much. Just something like, "How are you, Bobby?" '

'Ah. Since Mr Hutton called Day by his first name, they were obviously on sociable, even intimate terms, weren't they?'

'I . . . yes, they seemed to know each other.' Randall, suddenly, was not enjoying this line of questioning. Not at all.

'Mr Randall, I'll ask you again. Why did you choose to move to the Caxton International?'

Randall didn't reply.

'It was because of Bobby Day and the personal service he provided, wasn't it?'

Randall looked trapped. 'I wouldn't know,' he mumbled.

'It wasn't the first time Patrick Hutton had been with a prostitute in this hotel, was it?'

Again Randall made no reply. He is, thought Julia Piper with satisfaction, incriminating himself with his silence.

'You've done all this before with him, haven't you, Mr Randall?'

Randall was now positively squirming. 'I personally', he said at last, 'never had anything to do with prostitutes.'

'But Mr Hutton did, didn't he?'

'Yes, he did.' At that admission, a buzz went round the court. This was the first real point the defence had scored – and the first indication that there was far more to this story than met the eye. In the public gallery, Matt Kavanagh leaned forward. This, he thought, was brilliant. Thank God his parents had decided that – suitably enough – the best way to keep him out of trouble was to let him come to court once more.

'And on those other occasions,' Kavanagh continued, 'the women were supplied through Mr Day, weren't they?'

Randall, hating Kavanagh, looked straight ahead. 'I believe Pat and Day had an arrangement, yes.'

'The difference this time was that Mr Hutton brought a woman with him, wasn't it?'

'Yes. In the past we would always go to the hotel and women would arrive later.'

'Women? More than one?'

Randall nodded miserably. 'Sometimes.'

'Was Mr Day paid for his services as middleman?'

'I assume that there was some form of financial understanding between Pat and Day, yes.'

Kavanagh stopped for a moment to let the jurors contemplate the notion of Patrick Hutton, public figure, as a liar and an adulterer. 'As a wealthy, high-profile figure,' he continued, 'did Mr Hutton employ anyone to look after his personal safety?'

Randall, heartily relieved that Kavanagh had changed tack, nodded vigorously. 'Yes. His driver was trained in security areas.'

'And was his driver present that night?'

'No, Pat let him go for the night when we got to the hotel.'

'Did he always do that on these occasions?'

'Yes.'

'So,' continued Kavanagh with hardly a pause for breath, 'Mr Hutton was in the habit of allowing complete strangers into his hotel room in the dead of night, without taking any precautions for his own safety?'

Randall, to his intense irritation, hadn't seen that one coming. 'Er . . . yes.'

'Given what you know of him, it's possible, isn't it, that Mr Hutton would have invited another woman up to his room after Miss Lewis left?'

'It's possible.' Randall's expression, however, indicated he thought it was highly unlikely.

'A woman arranged for him by Mr Day?'

'Yes.'

Kavanagh drew himself to his full height and looked Mark Randall in the eye. 'Anything, in fact, could have happened in that hotel room after my client left, couldn't it?'

'No,' Randall returned the piercing gaze, 'because Patrick was dead.'

Bobby Day oozed confidence. His rather ordinary looks were enhanced by a beautifully cut suit; his hair was perfectly styled; his hands were manicured and his skin, no doubt, was testament to the efficacy of a whole range of products designed to flatter male vanity. Vain, in fact, was the word Kavanagh would have used to describe the man. Vain – and smug.

'Mr Day,' said Foxcott as he rose to question him, 'when did you first see the defendant on the night of September the tenth?'

'I saw her come in at about twelve-thirty.' Day, having rehearsed his evidence many times, spoke with both authority and conviction. 'I had a brief conversation with Mr Hutton. Then they took the lift together.' The last words were uttered with just the merest hint of disapproval.

'Mr Day, did you see Annie Lewis again that night?'

'Yes. I was in my office. I looked up and saw her running across the lobby. She went out and through the main doors.'

'Are you sure it was her?'

Day nodded. 'There is no doubt in my mind. I only saw her from behind, but it was definitely her.'

'And you say she was running?'

'Yes. There was something panicky about it. Running away might be a better way of putting it.'

Foxcott smiled. That, he thought, had gone well. 'What time was this?'

Day too smiled. This was the clincher. 'Just after three o'clock.'

At that, Annie Lewis, hitherto calm and expressionless in the dock, sprang to her feet. 'That is a bloody lie!' she shouted.

Judge Trafford was on to her like lightning. 'Unless you can control yourself, Miss Lewis, you will be taken down.'

Annie, furious, shrugged off the attentions of the policewoman beside her. Reluctantly, she sat down again: but this time there was no lack of expression on her face. Lips set in an angry line, eyes flashing with hatred, she looked straight at Bobby Day.

Foxcott, rather than being annoyed, was pleased at the interruption. It would serve to emphasize to the jury the time of night that Annie had left the hotel. 'Are you certain,' he continued, 'that was the time, Mr Day?'

'Yes. I am. I remember looking at my watch.'

As Foxcott sat down, Day looked at Annie. The look on his face said it all: 'That's fixed you,' he seemed to be saying. 'Who do you think they're going to believe – a prostitute or an experienced hotelier?'

Kavanagh, however, was determined to 'fix' Bobby Day. 'Mr Day,' he said as he got to his feet, 'in your statement to the police, you said that Mr Hutton had stayed at your hotel in the past, and that you recognized him, but that was the extent of your acquaintance. Is that correct?'

Day smiled at the defence counsel. 'Yes, that's what I said.'

Kavanagh was quick to wipe the smile off his face. 'But that wasn't entirely true, was it?'

'Yes, it was.'

'Mr Hutton called you "Bobby" when he arrived at the hotel that night, didn't he?'

Day looked evasive. 'I don't remember.'

'We have just heard Mr Randall say that he did.' And who, his expression said, do you think the jury are going to believe – an international businessman or a hotel night manager of dubious morals?

Day shrugged. 'He may have done.'

'But if you didn't know him, why would he address you in such a familiar way?'

'I dare say he might have heard the staff using my name . . .'

'And you knew him well enough to feel able to protest to him about the woman he brought back to the hotel, didn't you?'

Day, completely thrown, didn't know how to reply.

'You knew who that woman was, didn't you?' prompted Kavanagh.

Day, still wary, replied that he knew the *type* of woman she was.

'What type was that?'

'A prostitute.'

'I put it to you, Mr Day, that you objected because she was not one of your prostitutes. You have a lucrative sideline in arranging girls for clients at your hotel, don't you?'

Day puffed out his chest in outrage. 'I deny that.'

'What are you denying? That this was the reason why you objected to her, or that you arrange prostitutes?'

'I deny that I arrange for prostitutes to ply their trade in my hotel.'

'You've never done that?'

'Never.'

Kavanagh paused and looked at Bobby Day. While the man still looked outwardly calm, there was a certain tension in his face – and the confident swagger of a few moments ago had vanished. 'You did,' he continued after a moment, 'know Miss Lewis, then?'

'Yes.'

'And you knew she was a prostitute?'

'Yes, I said so.'

Kavanagh smiled without even a trace of warmth. 'Then why didn't you want her to come in? Mr Hutton was a wealthy and powerful man. You couldn't stop him doing what he wanted.'

Day bit his lip – and failed to find a reply.

'You tried', continued Kavanagh, 'to stop Miss Lewis because she would not pay you a cut of her earnings in return for business you put her way. That's right, isn't it?'

'I haven't the slightest idea what you're talking about.'

'Haven't you? Mr Randall has just told this court that you arrange girls for clients at this hotel, and that you had performed that service for Mr Hutton in the past.'

But Day stuck to his guns. 'Then he is mistaken. That is rubbish.'

'So he's just making that up, is he?'

'He must be.' As soon as Day said the words, he knew how weak they sounded.

'It's your word against his?'

'Yes.'

Again Kavanagh paused – and again his expression suggested that not many people would find Day's argument entirely convincing. In case anyone was still in any doubt about the reliability of Day's evidence, he pressed on. 'You told m'learned friend that it was three o'clock when you saw Miss Lewis leaving the hotel, didn't you?'

'Yes.'

'Miss Lewis says it was one o'clock.'

'She's lying.'

Kavanagh stopped to let Day's words echo round the court.

Then he smiled. 'Your word against hers?'

Day looked thoroughly miserable. 'Yes,' he said quietly.

CHAPTER TWENTY-SEVEN

The headlines in the morning tabloids were, as they had been from the beginning, full of news about the Annie Lewis trial. Most of it was selective – some of it was untrue – but what every paper carried in common was the opinion that Bobby Day wasn't going to be holding on to his job for very long. Whether or not he had been lying about arranging prostitutes for guests, it was a pretty safe bet that the directors of the chain which owned the Caxton International would decide that, whilst the headlines about their hotel were inevitable, its continuing employment of Bobby Day was not. Yet, while the general public digested yesterday's news – and the particularly hard, unflattering photograph of Annie that accompanied it – the reporters who had written that news were back in the Old Bailey watching, as far as they were concerned, a rather more interesting witness than Bobby Day.

He was Des Carter, the man who had lived with Annie Lewis for four years, who had fathered a child by her, been abandoned by her, and who was now – far more importantly from the reporters' point of view – in possession of the sensational diaries Annie had left behind. The diaries were now tagged as evidence, but Des Carter had made more than a few hints that they would, when the trial was over, be for sale.

Carter, a chirpy and cocky individual most of the

time, was evidently intimidated by his surroundings. He had never been in a building quite so grand and forbidding as the Old Bailey, and he had never stood facing so many serious-looking people. Looking respectable if slightly furtive, he was now, thanks to Peter Foxcott's careful questions, beginning to enjoy himself. He was even picking up the theatricality of his environment: his last statement about how he had – only a few weeks ago – finally found and read the diaries had gone down extremely well. There had been an audible gasp in the court when he had said that he had gone straight to the police because their contents had made him 'unable to sleep'.

'I see.' Peter Foxcott's reply was non-committal; the diaries, he knew, were about to speak for themselves. 'Mr Carter, could you please take the 1989 diary and read from the entry Miss Lewis made on June the fifth of that year?'

Carter, unused to reading out loud, knew he had to make a good impression. He couldn't give a stuff if they incriminated Annie or not: all he was interested in was making them sound as riveting as possible to the journalists in the gallery. Opening one of the photocopied diaries at the requested date, he began to read:

'*They're all liars and cheats, all the husbands and fathers, all so bloody respectable, but underneath, the same stinking hypocrites. One day I'd like to get one and do him, just like slaughtering an animal.*' As instructed by Foxcott, Carter stopped here and looked up: every pair of eyes was fixed on him – and Annie's eyes were the only ones without expression. There was not a sound in the whole room as he continued:

'*I'll wait until he's asleep and then stick the bastard in the*

258

guts. And I'll want him to wake up then, so the last thing he sees is me watching him bleed to death.'

As Carter finished quoting from the diary, several of the jurors turned to Annie. With enormous effort, she managed to retain her composure and mask whatever was going on in her mind. Yet she knew that both the spectators and the jurors were now, for the first time, wondering if they were in the presence of a monster.

Foxcott, aware of the emotions running through the court, asked Carter to read another extract, and then yet another. The effect was as he wished: it proved that the first had not been an aberration; an idle, if rather violent, isolated thought. It was clear that Annie Lewis had harboured murderous thoughts about her punters for many years.

During Foxcott's examination of Carter, Kavanagh and Julia exchanged worried glances. The diaries were, from prosecution's point of view, the ace of trumps. Yet, even though defence had had less time to examine them, Kavanagh had found within them a few high cards in his favour. Des Carter, he mused, ought to have read them more carefully.

'Let's look', he said as he began his cross-examination, 'at some alternative entries in this diary, Mr Carter. Could you please read from September the twelfth, 1987?'

Carter duly did as he was bid. The moment he started reading, his voice betrayed a different emotion – extreme reluctance:

'Des came back today, thank God. Two days. I was terrified he'd gone for good. He said I'd really upset him, and why was I giving him so much grief about it? I asked him if he *loved me and he came straight out and said of course. So in the end I said I'd do it. He was really chuffed.'*

'Could you explain', asked Kavanagh when Des finished reading, 'what Miss Lewis was referring to in that entry, Mr Carter?'

'No.' Carter was defiant. 'Doesn't mean a thing to me.'

'All right.' Kavanagh didn't look in the least put out. 'Let's turn to a week later, the nineteenth.'

Carter, with even greater reluctance, turned the pages. *'Des brought H. back from the pub. Not too bad. £100. Kept £20.'*

Again all eyes were fixed on Carter. But this time they were looking at him with contempt.

'Can you tell us who H. was, and what the £100 was for?'

Carter shuffled uneasily and refused to look Kavanagh in the eye. 'I don't know.'

Undaunted, Kavanagh pressed on. 'Would you read the extract from February the seventeenth, 1988, please?'

'Had 'flu. Told Des I couldn't go out. Gave me one of his little talks. Worked Knightsbridge later. Felt sick. £280.'

'What did she mean by "a little talk", Mr Carter?'

Carter, now looking thoroughly miserable, avoided his eye. 'I dunno what she's on about.'

You must, thought Matt Kavanagh as he watched his father with admiration, be the only one in court not to.

'Very well.' Kavanagh, still unfazed, asked Carter to read out the extract from 5 March, 1988.

Carter duly flicked through the photocopies until he found the place. Then, puzzled, he looked up. 'There's nothing written. Just a drawing.'

Kavanagh asked him to hold it up. Only the legal teams and the jury were close enough to get a clear view of the large, crude drawing of a face. It resembled a child's drawing of a 'happy' face – except that the smile was upside-down.

'Do you know what that means?' asked Kavanagh.

'No idea.' Des, for the first time during the cross-examination, sounded genuinely in the dark.

'When you read these diaries, did you find this drawing often?'

'Sometimes.'

Kavanagh took a deep breath and adjusted his glasses. 'Mr Carter, throughout the period of your relationship with Miss Lewis you repeatedly assaulted her in order to make her earn money for you as a prostitute, didn't you?'

'No way. I paid the rent, bought her gear, the lot. She did all right out of me. If she didn't want to be a tart, why's she still doing it now?'

The jurors, and the women of their number in particular, looked horrified, both by Carter's words and by the fact that he so obviously believed what he was saying.

'Mr Carter, how long were you and Miss Lewis living together?'

'About four years. From March '87 to Christmas '91.'

Kavanagh gestured towards the diaries. 'How far back do these diaries go?'

Des knew the answer to that one by heart. He had been calculating how much twelve years of Annie's thoughts would earn him. 'The earliest ones are from 1983,' he replied.

'And there isn't any violent material in the early years of these diaries, is there?'

Carter shrugged. 'There might be.'

'Well, you've read them. Find it for us.'

Carter flicked miserably through the diaries. Judge

Trafford was almost on the point of intervening when, at last, he raised his head and admitted defeat. 'I . . . I can't see anything.'

'It doesn't start, does it, until after both of you moved in together in 1988?'

Carter, genuinely perplexed, looked up at Kavanagh. 'I can't see what that's got to do with it.'

Kavanagh smiled. 'Well, some people might think, Mr Carter, that the violence was directly linked with the time Miss Lewis spent with you, mightn't they?'

Peter Foxcott cast an annoyed glance in his opponent's direction. If people hadn't been thinking along those lines, they certainly would be now. Des Carter, unfortunately, was one of those people. It simply hadn't occurred to him before – and he was damned if he was going to believe it. 'It's nothing to do with me,' he said.

Kavanagh put his hand to his chin and, after a moment, added, almost as an afterthought, 'Where did the newspapers get hold of this morning's picture of Miss Lewis, Mr Carter?'

'Mystery to me.'

'Have you agreed to sell your story to a newspaper at the conclusion of this trial?'

'I've had offers,' conceded Carter, 'but I wasn't interested.'

It was the last thing he said in court – and the least convincing, by far.

Annie Lewis knew a thing or two about dressing for the part. Generally, she dressed 'up', but Kavanagh's advice about the effect she could create on the jury had not fallen on deaf ears. She had, she knew, already created a favourable impression in that respect – and today she had made an even greater effort. Head held high, she walked to the witness box in her demure and not too expensive tailored suit and her low-heeled court shoes. Her make-up was so discreet as to be almost invisible: it served merely to accentuate her natural good looks. As she was sworn in, she cast a quick look at the jury. They were, without exception, looking at her with interest, even appreciation. There was, however, a palpable atmosphere of excitement in the court – and particularly in the public gallery. The pressmen were scribbling descriptions of Annie's appearance, a few people made whispered, flattering remarks about her – but one person simply stared at her. Susan Hutton, utterly mesmerized by the woman who had allegedly slept with her husband for money and then killed him, seemed unaware of anything or anyone else.

Kavanagh, now that the case for the prosecution and its calling of witnesses had been concluded, rose first to conduct his examination-in-chief. Leading Annie towards the events of the night in question, he asked her how she had established that Patrick Hutton was interested in her.

'He made it clear,' replied Annie, 'that he wanted me from the moment he walked in. He called me over to his table.'

'Did you recognize him?'

'He made a big thing about not using his full name, but I knew who he was. I nearly didn't go with him,' she added. 'There was something about his mood I didn't like. I've seen it before. The kind of mood that can turn ugly.'

In the gallery, Susan Hutton slowly shook her head in disbelief.

'But,' Kavanagh pointed out, 'you did go back with

263

him to the Caxton International Hotel. What happened when you got there?'

'As we came in we saw Bobby Day.' At her own mention of the name, Annie's expression darkened. 'I could tell he wasn't happy. I was working on his territory. He'd told me before he'd put me out of business.'

Leaving a few seconds for that to sink in, Kavanagh then proceeded. 'So you went up to Mr Hutton's room?'

'Yes. I should have seen the signs then. It was obvious what he really wanted.'

'What was that?'

'He wanted to hurt me.' Annie's voice, low and even, seemed to plunge the court into a deeper silence.

'What happened then?'

'After we'd fixed the price I turned towards the door, and then he hit me. He went mad. He tore my dress, then threw me on the floor and hit me again. He started punching and slapping me, calling me all the usual names, like bitch and slag.' While Annie recalled the events in a distant, far-away voice, her words had an immediate effect on the court. Horror, Kavanagh noted, outweighed disbelief. Far behind him, Susan Hutton began to shake.

'I struggled as hard as I could,' Annie continued. 'I think I hit him, because his nose was bleeding. Some of the blood must have got on my dress. He put his hand to his face, and I got to the door and ran out.'

'And what did you do next?'

'I got a cab home, cleaned myself up and went to bed.' The matter-of-fact delivery and the mundane words made their context all the more shocking.

'Can you explain', asked Kavanagh, 'how Patrick Hutton's cigarette-lighter was found in your possession?'

'Yes.' Annie looked him straight in the eye. 'I stole it.'

'Why?'

'It's just a way of letting the punters know what I think about them.'

'Did you steal his briefcase?'

'No.'

'Did you steal his wallet?'

'No.'

'Can you explain how your fingerprints came to be on the glass ash-tray in his room?'

'Yes. I had a cigarette while I was waiting for him to get changed. I must have touched it then.'

'The court has heard Detective Inspector Wilton claim that you had hidden the blood-stained dress. *Did* you hide it?'

For the first time, Annie smiled. 'No. I just put it by the sink because I was going to wash it by hand in cold water.'

Kavanagh then nodded in the direction of one of the court ushers. The court watched intently as the usher brought him the infamous diaries that had caused such a stir during the testimony of Des Carter.

After they were deposited in front of him, Kavanagh looked back towards his client. 'Miss Lewis, why did you keep a diary?'

'To begin with, for the same reason that everybody else does.' Annie shrugged and added, 'Just to keep a few secrets. Kid's things, ordinary stuff.'

'And later?'

'I was confused. I ... . I didn't understand everything that was happening to me.'

'When was this?'

Again Annie's face darkened. 'After I met Des Carter.'

'Were you in love with him?'

Only those closest to Annie could see a muscle twitching in her cheek as she answered, 'I thought so at the time.'

Now Kavanagh looked at the notes he had made during Foxcott's examination of Des Carter. 'On September the twelfth, 1987, you wrote that Des had come back and that you had agreed to do as he suggested. What had he suggested?'

'That I go on the game to earn some money.'

'What was your reaction?'

'I didn't want to do it. We had a row. I was frightened he was going to leave me, so eventually I said I would.' Annie's next words were leaden with irony. 'He said it would only be for a while.'

'And then what happened?'

'He brought a mate of his back from the pub, a bloke called Harry. That was my first time.'

'And afterwards?'

'It was still once in a while at first, but Des kept going on at me, so I started going out more often.' Annie had reverted to the dispassionate tone she had started with. As Kavanagh had pointed out, she would be doing herself no favours by pleading the poor abused innocent. Much better to let the jury make their own deductions. And it was an extra bonus that Des Carter had, earlier in the day, made such a poor impression.

'What did you do with the money?' asked Kavanagh.

'Most of it went to Des. I kept a few quid back when I could.'

Here, Kavanagh held up the diary. 'Can you tell us what this drawing means, Miss Lewis?'

'Yes.' Annie smiled grimly. 'It means it was a day when Des had beaten me up.'

'Why didn't you just write that?'

Annie shrugged. 'I was frightened he'd see the diaries. If he'd read something like that he'd have gone mad, especially after a drink.'

'Why didn't you just leave him?'

'I don't know. To begin with I still thought I needed him. Later I was frightened of what he might do.'

'Were you working regularly as a prostitute by this time?'

'Six nights a week. Seven sometimes. Des took virtually everything I earned. In the end I got out because I knew I could do better on my own.'

Kavanagh paused and then asked the question that was on everyone's lips. 'Why did you write about killing men in your diaries, Miss Lewis?'

'Because I was sick of feeling scared. Somehow imagining something like that made me feel safer and more powerful. It was a safety valve, that's all. I never meant,' she added with vigour, 'that I was actually going to do it.'

'Do you still keep a diary?'

The faint trace of a rueful smile played on Annie's lips as she replied, 'No. I don't need a diary any more.'

'Why not?'

'Because I'm not scared or angry any more. I haven't got anything else to say.'

Once more, Kavanagh reached for the diaries. Opening one at a pre-arranged place, he asked the court usher to hand it to Annie. As she took it from the usher, Annie's hand shook almost imperceptibly. She had known this was coming: she had rehearsed this with Kavanagh. Yet doing it in court, especially in this grand and intimidating court, was quite a different matter.

'Could you read one final extract for us, Miss Lewis,' requested Kavanagh, 'from August the seventh, 1990?'

Annie bowed her head and took a deep breath. '*Tracy*', she read, '*is one month old today. She is the most beautiful thing I have ever seen. The only good thing in my life. One day, when I've made enough money, I'll take her with me somewhere else, to another town, or maybe even another country. Away from all this, anyway.*' To her credit, Annie didn't falter as she read the extract. Yet as she looked up and straight at Kavanagh it was clear for all to see that the words had affected her deeply. A tiny, solitary tear trickled down her left cheek.

As a finale it was, from Kavanagh's point of view, a triumph. Thanking Annie, he then bowed to the judge and sat down.

Peter Foxcott began his cross-examination as he meant to go on – by firing questions at Annie in a manner that only just stopped short of aggressive. 'Miss Lewis, if you didn't take Mr Hutton's briefcase and wallet, who did?'

'I have no idea.'

'Was anybody else with you in the room?'

'No.'

'Did you see anybody else go in when you left?'

'No. I was running away.'

'If this man beat you up as you described, why didn't you go to the police?'

Annie looked at the prosecution counsel with something like contempt. 'Who do you think they would believe?'

It was the perfect reply. Unlike the question. Yet Foxcott remained unruffled as he continued, 'This story of an unprovoked attack by Mr Hutton is not true, is it?'

'Yes, it is.'

'What actually happened was that you waited until he was asleep and then set about stealing his belongings. But he woke and surprised you, didn't he?'

'No.'

'There was a struggle during which you received your injuries, but he was sleepy and defenceless and in the end you picked up the ash-tray, and driven by fear and hatred, you beat him to death, didn't you?'

'No. When I left he was alive. I don't know how he died.'

'Mr Hutton', persisted Foxcott, 'represented everything you hate and detest in men, didn't he?'

Annie, still composed, was even managing to treat her interrogator with mild deference after her brief, contemptuous outburst. 'He was arrogant and brutal, if that's what you mean.'

'And that enraged you, didn't it?'

'No. Not any more. It might have done once.'

'You mean in the days when you were writing in your diary about taking revenge on the men who abused you?'

'Yes.'

'That was only a few years ago, wasn't it?'

'Yes.'

'And you still have the same self-pitying vision of yourself as some sort of victim, and you still want your revenge, don't you?'

'Self-pity?' Annie sounded genuinely surprised. 'I have been beaten up more times than I can remember, I've been raped and half-strangled, and smashed in the face with a bottle. Every time I go out I wonder if tonight's the night I end up dead in an alley somewhere.' Once more there was a trace of contempt as she added, 'But no, I do not pity myself.'

'But you hate and fear men, don't you?'

'Yes, I do. And with good reason . . .'

'You hated and feared Patrick Hutton that night, didn't you?'

Now visibly riled, Annie glared at him. 'Yes, I did . . .'

'And that is why you killed him, isn't it?'

Annie was still looking in Foxcott's direction as she replied, yet she seemed somehow far away; back in a different place at a different time. 'I wanted to kill him. When he started hitting me, I wanted to see him dead. He deserved it. I knew there would never be a single moment's guilt or regret if I did it.' Bringing herself back to the present, she focused on Foxcott. 'I wanted to kill him. But I didn't.'

CHAPTER TWENTY-EIGHT

By the time the jury reached their verdict the nerves of everyone connected with the trial of Annie Lewis were strained to breaking-point. Annie herself was at the end of her tether: the waiting in jail for the trial to begin was as nothing compared to this. Now, it was out of her hands; there was nothing more she or Kavanagh could do to influence the verdict.

As she whiled away the hours – the hours that turned into days as the jury failed to reach a unanimous decision – Annie cast her mind back to her final appearance in court and to the last words she had spoken: 'I wanted to kill him. But I didn't.' Had she been naïve? Had it been misguided of her to be so honest about her feelings towards Patrick Hutton? She had admitted she wanted to see him dead: was it too much to expect a jury to believe it was complete coincidence that he had been killed – by someone else – after she had fled, covered in blood, from his room? Annie nearly tore herself apart as she waited for the jury to decide her fate. She also nearly tore apart the only thing that kept her going throughout those dark, lonely days: her daughter's drawing of a house, the child's vision of a happy family outside their house in the sunshine.

The tabloid press were also busy during the days of deliberation. Des Carter, inevitably, was keen to make arrangements to sell the diaries for the highest price possible – but there were no takers. Yet. The papers refused to negotiate a sale until – and unless – Annie was found guilty of murder. Des couldn't understand it: there was, as far as he was concerned, not even the remotest possibility that Annie would be found innocent. It would have enraged him even more if he had stopped to consider what the press were going to do if Annie *was* acquitted: already her solicitor had been approached about her selling her story – for a great deal more money than Des could hope to get for the diaries.

James Kavanagh, too, was under a great deal of stress, but not just because of Annie Lewis. Yet, like Annie, he was forced into the contemplation of the future. A future that was very much in Lizzie's hands.

Lizzie, as James knew she would, had accepted the job. Her husband's reaction had surprised her.

'There's a British Airways flight', he said, 'every hour on Fridays. Going both ways.'

'You mean you don't mind?'

'Mind?' Kavanagh grinned and hugged her. 'The way I look at it, the happier and more fulfilled you are, the stronger we are together. Spending more time apart isn't going to touch that. If you didn't take this chance, you'd never forgive yourself.' Looking into her eyes, he added with a grin, 'Or me. We'd just be feeding the fear and insecurity we thought we were avoiding.'

'That', replied Lizzie, 'was my speech, wasn't it?'

'If you were listening carefully, there was an apology in it somewhere.'

They looked at each other in silence and perfect understanding. The uncertainties of the past few months were behind them. Now it didn't matter if they were going to spend most weeks apart – they were together in their minds.

There was, however, one little problem that wouldn't go away – at least, until it grew up.

'In the meantime,' said Kavanagh, 'what the hell are we going to do about Matt? About the weekends?'

He should have known that Lizzie already had the answer. She laughed and told him that she already had that one sorted out.

'Matt's agreed', she said, 'to my little plan.'

'Oh? And what's that?'

'To spend the weekends we can't be with him at my mother's.'

'Oh, God!' Jim put a hand to his head in horror.

'What on earth's wrong?' Lizzie, sensing dissent, was ready to do battle.

But she had missed the expression on her husband's face. He was grinning as he looked up at her. 'I thought the idea was to keep him out of trouble. Sending him to your mother's, my darling, is like forcing him to become an alcoholic. Or', he added with a glint in his eye, 'a sex maniac.'

'Well,' Lizzie looked mildly flustered, 'one has to learn *sometime.*'

'And,' Kavanagh replied as he drew closer to her, 'one has to practise. Often.'

There was pandemonium both inside and outside the Old Bailey after the forewoman of the jury delivered the verdict. The press, suddenly, were everywhere. Foxcott and Kavanagh, opponents in this case, friends outside it, just looked at each other. Matt Kavanagh, who wouldn't have missed the verdict for anything – and certainly not for seeing his mother off at the airport – was nearly knocked over as the public gallery erupted.

Annie Lewis went white. As she stood in the dock, her legs began to shake. She felt suddenly old and weary. Tracy's drawing, until now clenched tightly in her fist, fell to the floor. And then she looked up at the sound of hysterical sobbing. Susan Hutton, even paler than Annie herself, came stumbling towards her, brushing angrily past Kavanagh as he tried to restrain her.

'Tell me it's not true!' yelled Susan. 'Tell me my husband wasn't like that, that he didn't do those things to you! Tell me you made it up to save yourself!'

Annie, horrified by the intensity of the woman's distress, shrank back in the dock.

'I don't care who killed him,' sobbed Susan. 'I don't even care if *you* killed him. But just tell me you were lying. Give him back as I knew him. Give him back. Tell me you were lying. Please. *Please!*'

As two policewomen approached at the run, Annie stared at the sobbing, broken woman. 'I'm sorry,' she said. 'I'm sorry, Mrs Hutton. I can't. I wasn't lying.'

Annie herself started crying as Kavanagh, appalled by Susan's scene, came up to her. 'You all right?' he asked gently.

Annie looked up at him and smiled through her tears. 'Yes. It's just . . . it's just the shock, the relief . . . the . . .'

Then, not knowing whether to laugh or cry, she grinned. 'Would you escort me down from this box, please?' Dabbing at her eyes with a little handkerchief, she added, 'I've got to go and meet my public.'

Annie's public were creating chaos outside the Old Bailey. Journalists were competing for space with several TV crews – and the real public, ever eager for sensation and scandal, watched in fascination as Annie Lewis walked to freedom. She was laughing, smiling and crying, and was flanked by Kavanagh and the journalist who had been negotiating with her solicitor.

Her smile faltered only once, when she spied a pale and tense Bobby Day in the crowd. For a moment his eyes met hers. 'They come early in the morning, Bobby,' she said. 'I'd be waiting for the knock on the door if I was you.' Then she turned away from him. She never wanted to see him again. She never would.

Jostled by the enthusiastic, cheering crowd, they reached the pavement. Annie turned to Kavanagh. 'Have you met my new friends from the newspapers, Mr Kavanagh?' She gestured towards the dark limousine waiting for her. 'They're going to give me a lot of money.'

Kavanagh smiled broadly. He was glad. Immensely glad. So, standing beside him, was Matt. He had decided Annie was a complete star.

'And all I have to do', continued Annie, 'is talk.' She sighed as if she could not believe it was all that was now required of her. Then she took a deep breath and, serious and a touch embarrassed, addressed her barrister once more. There was moisture in her eyes as she looked at him. 'I've known an awful lot of men, Mr Kavanagh . . . but . . . but . . .' But suddenly she could take no more emotion and the tears began again.

Kavanagh, touched, smiled and reached out for her hand.

'Thank you,' said Annie as she shook it. 'Thank you.' Then she was gone, ushered into the waiting limousine and out of the sordid debris of her past.

It was Matt who broke the silence. 'I think Bobby Day knows what happened, Dad.'

Kavanagh shrugged. 'You could be right, Matt. I don't know.'

'But aren't you curious?'

'I can't allow myself the luxury.' Kavanagh turned to his son and put his arm round his shoulders. 'As it turned out, the evidence wasn't enough to convict her. And that's my job done. The rest, thank God, is for the police.'

'I'm glad', said Matt as they walked in the direction of Kavanagh's car, 'for Annie.'

'Why?'

'I liked her.'

Oh dear, thought Kavanagh. But he noted his son's serious expression and chuckled. 'So did I, Matt. She was a real trouper.'

'Talking of which,' said Matt with a grin, 'I'm really looking forward to spending the weekend with Granny.'

'Are you? Oh. . . . good.' Visions of empty gin bottles swam before Kavanagh's eyes.

'Yeah,' said Matt. 'It's kind of cool. New. Different. It should be fun.'

High above them, a plane, heading south, appeared through a break in the clouds. 'Yes,' Kavanagh said as he watched it. 'New. Different. It *will* be fun, won't it?'